PRAISE FOR KERI

No More Words

"Lonsdale expertly maintains suspense throughout. Psychological-thriller fans will be well satisfied."

—*Publishers Weekly*

"A perfect summer read."

—Red Carpet Crash

"[A] mesmerizing first installment in her newest No More series . . . *No More Words* simmers with drama and secrets, sure to dazzle readers as an unmissable summer read."

—The Nerd Daily

"Lonsdale's first book in a new trilogy about love, betrayal, and the secrets families keep. Read in one sitting!"

—Frolic

"[Lonsdale] creates stories that readers will want to read again and again."

—*Write-Read-Life*

"Lonsdale is at her best with this multilayered story about three dysfunctional siblings and the secrets they keep. What a ride. I'm still a little breathless. This one was an addictive page-turner—impossible to put down. Fans of domestic suspense will EAT THIS UP."

—Sally Hepworth, bestselling author of *The Good Sister* and *The Mother-in-Law*

"Kerry Lonsdale is back and better than ever with this multilayered tale about three siblings torn apart by a series of tragic events. Nuanced and smart, filled with characters with real emotion and depth, *No More Words* is everything you've come to love from the master of domestic drama. A mesmerizing beginning to a new trilogy that will have you one-clicking the next in the series."

—Kimberly Belle, internationally bestselling author of *Stranger in the Lake*

"Full of suspense, romance, and drama, *No More Words* is a powerful story about what it means to be a family. Emotional and honest, it tells the story of three siblings, each dealing with demons from the past. I fell in love with all three Carson children and look forward to the second and third installments of this series. Kerry Lonsdale is a master storyteller of family drama, and this is Lonsdale at her best."

—Suzanne Redfearn, #1 Amazon bestselling author of *In an Instant*

"Kerry Lonsdale starts her latest trilogy off with a bang! Brimming with drama, suspense, and family secrets galore, *No More Words* will have you tearing through the pages to figure out what really happened to this broken family, and who is playing whom. With beautifully drawn, complex characters and a twisted plot that reveals itself layer by layer, *No More Words* is a stunning thriller that deserves a top spot on your 'to be read' list."

—Hannah Mary McKinnon, bestselling author of *Sister Dear* and *You Will Remember Me*

"*No More Words* burns and smolders with the tension of a lit cigarette. Kerry Lonsdale has created a page-turning story of family secrets and assumed truths that forces readers to ask what they would do if the buried past came calling at their door. Nothing and no one can stay hidden forever."

—Amber Cowie, author of *Rapid Falls*

"Every family has its secrets, and the way Kerry Lonsdale twists the truths in *No More Words*, you're guaranteed to lose sleep over this perfectly blended tale of suspense, intrigue, and emotional betrayal. Lonsdale has done it again, gripping the hearts of readers with her complex characters and layered storylines. This is a must-read thriller that will leave you stunned at the end!"

—Steena Holmes, *New York Times* and *USA Today* bestselling author of *Lies We Tell Ourselves*

Find Me in California

ALSO BY KERRY LONSDALE

THE EVERYTHING SERIES

Everything We Keep

Everything We Left Behind

Everything We Give

STAND-ALONE NOVELS

All the Breaking Waves

Last Summer

Side Trip

THE NO MORE SERIES

No More Words

No More Lies

No More Secrets

Find Me in California

A Novel

Kerry Lonsdale

Published by Lake Union Publishing, Seattle

www.apub.com

Amazon, the Amazon logo, and Lake Union Publishing are trademarks of Amazon.com, Inc., or its affiliates.

ISBN-13: 9781662514821 (paperback)
ISBN-13: 9781662514838 (digital)

Cover design by Ploy Siripant
Cover image: © Quirex, © andipantz / Getty

Printed in the United States of America

For Orly:
to a friendship founded on words that's as lasting as
language itself

Friday

CHAPTER 1

—

MATT

Matt turns his Porsche into the driveway and stops at the sight before him. Fifteen large boxes stacked five across in towers of three block his garage. Bleary eyed and exhausted from his flight, he stares. Somebody screwed up a delivery, because this is too large of an online order to forget. These boxes aren't his.

Sucks for whoever they do belong to. It's monsoon season.

He glances up at the sky. Bloated clouds are moving in fast and he's not leaving his silver metallic baby outside overnight. The boxes, however, will remain in the driveway unless the owner lives nearby and can pick them up before the rain starts. There's only so much space he's willing to give up in his garage.

Grabbing his phone, he unfolds from the car, intent on moving the boxes out of the way and calling the number on the shipping label. But what he reads stops him cold. SHIP TO: MRS. ELIZABETH HOLLOWAY C/O MATTHEW GATLIN.

His grandmother. What the fuck?

He hasn't seen or heard from her since he was eighteen, when he moved out of her house and left California. That was twelve years ago. Alarming that she knows where he lives. But not as disturbing as the boxes being left in his care.

Matt grips the back of his neck and looks up and down the street. Please don't tell him she'll show up next.

To say they have a complicated relationship is an overstatement. Their relationship is nonexistent. Elizabeth Holloway made sure of it after his mom's death. Which prompts another thought . . .

Maybe Elizabeth finally croaked.

For one glorious, fantastical second, giddy satisfaction explodes inside him. God rest her soul, but trust him: ever since he moved away, his life has been better without her in it.

But the feeling doesn't last long. If she were dead, the boxes would have been addressed specifically to him and sent with an explanation. A phone call giving him a heads-up that he had inherited her belongings would have been nice. A letter informing him of her passing would have been sufficient. Anything but this inconvenient and unwanted surprise.

Only one way to find out what's going on and stop this impending train wreck.

He calls the number on the label, reading the return address. Weird, they were shipped from Pasadena. His grandmother lives in Beverly Hills. She inherited her house from Matt's great-grandfather, a producer who made his riches during Hollywood's golden age. Matt can't imagine she would have sold the place and moved out.

A woman answers after the fourth ring. "Rosemont Assisted Living and Memory Care, this is Julia. How may I direct your call?"

Ah, that explains the address.

Matt mentally calculates Elizabeth's age, putting her at eighty-three. He wonders what she did with the house.

"Elizabeth Holloway." Matt keeps his tone neutral. Inside, his stomach churns at the thought of having to speak with her. This is not how he planned to start the evening. He's starving and has to curate the several thousand photos he took at the International Auto Show. After a seventy-two-hour, whirlwind trip to New York and back to Santa Fe, he still has a long night ahead.

"We don't have an Elizabeth," says the woman on the other end of the line.

"You sure? Because someone there sent me—"

"Wait, do you mean Liza? We have a Liza Holloway."

"Yeah, that's her."

A light, self-deprecating laugh comes over the line. "I blanked out there for a second. Long day. Forgot Liza and Elizabeth are the same. She goes by Liza here."

He should have remembered that. Everyone called her Liza. Everyone but him. He wasn't allowed. To him, she was Grandmother Holloway. Always formal, never familiar.

"One sec. I'll transfer you." She puts him on hold.

Matt switches the phone to his other ear, ruminating on how succinctly he can tell his grandmother that she isn't welcome at his house and neither is whatever's inside the boxes.

He doesn't have to wait long before the line connects. But his grandmother isn't the one who picks up.

"Liza's with her nurse at the moment. May I take a message?" says the woman he was speaking with. "She'll call you back."

"Who's in charge?" Maybe he doesn't have to speak with his grandmother at all. Surely whatever's going on has to be some mix-up on the center's part.

"That would be Lenore Pullen, the facility director."

"I'll speak with her."

"She's in a meeting right now. I'll transfer you to voicemail."

Slumbering memories from when he was first sent to live with his grandmother begin to wake. Choppy water. Small boat. An empty stomach. A heartache that stole his breath and almost his life.

His answer is sharp and short. "No." He can't revisit that time.

He then pushes out a long stream of air. He didn't mean to snap. But he does need this resolved *pronto*. "What did you say your name is?"

"Julia."

"Hi, Julia. Matt."

"Hello, Matt." Her voice is pleasant with an undercurrent of cheer. It helps calm his nerves. "Is there anything else I can do for you?"

"I'm hoping there is. I'm tired and I've got a long night ahead." He pushes a thumb into his temple where his head aches the most. If he doesn't pop an edible soon, that throb will turn into a full-blown migraine within an hour. His photos won't get edited. He'll miss the deadline with *Road & Track*. Dave will be furious.

"I'll try my best to help, sir."

"I just returned home to find fifteen boxes left on my driveway. Do you have any idea why Elizabeth sent them to me?"

A gasp. "You're Matt, her grandson."

Unfortunately. "That's me."

"I can't believe I didn't make the connection when you first asked for her. I'm more tired than I thought. I'm so glad you called."

"So what's up with the boxes?"

"She didn't send them. I did."

"Come again?"

"I helped her pack and arranged the delivery."

He has so many questions about that statement. One makes it to the front. "Why didn't you call ahead and warn me? A heads-up would have been nice."

"Lenore did call. Quite a few times."

"When? Never mind." He doesn't need to look at his call log to know there are likely many missed calls from Rosemont's director. He doesn't listen to voicemail and rarely answers calls from unknown numbers. That's why he has Dave. His partner handles the business end of things, books Matt's shoots, and negotiates the contracts.

"She has no one else, Matt. She wanted me to throw everything away. I get that she isn't sentimental, but I couldn't bear for her to let everything go because she has to move out, so I convinced her to send her things to you."

"You lost me." He's so confused. None of what she's said makes sense, especially the part about his grandmother having no one else.

She had tons of friends, people she regarded as more deserving of her attention than him.

"I shouldn't share this. It isn't my place." Her voice lowers conspiratorially. "Liza is broke."

He scoffs. "That's absurd." His grandmother descended from Hollywood royalty. He can still recall being awestruck when he first entered her palatial two-story estate. Her wealth was beyond the imaginings of his ten-year-old self.

"She's only been with us for a year, and granted, she isn't the most pleasant resident we have. But nobody deserves to be homeless, not even Liza."

"What are you talking about?"

"Liza is out of money, and the man she appointed as her power of attorney has gone missing. The center's evicting her in five days."

Five days?

Empathy floods his chest, but he immediately shuts that shit down. He will not feel sorry for her.

"What does this have to do with me?"

"You're listed as her secondary power of attorney, and you're her only living relative. You have to come get her."

"Like hell I do." The thought escapes before he can censor it.

"Matt," she pleads, and he instantly feels the guilt. Not because of what he said, but because of what Julia must think of him. He sounds like an asshole. He probably is one. But Elizabeth always brought out the worst in him. "She has no one."

He swore he'd never sacrifice his sanity for her peace of mind again. He's kept the memories from that period of his life locked away for years. He can't lower his guard and risk Julia's bleeding heart—or his grandmother—letting them out.

"Why am I hearing about this now? What happened to thirty days' notice?"

"Mrs. Pullen has been trying to reach you."

Right. The missed calls.

"Can I tell her you're coming?" Julia asks.

Matt's gaze drifts over the boxes hogging up driveway real estate, and his mind reels back in time. He remembers all the things Elizabeth didn't say to him and didn't do for him. The comfort she didn't give, and the love she withheld when he'd been his most vulnerable self.

No, he isn't coming to get her.

"Elizabeth Holloway is a resourceful woman. She can figure out where she's going to live, so long as it's not with me."

That said, he ends the call.

CHAPTER 2

JULIA

Julia gapes at the phone's receiver. The grating dial tone from Matt's severed call loud enough to hear despite her holding the earpiece away from her head.

Liza mentioned she and her grandson are estranged, but she didn't tell Julia that he is downright rude.

She'd like to add *inconsiderate*, *ungrateful*, and *disrespectful* to his list of flaws. He abandoned a frail eighty-three-year-old woman and has no issue admitting this to Julia's face. Or, more precisely, her ear.

Julia plunks the phone in its cradle, miffed. That must be some rift between the two of them.

She waffled about asking Liza what had happened between them because she didn't want to pry. Liza wouldn't hesitate putting Julia in her place. But she does feel sorry for the woman. From what she's seen, Liza doesn't have any regular visitors other than her missing power of attorney.

It makes Julia all the more grateful for the relationship she used to have with her grandmother, Ruby Rose Hope. She was fortunate to have been raised by the free-spirited and passionate woman, and she appreciates every hour she volunteers as Rosemont's in-house massage therapist so she can be close to Mama Rose, even if her grandmother rarely remembers who Julia is nowadays.

"Any calls come in?" Shelly asks, returning to the reception desk after her break.

"A few that I forwarded. Nothing urgent. You'll see them in the log." Julia stands, giving up Shelly's seat. She almost tells Shelly about Matt's call but decides against it. That's between Matt and Lenore. And Julia. Liza's financial and living circumstances are confidential. Julia only knows Rosemont is giving the elderly woman the royal boot because Liza complained to her during her massage session. She asked Julia for assistance to bag and toss her personal possessions. She said she has no use for them if she'll be homeless. Initially, albeit reluctantly, Julia cooperated. But when she came across Matt's birth certificate and asked Liza about it, the older woman admitted Matt is her grandson. When Lenore confirmed Matt is Liza's backup power of attorney and that her calls to Matt had gone unanswered, Julia convinced Liza and Lenore to allow her to box and ship Liza's possessions to Matt. She hoped the delivery would prompt Matt into action.

It did, just not in the way Julia had expected. A resounding *no*. He's not going to help Liza.

What a mess she caused. She took a risk and it backfired.

She should update Lenore. Judging from the phone conversation, Matt won't be calling back.

"Jules, do you have a moment?"

Julia glances over her shoulder at Lenore Pullen. Just the woman she needs to speak with. "Sure. One sec."

"Are you here tomorrow?" Shelly asks.

"You know me. Every day after my shift ends at the club. Like clockwork."

"I have an extra ticket for Margaret Cho at the Ice House. Starts at eight. Come with me? Dale's going to the Dodgers game." Her husband lives for baseball.

"I wish, but I'm here past nine tomorrow night."

Shelly's bottom lip curves into a dramatic pout. "You need a life, girl."

Julia works a full shift five days a week at the Pasadena Country Club spa, then puts in a four-hour shift volunteering at Rosemont. She also spends her days off from the spa at Rosemont, to upward of twelve hours a day.

What Julia needs but can't manage is a social life. With her disastrous record with romantic relationships plus her mounting debt, she can't afford one—emotionally or financially. Whenever she feels lonely, she overcompensates by working. So far, she's never felt alone. But that feeling has an expiration date. Once her grandmother passes, Julia will truly have no one. She tries not to think about it.

"Next time." Julia's smile is apologetic. She hopes there will be a next time, one day. But that day is far off, and after repeated rejections, Shelly will likely stop inviting her out. Her invitations will dry up like Julia's other friendships.

Shelly wiggles her fingers goodbye, and Julia follows Lenore to her office.

Lenore's private space overlooks Rosemont's side yard garden, a beautiful display of foliage and color. The facility's grounds solidified Mama Rose's decision to move in during the earlier stages of her dementia. This is where she wanted to be when Julia could no longer care for her. The cordial and experienced staff impressed Julia. She believed they'd treat her grandmother as family. But she wasn't entirely sold on the idea until she crunched the numbers. Between Mama Rose's social security and portfolio disbursements, and how long the doctors expected her to live, they could afford Rosemont. Barely. Julia would have to volunteer at least thirty hours a week in exchange for a reduced monthly fee. That was on top of her full-time job to keep herself fed and not lose Mama Rose's house, which she had to mortgage to cover her grandmother's expenses after they exhausted her retirement savings.

"Have a seat." Lenore gestures at the chair before her desk. Her features look strained behind her sapphire blue–framed glasses, her expression guarded underneath the Chianti-red lipstick as she settles in her own chair.

Julia suddenly has the distinct feeling she's being laid off. Silly, given she's a volunteer.

She warily sits across from Lenore. "Is something the matter?"

Lenore folds her sturdy hands on the desk. Doe-brown eyes rove across Julia's face before lowering. "This isn't easy, so I'll get right to the point."

"Okay." Julia tugs at her hot-pink Dickies pants. This isn't good if Lenore can't make eye contact.

"Not many people know yet. It hasn't been officially announced. Rosemont has been purchased by a larger corporation. Effective immediately, we are under new management."

Julia's mouth parts. "Oh." Maybe Lenore's being laid off. "Have you been let—"

"No." Lenore shakes her head. "Not yet anyway. I've been told they intend to keep the existing staff. Our new parent company will act more in the capacity of oversight. It's one of the reasons the board agreed to the terms. We don't want disruption in care."

"That's good." Julia slouches with relief, but she wonders how this could affect her grandmother's care. Lenore's gaze turns troubled. "That is good, right?"

Hands steepled on the desk, Lenore taps her fingertips together. "I know we have an arrangement for Ruby."

Their arrangement has been a lifesaver.

Julia's knee starts to bounce. "Yes, and?"

"We can't honor it anymore."

Her knee stops, and Lenore's announcement sinks in. "What do you mean?"

"They're cracking down on our finances. All residents must pay their full contracted fee."

Their agreement to exchange Julia's volunteer hours for a discount on Mama Rose's fees isn't in writing. It's between her and Lenore, who's become a dear friend. As long as Lenore worked at Rosemont and Julia volunteered, they would be good. Julia knew Lenore could renege on the monthly discount and the fee could revert to the contracted rate. But thinking something could happen is not the same as it actually happening.

"You swore you—"

"I swore I'd honor Ruby's discount as long as I could. There was always the possibility rates would increase or the board would crack down. I made that clear in the beginning."

Julia chides her selective memory. Lenore had explained all this and more. She was just in denial this day could come. Ignorance is bliss until it rains on your parade.

"I don't have the authority I once had, and I no longer have sway with the board, not under the new management structure. I can't make exceptions, Jules. I'm sorry."

"I'll volunteer more hours."

"When?" Lenore peers at her through thick lenses. "You're already putting in twelve-hour days."

Julia throws up her hands. "I don't know. I'll figure something out." She has to—she doesn't have other options. She's exhausted her income sources.

"Even if you could find the time, I still can't honor our deal."

"Lenore . . ."

Lenore slumps over her desk. "Jules, please. I love your grandmother. Don't make this harder for me than it already is."

Harder for her? Lenore's grandmother isn't the one getting evicted if Julia can't make the full payment.

"How much time do I have?"

"End of the month."

Five days until the full fee kicks in. And not for just the upcoming month, but for every month thereafter. They'll burn through the remainder of the cash Julia put aside when she mortgaged Mama Rose's house.

"And if I can't make the payment?"

"We're left with no choice but to give her notice. We have several others on the waiting list."

And the center's new parent company sees only dollar signs on the ledger.

"We'd hate to lose Mama Rose, but I understand if you see fit to move her to another facility." Someplace more affordable. Lenore's suggestion goes without saying.

As much as Julia would love to save money and cut back on her hours, she can't. She can't move Mama Rose. For reasons her grandmother refused to share, Mama Rose insisted she spend her remaining days at Rosemont. She begged Julia to promise that under no circumstance would she move her elsewhere unless it was back home for hospice care. She has to live here.

Julia pushes up from the chair. "She's not moving out."

"Julia." Lenore rises with her. "Please listen to me as your friend. You're already overextended, and you're practically broke. You told me yourself. You're also not being fair to yourself."

A small price to pay. She made Mama Rose a promise and she intends to keep it.

"I'll come up with the difference." Who knows how.

Julia leaves Lenore's office in a daze, her mind grappling for solutions and coming up empty handed. It isn't until she reaches her grandmother's room that she remembers. She forgot to tell Lenore about her conversation with Matt.

CHAPTER 3

—

MATT

Dave wraps a putrid yellow scarf around his neck. "Your grammie has some wild shit."

"Get off her stuff." Matt yanks the scarf from Dave and shoves it in the box. Dave showed up twenty minutes ago, as Matt brought in the last of Elizabeth's boxes, stacking them on the side of the garage opposite his Porsche 911, between the side wall and the '67 Chevy Chevelle he's rebuilding. He sliced open and dug through a few boxes. When he couldn't find a note from her, he gave up on the rest. Childish of him to think *Grammie* cared enough to write him a letter explaining how she got into this scrape.

He closes the box flaps. "Don't ever let her hear you call her that." Matt let slip "Grandma" once and *Grandmother* Holloway grounded him for the weekend.

"Until a hot minute ago, I didn't know you had a grandmother. You never mentioned her."

"Nothing worth mentioning." Ten-plus years of friendship with Dave probably does warrant a mention or two. But Matt chooses not to talk about the eight years he spent with Elizabeth or why he had to move into her house, because he'd rather forget it ever happened.

Dave leans against the workbench where Matt stores his tools. "When do I get to meet this mystery woman?"

"Never. And consider yourself lucky," Matt adds when Dave screws up his face. "Toss me the packing tape. It's behind you."

Dave tosses over the tape and nods at the boxes. "What are you going to do with those?"

"Ship them back." He'll put in a UPS pickup order first thing on Monday.

He reseals a box and moves to the next one he opened.

"I thought she was being evicted."

"Yeah, so?" He casts Dave a sidelong glance.

"Dude." Dave gives him a pathetic look. Matt knows he's being selfish. In his defense, his attitude isn't any different from hers toward him.

"Whatever she's gotten herself into isn't my problem."

Dave snags the tape from him. "This is your grandmother."

"Give it back."

"Your flesh and blood."

Matt holds out his hand, waving his fingers for the tape.

"Not until you talk to me," Dave says.

Elizabeth is the last person he wants to talk about.

"There's nothing to discuss." Matt grabs for the tape.

Dave moves out of reach. "She's old, you freak."

Matt grunts with annoyance. Hands on hips, he stares at Dave, his expression flat. "What do you want?"

"A bedtime story. Whatever this is"—Dave waves the tape at the boxes—"it's fucking with your head."

Matt's head is already a lost cause, and so might be his plans for working tonight. His migraine is now full blown, making him edgy and irritable. Not an ideal state for editing photos. He can't let his attitude bleed over into his work, especially with this job. He wasn't at the auto show for only *Road & Track*. It was his first assignment with Ford shooting their concept car for an upcoming marketing campaign.

"Spill," Dave says, folding his arms and tucking the tape under his bicep. His posture signals that he won't back down until Matt relents.

People have described Dave as bullheaded. Matt prefers "determined and persistent." It's why Matt agreed to partner with him. They met in New York in their early twenties, when they worked ungodly hours freelancing and trying to make names for themselves. Dave is a skilled photographer in his own right, but something about Matt's style landed his photos on more magazine covers and featured articles.

But Matt's work record wasn't perfect. He'd been in such demand at one point that he started missing jobs, running late or not showing up at all because he couldn't manage his schedule. And Matt learned he could fall quicker than he'd risen. He gained a reputation of being unreliable, and the good offers, the lucrative ones that helped him maintain a living wage, dried up. He was back to seeking assignments like a rookie. Like Dave, whose photography lacked Matt's X factor. Dave treated photography more like a hobby, and he had a second hourly wage job as a staffing assistant to make ends meet. But he knew how to manage his assignments and pitch his skills.

One night over old-fashioneds at a dive bar with sticky tabletops in lower-end Manhattan, Dave and Matt came to an agreement. With Dave's business savvy and Matt's prowess behind the lens, they'd make a formidable team. And they have. When Dave tired of the big city, he moved back to his hometown of Santa Fe, and Matt, weary of crowds and noise, followed.

Matt drags his hands down his face and blows air into his palms. "I was sent to live with Elizabeth after my parents died. Never met the woman until a neighbor put me on a plane for Burbank."

"Mom's or dad's side?"

"Mom's. My dad's parents died before he married my mom."

"What happened between you and your grandmother?"

Matt keeps his tone neutral so he doesn't feed into the memories. "She blamed me for my mom's death, so she didn't want anything to do with me. She took me in but ignored me." He lived in her house, but not with her.

Dave's face falls open. "Shit. Dude. What a—" He presses his lips tight.

Matt shakes his head. "Don't say it." He doesn't need to hear what he already knows about her.

"How old were you?"

"Ten."

"And you lived there how long?" Dave gives back the tape roll.

"Eight years." He left on his eighteenth birthday. The only good thing that came out of his time in California was his love for cars and photography. Elizabeth lived in an exclusive neighborhood in Beverly Hills, so he washed and waxed some very expensive vehicles after school, and the neighbors tipped well. One gifted him his first Nikon camera, which Matt took with him everywhere.

Dave whistles. "That's brutal."

Matt seals a box. "Now she's apparently broke and her power of attorney is AWOL. Some woman at the assisted living facility convinced Elizabeth to ship her things here thinking I'd come deal with her before they kicked her out."

"Some bedtime story," Dave scoffs.

"Mm-hmm."

Clouds split open, dumping rain. In seconds, the garage feels like a sauna. Dave picks up his helmet.

"Don't ride in that mess," Matt says.

"Not going far. Meeting my sis for dinner down the street." He zips his leather bike jacket.

"Did you have a chance to pick up my orders?"

Dave reaches into his backpack and tosses him a crumpled paper bag. Matt upends the contents on a box top. Two metal tins of gummies roll out.

"Chill your nerves and kill your migraines. They're both there." Dave points them out and slides one from his pocket, waves it in Matt's face. "These cubs, I had Doc toss in for me, but I'm giving them to you. They're homemade and they'll take you anywhere you want to go. Straight down psychedelic lane to funky town if you so choose."

Given that his day has gone sideways, Matt grabs for them. Dave moves his arm back, wags a finger. "Nuh-uh. Doc said this is some good shit but it's potent. No clue what's in them, but consider yourself warned. Watch the dosage."

Doc isn't a real doc. It's the nickname of the guy who owns the dispensary Matt frequents. Knowing Dave and his relationship with Doc, Matt wouldn't be surprised if the edibles are homemade.

Dave gives Matt the tin, and Matt returns everything to the paper bag after popping a gummy for his headache.

Dave holds up a fist for a bump and starts to leave. "Oh." He snaps his fingers and turns back. "How was New York?"

"Great. Took almost three thousand shots. They're due Wednesday?"

"*R&T* wants theirs Monday. Ford's aren't due till Wednesday. Speaking of which, you all set for Le Mans?"

"Waiting on a new lens and a couple filters. But yeah, good to go." Shooting the twenty-four-hour auto race in France has been a dream since he first fell in love with auto photography in his teens.

"Excellent. We leave Thursday. Plenty of time for you to deal with Grams."

"Hell no."

Dave grips his shoulder and gets in his face. "I wasn't asking. We worked our asses off to get Ford's invite. You need to be on and fired up to shoot for seventy-two hours straight. You miss a shot, you screw us for next year. We can't have you getting rando calls from California because the old folks' home gave your grandmother the boot and she's wandering the streets in a bathrobe and rollers. I need you in the right frame of mind."

"She won't be a problem."

Dave pokes his chest. "You're right, because you're going to call that woman who packed all this and tell her you'll pay for your grandmother to stay until you return and can sort everything out."

Like hell he is. The last thing he wants is Elizabeth to be dependent on him.

He shoves Dave aside and moves toward the door into the house.

"Matt."

"I'll deal with it," he snaps over his shoulder to shut Dave up.

"Now you're talking." Dave's grin disappears under the helmet he slaps on his head. He throws a leg over the seat and revs the bike he parked in the garage when he arrived. With a two-fingered salute, he's off.

Matt scowls at his grandmother's boxes and considers popping another gummy. *Chill your nerves* should do the trick.

CHAPTER 4

JULIA

Her stomach knotted like the tangled wad of bras she removed from the washer this morning, Julia tables her worries and knocks on her grandmother's door in Rosemont's memory care unit. She can't discuss finances and brainstorm options with Mama Rose. Rarely does her grandmother remember who Julia is, and several months back, when Julia mentioned money to her, Mama Rose believed she still had a nest egg. She can't comprehend it's already been exhausted. Julia's on her own with this dilemma.

"It's open." Her grandmother's voice comes through the thick door. A soft chime sends a signal to the caretaker's station when Julia enters. She quickly punches in a code on the keypad to silence the alarm and stops short with a look of horror when she sees her grandmother. Mama Rose stands amid a pile of blankets, her wheelchair on the other side of the room. She clutches a thick green-and-pink knit throw.

Panic explodes in Julia's chest as a likely scene plays out in her head. Mama Rose will forget why she's doing whatever she's doing. She'll forget about the blankets on the floor. Her foot will tangle in the wool and fleece. She'll topple over and break her hip. Again. She's been using the wheelchair because of a previous fall.

Dropping her shoulder bag on the table, Julia rushes to her grand-mother's side and gently grasps Mama Rose's shoulders so she doesn't lose her balance as she folds a blanket. Her grandmother's face lights up at the sight of her.

"Have you come to get me out of this dreadful place?"

"You love it here," Julia says. "You told me you wanted to stay." It's far more pleasant than other facilities.

"I said no such thing."

Julia hums under her breath and resists getting sucked into this conversation. It's old and repetitive, a symptom of Mama Rose's condition. "What are you doing here?" She gestures to the pile on the floor.

"I'm . . ." Mama Rose smiles apologetically. "Forgive me. I can't remember your name."

Julia deflates. She'll never get used to Mama Rose not recognizing her. "Call me Jules."

Mama Rose pats her arm. "Beautiful name. My granddaughter's named Julia. Have you met her?"

"I haven't, but I'm sure she's lovely. May I help?" She breathes through the hollowness in her chest. Reassured that Mama Rose is steady on her feet, she picks up the other end of the blanket and helps her fold. "Were you looking for something?" Her grandmother is always searching for objects from her past, be they keys or seeds or mail.

"A book."

"In your blanket chest?" Julia sweeps the blankets off the floor to get them out of the way and drops the pile on the bed to fold.

"I found a toothbrush in there, so it's possible." Mama Rose puts the folded green-and-pink knit blanket into the chest and shuffles to the table.

"Tell me about the book. Is it one of those?" Julia asks of the books shelved above the dresser. Paperback mysteries and romances, their covers and spines creased from age and love. Books her grandmother read repeatedly before her eyesight deteriorated and Julia introduced her to audiobooks.

"No, none of those." Mama Rose digs through Julia's shoulder bag. "Now what are you looking for?"

"These." Mama Rose jingles Julia's keys like she won a round in *The Price Is Right*. "We're bugging out."

"No, we're not."

"I'm driving." Mama Rose shuffles to the door, or what she thinks is the door. The entire wall has been painted to look like a scene out of Monet's garden, camouflaging the door. "I always get turned around. Where's the door, love? You can't keep me here forever. I'll call the police. Soon as I get out of this dreadful place." She runs her hands along the wall in search of the door, and the keys drop on the floor. "Oops."

Julia is at her side and snags the keys before her grandmother has the chance.

"How about we go for a walk instead," Julia says and gently takes her arm.

"I don't want to go for a walk." Mama Rose yanks her elbow away. "I want to go home."

Moisture bites Julia's eyes. "But you are home. You love it here. This is where you want to be."

"Stop telling me what I want. Lies! All of them." Mama Rose's face flushes with her ire, and she wags a finger in Julia's face. "I see right through them."

"How about we see the garden instead? You always enjoy the gardens this time of evening."

Mama Rose's lips pinch. She rubs her thumbs across her fingertips over and over, her gaze darting around the room. "Yes, yes, you're right. We'll go see the garden. Maybe the book will be here after."

"A wonderful plan." Julia despises the relief that floods her forced calm. She's curious about the book and wouldn't mind helping her grandmother search for it later, but a visit to view Rosemont's gardens is the distraction Mama Rose needs. Some days, Julia can't derail her grandmother from her quest for some random object or her determination to break out of Rosemont until her frustration violently escalates and her caretaker has to medicate her.

"Hurry. The sun is setting." Mama Rose pads to the wheelchair with Julia at her side.

Julia drapes a blanket over her grandmother's legs once she's settled in the chair and wheels her to the common room the memory care unit shares with the assisted living wing that overlooks lush gardens of roses, geraniums, and fuchsias in full bloom. The sun has all but set, blanketing the flowers in shadow. But it's the scents of violets and begonias her grandmother loves.

She parks Mama Rose before an open window beside a rocking chair already occupied by Liza Holloway. The sight of the willowy woman reminds Julia of Matt's call and that she needs to update Lenore before she leaves for the evening.

Upon noticing Mama Rose, Liza lifts her chin so she's looking down her nose at Julia's grandmother. "I don't want company. Put her elsewhere."

"The common room is for everyone, Mrs. Holloway." Julia winks at the surly woman.

"Doesn't it smell lovely?" Mama Rose asks.

"Do be quiet. I'm trying to read." Liza flips a page in her hardback with enough flair to prove her point.

Julia pulls up a chair on the other side of Mama Rose. "We're here for the sunset; then we'll go."

"Have I told you about the garden I tended in Beverly Hills one year? The roses were magnificent. I'd just moved to California and had never seen a multicolored floribunda until then."

"Not this story again." Liza snaps her book closed. "Can't you talk about something else? And what's with that you've got on? Weren't you wearing that yesterday?"

Mama Rose glances down at her maroon tracksuit with a confused smile. Julia bought her several sets in various colors when her grandmother insisted on wearing them daily. Maroon is her favorite, and she has two in that color. Julia doesn't think it's the same set she wore yesterday until she notices something crusted on Mama Rose's chest, a dribble of food alongside the zipper. It looks like yesterday's corn chowder.

Julia touches her grandmother's knee. "I like this story." She'll listen to anything Mama Rose says, even if it's the same tired story she repeats each time she gazes at the garden. Julia knows that the day will soon come when she aches to hear her grandmother's voice.

Upon Julia's smile of reassurance, Mama Rose prattles on about every plant varietal she recalls from Rosemont's garden and compares them to that mysterious Beverly Hills garden. It always strikes Julia how much her grandmother remembers about her earlier life and her present surroundings, yet she can't recall who Julia is to her.

Julia blinks away a flash of hopelessness when Liza barks, "Would you shut up?"

Mama Rose turns to the woman beside her, startled to see her sitting there, so consumed she'd been with her storytelling. She never seems to recognize Liza, which gives Julia a perverse sense of pleasure. She isn't the only one her grandmother can't place.

When the sun has set, casting the garden's far corners into darkness where the landscape lights don't reach, Julia rises to wheel Mama Rose back to her room. Even she has her limits when it comes to spending time around Liza. But before they depart, Mama Rose's caretaker Trevor appears. He grasps the wheelchair handles. "Time for your meds, Ruby Rose." Soft, tender eyes fall on Julia. "Get yourself home, Jules. I've got her."

Julia suddenly feels the full weight of her weariness. She's been up since four thirty this morning. She touches Trevor's arm. "Thanks."

"Got plans for tonight?" He unlocks the wheel brakes.

Had her ex-boyfriend Nolan not run scared a few years back, she might have been meeting him for dinner. She certainly wouldn't be as paranoid about running out of money if he'd stuck around. He paid half the monthly mortgage when he lived with her.

"Does a hot date with my laptop count?" She intends to spend the evening trying to mold their minuscule savings into a workable solution. An impossible feat that only magic could accomplish, a talent—aside from money—she sorely lacks. Still, she needs to do something, and staring at their account balances may coax forth an answer.

Trevor offers her a sad little smile. They both know she works herself to the bone and has a nonexistent life outside of work, volunteering, and spending time with Mama Rose.

"At the very least, pour yourself a glass of wine." Trevor swings Mama Rose's chair around.

"I will."

Mama Rose looks up behind her. "There you are, Trevor. Looking like the sexy hunk you are."

Despite how many times he's heard it, Trevor still blushes. "Now, now, Ruby Rose. You know I'm already taken." He grins at Julia, and she secretly hates him. Mama Rose always recognizes him.

"Well, you're still good looking. Just not as handsome as my Matty."

Beside her, Liza hisses, "He's not yours."

"Testy, testy." Julia clucks her tongue, sharing a look with Trevor. From the day she moved in, Liza's always had something against Julia's grandmother. Julia's never been able to define what, and Liza wasn't forthcoming the single time she had the courage to press her on it.

Trevor starts to leave with Mama Rose when she snatches Julia's wrist with startling strength. With a soft gasp, Julia lifts her gaze from her grandmother's veiny hand to her faded blue-gray eyes. They shine with focus.

"Find my diary, Jules. The light-blue one with gold embossed lettering. You know the one. I need it."

A sharp inhale from Liza. Julia spares the woman a glance. She has no idea what her grandmother is talking about. She's never seen such a diary in her possession. She didn't know her grandmother had kept diaries. But Liza's complexion has gone ghostly white.

Trevor wheels Mama Rose from the room, and Liza stands with the assistance of a cane, collecting her book and readers. "All those secrets."

"Excuse me?" Julia's head swerves toward the woman.

"She was very good at keeping them."

Shock immobilizes Julia. Did Liza just admit she'd known Mama Rose from before?

"What do you mean by that?" Julia asks. "What secrets?"

"That's not a question for me."

But Julia can't ask her grandmother. Mama Rose has likely already forgotten she wants the diary.

"What do you know of her diary?" Julia asks. Now she must find it.

Liza's thin, faint brows bob once before she leaves the room, stunningly quick for her age.

CHAPTER 5

—

MATT

Seated at his desk in his office, Matt can't focus. He thought dinner and an old-fashioned would put him in the right mood to work on the RAW images. He's on deadline. But he's irritable and distracted. His mind keeps drifting to Elizabeth. He never thought she'd end up destitute and alone. How did she manage that?

From what Matt knows of his mom's side of the family, which he only learned of in sound bites from Adam, Elizabeth's butler, they had been wealthy. His great-grandfather started in the movie business as a cameraman in the 1930s and worked his way up to producing films. Elizabeth inherited the house in Beverly Hills when he passed. Her mother, Matt's great-grandmother, died in the fifties. Elizabeth was raised on movie sets and back lots and often regaled friends and acquaintances with stories of Gary Cooper and Rock Hudson. Her garden parties had been legendary. Matt witnessed many of them from his bedroom window, which overlooked the sprawling backyard. She was married to Matthew Holloway, a 1960s heartthrob and actor, for a short time. They had one daughter, Aubrey, Matt's mom. She was born in 1973 and quickly followed in her father's footsteps, starring in movies until she turned seventeen, when she met Matt's dad and left the industry.

Matt avoids thinking about his mom. He can't remember her without remembering how she died. He can't even bring himself to watch the movies she starred in. He also doesn't go out of his way to think about his dad, because it always makes him think of his mom. In turn, he barely remembers what his parents look like when he closes his eyes.

Estranged from their families, Matt's parents seldom spoke about their childhoods or how they met. Matt was quite young when his parents died, so he doesn't remember hearing much about his relatives other than generic highlights. Which only makes him think how little he does know of his parents. He had only ten years with them.

He then had eight drawn-out years with his grandmother, the reluctant guardian. The woman who blamed him for her only daughter's death, completely disregarding Matt's feelings on the matter. Completely ignoring that he was devastated, grieving, and had PTSD. He couldn't talk about what had happened. Elizabeth took his silence as a personal affront and, other than advising her butler, Adam, to watch over him, left Matt to his own devices.

So why would she appoint him as her secondary power of attorney? Surely there must be someone more suitable. What will happen to her if he doesn't step up? Will the government intervene? His knowledge is limited, but he assumes she'll become a ward of the state. She'll be assigned a guardian, who'll move her to a state-run facility. She'll be fine. Won't she?

Unless she's psychologically and physically sound and doesn't need a guardian. She's just broke.

Would Rosemont unload her at a nearby motel? Would they give her a one-way bus ticket to a destination of her choice like a prisoner who's served their term?

He doesn't like how that makes him feel: guilty, neglectful, and regretful. Because he could do something. He *should* do something.

Elizabeth didn't take him under her wing by any means, but she did allow him to stay under her roof.

Damn moral compass.

Matt shoves away from his desk and rolls his chair to the center of the room. Leaning back, he stares at the ceiling fan overhead, drumming a pen on his thigh. Dave was right. Elizabeth is messing with his head.

He drags his hands down his face and sits upright. "What would you do?" he asks of the woman in the photo on his desk. In the picture he stands between his parents on his dad's charter boat, *Key to My Heart*. Matt was nine when the photo was taken. It's the only picture he has of his parents. Their neighbor, a Mrs. Kinsley, had the good sense to pack it in his luggage when she put him on a plane to California.

Aubrey Gatlin was one of the most generous souls Matt had known. Even at ten, he understood his mom was different from others, a childhood star who abandoned Hollywood's glitz and glam for a more private and emotionally rewarding life, a life she really wanted. She collected used shoes and books for students in schools in lower-income districts. She invited neighbors who didn't have family over for the holidays. One fall, she volunteered at the homeless shelter and brought home a woman and her son to stay in their guest room through the New Year.

His dad often said his mom's heart was the key to their love, that it was too big to break. He didn't live long enough to witness her heart shatter.

It confounded Matt how someone as warm and giving as his mother could come from a cold, insensitive woman like Elizabeth. Would Aubrey look past their estrangement to help her mom if Elizabeth needed her?

"You would, wouldn't you?"

Sea-green eyes that are an exact match to his own stare back at him. Yes, she would.

He frees a long stream of air and pushes up from the chair. He grabs his phone and takes it to the great room, where he folds open the doors in the glass wall that overlooks his patio and the lights of Santa Fe. The rain has tapered to a drizzle, the air ripe with humidity. He calls Rosemont, figuring he'll do as Dave suggested: pay this month's fees and handle the rest later when he returns from France.

A man answers after the second ring. "Rosemont Assisted Living and Memory Care. How may I direct your call?"

"I can't remember her name. Linda, I think? The director? Is she available?"

"Lenore Pullen, and she's left for the evening. One sec—I'll transfer you to voicemail."

A few clicks and a prerecorded message. Matt waits for the beep. "Hi, this is Matt Gatlin, Elizabeth Holloway's grandson. I understand you've been trying to reach me. I leave town in a week. Call me back. Thanks." He leaves his number and hangs up, only to redial Rosemont. He's busy, the director is probably busy. Who knows when she'll get back to him. Matt wants to get this worked out tonight.

"Rosemont Assisted Living and—"

"Hi, this is Matt again," he interrupts. "I spoke with a Julia earlier. Is she there?"

"Julia who?"

"I don't know. She didn't give me her last name. She answered the phone when I called this afternoon."

Matt hears mouse clicks.

"The only Julia we have is our massage therapist. She's a volunteer. She wouldn't have answered the phone."

"That's her," he says, without knowing whether it really is her. How many Julias could there be? He'll take his chances. "Can you transfer me?"

"She's left for the evening, and we don't have a voicemail box for her."

"What's her cell number?"

"I can't give that out, sir, but I'll take a message."

He rubs the back of his head, anxious to have his grandmother issue resolved. "Fine." He gives the guy his name and number. "Tell her I'd like a call back tonight, if possible. It's urgent."

"Uh-huh. Sure."

The guy doesn't believe him.

But it *is* urgent. Julia told him Elizabeth has only five days left at Rosemont, and today's already over.

CHAPTER 6

JULIA

At home, Julia stares at the sad selection in her fridge: wilted lettuce, oat milk, and an odd assortment of take-out containers. She goes with the vegetable chow mein she picked up earlier in the week and hip nudges the fridge closed. She eats straight from the carton at the counter, staring out the kitchen window into the darkness.

Out there lies Mama Rose's backyard garden, once vibrant with a multitude of rose varietals and citrus trees, now looking as pathetic as Julia feels. Julia tried to maintain it the first year after Mama Rose had moved to Rosemont, but she doesn't have her grandmother's green thumb. And she no longer has the time. The trees are overgrown, the rosebushes have lost their shape, and the lawn has dried up like Julia's relationships. Her grandmother would be disappointed with her. She promised to keep it up.

She also promised not to move Mama Rose from Rosemont, so Julia better get on figuring out how she'll manage that with the fee increase.

She drops the empty carton into the recycling bin and goes to the living room to retrieve her laptop. But the overflowing bookshelves that buttress the brick fireplace enchant her. Regency romances and coffee shop mysteries fill every nook and cranny. Worn landscape and gardening books tower in stacks on the floor, collecting dust since her grandmother's retirement. These books belong to Mama Rose. Julia keeps her collection of thrillers, up lit, and self-help upstairs in her room.

Could the diary Mama Rose mentioned be the book she was searching for under the pile of blankets in her room? From Liza's reaction tonight in the common room, it's clear she and Mama Rose have some sort of history. Julia's dying to know how Mama Rose knows Liza. What secrets has she been keeping?

Julia calls Rosemont. Likely her grandmother has forgotten she asked after the diary, but maybe Julia can spin her questions so Mama Rose will give her some clues where to look.

"Steve," she says after the night attendant answers with the canned greeting, "it's Julia."

"Who?"

"Julia Hope, the massage therapist. My grandmother is Ruby Rose Hope in room 115."

"Ah, right. It's late. She's probably asleep."

Julia glances at the old ticking clock on the mantel and deflates. It's already after 10:00 p.m. Mama Rose is definitely asleep.

"Want to leave a message?" Steve asks.

"No, thanks. I'll see her tomorrow." Just as well. Doubtful the diary exists. Julia would have come across it when she boxed her grandmother's belongings. Best she avoid that rabbit hole before she falls in. She has more pressing matters to contend with and can't afford the distraction.

She's about to say goodbye when Steve says, "You got a call earlier."

"I did?" That's unusual. Her Rosemont clients have her cell number. They or their caretakers call her directly to schedule appointments.

"Hold on." Papers rustle on Steve's end. "Some guy named Matt Gatlin."

Well, what do you know. He did call back.

"What time did he call?"

"Around eight forty-five."

Four hours after he hung up on her.

"Do you know if he spoke with Lenore?" She didn't get the chance to. Lenore had left for the day by the time Julia sought her out.

"No, but I transferred him to her voicemail. He might have left a message, but he called right back and asked for you."

"Did he leave a number?"

"Sure did."

She takes down the number Steve dictates. "Thanks."

"No prob."

Matt might have had a change of heart about his grandmother. Maybe he decided to handle her finances and will come to get her. Probably best to speak with him before she updates Lenore in the morning.

Taking Trevor's advice from earlier that day, she pours herself a glass of cabernet and, facing the bookcases, perches on the edge of the old couch with unforgiving cushions. She calls Matt only to reach his voicemail. A simple "Matt Gatlin—leave a message" plays, followed by a standard recording that states his voicemail box is full.

She disconnects and dictates a text instead: "Hi, Matt. This is Julia. We spoke earlier about your grandmother. I got a message you called. I tried calling back but got your voicemail, which is full, by the way. You might want to clear it out. I know Lenore tried to contact you recently, oh . . . so many times. Anyway, it's me. I'll be up for a little while longer if you need to reach me."

She reads the text back, cringing at the two-and-a-half-sentence rant about his voicemail. Deleting that. She corrects a few typos, adds punctuation, and sends it. After adding Matt's information to her contacts, she leaves her phone on the coffee table and, sipping her wine, peruses the bookcases on the off chance Mama Rose slipped her diary among the books. Assuming it exists. But several books on the shelf have light-blue spines and gold lettering.

She slides the nearest one off the shelf, and her phone blares Ozzy Osbourne's "Patient Number 9."

Julia jumps and the book drops to the floor. Wine sloshes onto the carpet. She scrambles for the phone and lowers the volume, chastising herself for not changing her ringtone back to Paratone's cover of "Time After Time." Mr. Myers, a seventy-four-year-old Rosemont resident who rocks out to heavy metal, asked her to show him how to personalize his daughter's ringtone this morning, which she demonstrated for him on her phone. Hence the Ozzy.

"Hello?" she answers, breathless.

"It's Matt."

"Hey, hiii." She looks around for something to wipe up the wine and settles on a roll of paper towels she gets from the kitchen.

"Thanks for calling me back. I wasn't sure you would." His voice is whiskey honey. He sounds as exhausted as she feels.

"Why not?"

"I hung up on you."

"You did." She sinks to her knees and blots the wine from Mama Rose's favorite area rug.

"I also think I came across as a bit of an ass."

"Is this an apology call?" she deadpans, but there's a smile in her voice. She did ambush him with Liza's boxes. Now that she's had time to think on it, if the same thing happened to her, she probably would have been outraged too.

A dry laugh. "Yes. I've probably already earned the world's-worst-grandson award, but I'm sorry. And I am an ass."

She crumples the soiled paper and sits back on her heels. "Apology accepted, and I'm not judging."

More chuckling. "Well, I am. And again, I'm sorry."

"I appreciate the call, but couldn't this have waited until tomorrow?"

"I'm calling about Elizabeth. You mentioned she's broke."

"Yes," she says, curious where he's going with this because there isn't much she can do for him.

"I leave for France next week. I'll wire money to cover her so she can at least stay there until I get back and have time to deal with this. I just need to know how much and where to send it."

"You know I'm a volunteer, right? I don't have those answers." She takes the dirty paper towels to the trash.

He sighs. "Yeah, I know. I hate leaving messages, and you already know I'm not good at listening to them."

"Your mailbox is full."

"See? I rest my case."

"You really need to speak with Lenore." She returns to the living room and meanders to the bookcases, picks up the light-blue book that she dropped. It fell open to pages covered in her grandmother's neat script. They don't teach penmanship like that anymore.

"I know. I'm pressed for time and don't want to miss her call or get stuck in a game of phone tag. Do you think you can ask her about it and have her text me the details? Better yet, you can text me. I'm sure she's busy too."

Right, because she's Lenore's girl Friday.

The nerve of this guy.

Julia bites the sharp retort that comes to mind, something about shoving his request up a dark crevice, and says, "I'm not privy to that information. I'll inform Lenore we spoke, but you really must talk with her directly. Maybe make the effort to pick up the phone when she does call?"

He draws in a frustrated breath. "I know, I know. I will."

"Sooner than later, Matt. Like tomorrow morning. Call her first thing." As of the stroke of midnight, Liza will have four days left at Rosemont.

"Will do. Promise."

"I'm serious."

"I get it."

"I—" She stares at the light-blue spine of the hardback in her hand.

"It's late. I should let you go before we start arguing. Are we arguing?"

Julia frowns at the book. "Maybe."

"You're supposed to say we're not. For what it's worth, thanks for returning my call."

"Sure," Julia says, distracted.

"Whatever." His tone goes flat. "Take care, Julia."

"Bye." She disconnects. Slipping her phone into her pocket, she flips the book to read the gold embossed title on the cover. *Magnolia Blu.*

Magnolia Blu was the name of the landscaping business Mama Rose started in her twenties and sold for a considerable amount in her early sixties. Her client list and the personal phone numbers that came along with it were Hollywood gold. Although similar looking to the dozens of ledgers Julia had boxed and stored in the attic, this book isn't filled with Magnolia Blu business orders, numbers, and accounting categories, but rather pages of journaling. Names leap out at her as she skims, and one in particular snags her breath. Liza Holloway.

Julia gapes at the bookcase. *Are you serious?* This couldn't be the diary. That was too easy. The book practically fell into her hands.

If Mama Rose were here, she'd make a quip about the law of attraction or shuffle her tarot deck to see what it all meant.

Julia and Mama Rose had been very close. She'd say that she knew everything about her grandmother. But the bold, provocative woman reflected in the few paragraphs Julia skims is not the same woman who raised her—a biscuit-scented, flower-loving, eccentrically dressed woman with an endless capacity to love.

She reads one particularly sordid entry and, eyes wide, slams the journal closed.

Jesus, Mary, and Joseph, Mama Rose.

Her skin flames from chest to forehead, and her eyes dart around the room as if Mama Rose might catch her reading her most private thoughts.

But Julia isn't going to read any more.

Okay, maybe a few pages, like a passage or two to find out how Mama Rose and Liza know each other. Then she'll stop. The diary is personal. It's none of her business. But it's tempting. By far more interesting than tonight's original plans of studying their bank accounts and revising their budgets.

She'll worry about their finances tomorrow.

Julia refills her wineglass, gets comfy on the unwieldy couch, and settles in to read.

CHAPTER 7

MAGNOLIA BLU

June 18, 1972

Five years ago, I left behind two things when I ran away from home in Arizona to a commune in southern Colorado with Sam: my name and my fiancé.

Ruby Rose Hope had been raised to be a good, obedient wife. She'd marry Benjamin Stromski, the freckle-faced boy next door who'd been admitted to Yale on scholarship and aspired to have a respectable career as an accountant. They'd have three children and raise them to be upstanding citizens. Ruby would be loving and supportive of her family. She'd be compliant and amenable toward her husband. In other words, she'd keep her opinions to herself and her sexual kinks . . . Well, she wouldn't have any.

That was the future my parents had planned for me.

I love my parents. But Blanche and Leonard Hope are the product of an obsolete generation and outdated mindset, and I am not, nor could I ever be, *that* Ruby Rose Hope. And much to my parents' disappointment, Benjie and I were not well suited.

Apparently, Sam and I weren't either. We only lasted five years.

Five years of sharing a bed, meals, weed, and partners. Life with Sam at the commune was filled with love and peace and pleasure until it wasn't. I'd left my home, my fiancé, and my name to find my true self separate from the person my parents had tried to mold me into, only to lose myself further.

Nothing had belonged to me in the commune. Everything was shared, including me.

So I took Sam's van—technically, it was my van too, because: communal ownership—and drove west. For five years I'd been dreaming of California, where I could freely express myself and love openly. Live by my rules. Five years and over a thousand miles later, I finally made it. Just me, my flute, and this journal that Sam found at a flea market. He thought the notebook's title, *Magnolia Blu*, was a more suitable name for me than Ruby Rose Hope.

Then, on my first day here, I met her: Elizabeth Holloway.

She blew into the Ralph's parking lot in her aquamarine convertible Mercedes and salon-colored platinum hair. I had heard movie stars shopped at this grocery store. Some were inside walking the aisles, pushing shiny carts, filling them with fancy foods. But I had no idea who this woman was as she hurried toward where I sat on the curb playing my flute with a small basket at my hip where several kind souls had parted ways with their coins. She wore tennis whites—a sleeveless knit shirt, pleated miniskirt, and sneakers just as bright—and an aura that beckoned the attention of anyone she rushed by on her way into the store.

She barely spared me a glance, yet like everyone else, I couldn't stop staring at her.

I couldn't stop thinking of her either while I waited for her to come back outside.

Everything about her was presented with intention—that was the impression she gave me. She was movie-screen ready, Hollywood dazzling, and Beverly Hills glamorous.

My parents would have loved her. They would have wished I'd grown into someone like her.

Maybe that was why I suddenly became obsessed with her. So many people had walked by me that day, ignoring me and my music, their faces unremarkable and their glances fleeting. But her . . . I had to know more.

Less than twenty minutes later, she flew out of the store, arms loaded with groceries. I watched her jog walk to her car. Then, mesmerized, I gathered my leather satchel, flute, and change, and followed her.

Fishing for her keys in her purse, she juggled the grocery bag, trying to jam the key into the slot to open the trunk. I could tell she was frustrated, and with one impatient heft of the groceries onto her hip, the bag tore. Tomatoes splatted at her feet. Soup cans rolled across the parking lot, and apples tucked under the car. The dozen eggs were lost on impact with the rear bumper.

She swore, throwing her keys onto the ground in a fit, and buried her face in her hands.

I ran to offer my help and collected what was salvageable. I could feel her watching me as I repacked the torn bag and gave her the keys.

Her sea-green eyes glistened when they met mine, and I wondered what had made her cry. It couldn't be just the damaged food. She accepted the keys with a glimmer of a smile and thanked me. As I put the groceries in the trunk, she said she knew I was the girl begging for cash at the storefront and that I probably wanted money in exchange for my assistance.

I needed cash for rent and a car. I couldn't live out of Sam's van forever. But I hadn't helped her expecting to be paid. I was only being kind. Although at her mention of money, my stupid eyes dropped right to her purse.

She muttered, "Figures as much," and her hand dived for her wallet. Right away I told her no. It didn't feel right taking money from her.

I scooped up the rose bouquet wilting at her feet. The plastic wrap crinkled as I inspected the dozen blooms. The petal edges had started to brown, and the stems were soft from too much water. They'd seen better days, but with a short trim at the base and a citric acid, sugar, and bleach blend in their water, the roses would perk right up.

I explained this to her, and she tilted her head, peering at me with fresh fascination. She asked if I was a gardener.

In a way, I told her. I was mostly self-taught from tending to the flower gardens at the commune. We'd grown an abundance of blooms that we bartered for rice and oats and other necessities. I was surprised she was even interested. I imagined from her perspective, and those of most of the people shopping here, I looked like nothing more than a hippie living off the land and freeloading off others, which wouldn't be an inaccurate assessment. But she listened to me as if I'd just revealed the secret to world peace.

Then out of the blue, she asked, "Would you join me for coffee?"

My rambling sputtered to a stop. I wasn't sure I'd heard her correctly.

"Coffee. You drink it?" she asked. The *L* script gold charm on her necklace shimmered in the sunlight.

I told her I drank coffee. But why the invite? She didn't know me. I also wasn't suitable company. My hair was greasy and clothes filthy. I hadn't washed my cutoffs and blouse in over a week, and I hadn't properly bathed since I'd left Colorado three days ago.

"I know you're hungry. I can hear your stomach." She tossed the flowers in with the groceries and slammed the trunk. "I also have a sneaking suspicion you're going to become a great friend."

That took me aback, and I warily asked what made her think so.

"I have a feeling about you. Call it women's intuition. A nose for smarts." She tapped her nostril. "Mine is very keen."

She got all that from looking at me and exchanging just a few words? I was doubtful. I also wasn't going to judge her. She was offering me coffee. There was a good chance food would be served along with it. She was right. I was hungry, and my stomach rumbled loudly.

I told her it would be a pleasure to join her for coffee.

"Wonderful." She thrust a hand at me. She had slender fingers, her nude nails filed into perfect half ovals. "I'm Elizabeth Holloway. Call me Liza. All my good friends do."

Her name resonated. I had the feeling I should know who she was, but I couldn't place her. I was also too intrigued by our exchange, too curious to find out exactly what she wanted of me. It had to be for more than a coffee date. People like her didn't pick up homeless strangers like me off the streets.

My rough palm clasped her delicate, smooth one. "Magnolia. But you can call me Mags. Everyone else does." Sam had. *Sure, Mags, whatever you want. Just kiss me, Mags. Suck me off, Mags. Now suck him off, Mags. Take a drag, Mags. Don't be a fucking drag, Mags. Wash my jeans, Mags. Get the fuck out of my van, Mags.*

She told me that I was too stunning to go by anything but Magnolia. "So that's what I'll call you."

I was shocked that she could see more potential in me than my parents ever could, despite all the grime, and felt something warm and delicious unfurled inside me. I felt a connection, to her and to this place, and was bangin' on my decision to move to California. It had been the right one.

"Come." Liza swung open the driver's door. "There's something I want to show you."

"What about coffee?" My stomach was growling. I hoped to bum a pastry off her or talk her into buying me a sandwich.

She told me that there was coffee where we were going and to trust her. Then she got into the car and revved the engine.

"You coming?" she tossed over her shoulder.

After the impulsive mistake I'd made running off with Sam, I was hesitant to ride off with another stranger. But Liza wasn't Sam, and my curiosity was greater than my hunger and my fear that I'd never find myself, or my place in life.

I spared Sam's van loaded with my meager belongings a fleeting look and left with Liza.

Saturday

CHAPTER 8

MATT

Awake with the sun, Matt calls Lenore first thing. He's told she isn't expected for another hour, so the attendant transfers him to her voice-mail box. Matt hangs up and calls back an hour later. She still hasn't arrived, so he waits an hour before giving her another try. He's informed she's in a meeting.

He impatiently tosses his phone onto the kitchen island. He learned at a young age to eat everything he's served, but he wants Elizabeth off his plate. He can't focus on his work.

He paces to the sliding glass wall and stands there, arms folded, staring outside. The sky is an ominous gray with the threat of thunderstorms. Rain is expected throughout the day. He rubs his eyes and yawns into his cupped palms. Up past two in the morning, he fell asleep at his desk. But he finished curating the *Road & Track* photos, whittling them down to ten, which he edited and sent to Dave for him to forward. He needs to start on the Ford photos. That will take several days and extra care since Ford's a new client.

He rubs the dull ache in his right temple. He already took an edible this morning and considers taking another when a memory sneaks up on him. He's on the deck of *Key to My Heart* with his dad and a few other men who chartered his dad's boat to deep-sea fish. His mom runs along the dock, waving for them to wait. She's wearing white shorts and a lime-green shirt faded from many washings. Her favorite because it brought out the green in her eyes.

"You forgot lunch," she said, breathless when she reached the boat. They were running late that morning, and in his rush to have the boat ready before his clients arrived, Joel had forgotten to pick up their order. "The deli called."

"You're a lifesaver, Aubs." Joel took the deli bags from her and handed them off to Matt. "Put these in the cooler, kiddo."

"Just a sec." His mom grabbed Matt's shoulders and before he could think *incoming*, she dropped ten kisses around his face. For as long as he could remember, she'd kiss him like that, starting at his forehead and circling from cheek to chin to cheek, ending on the tip of his nose. A kiss for each year. Every year he'd received one more kiss. Normally it didn't bother him. But his dad's clients were watching. "Mom, stop." He wiped his face when she let him go, scratching his nose and chin where her hair had tickled him.

She laughed, the faint freckles he could only see up close because she was always so tan crinkling on her nose. "Hurry up with helping your dad. I'll be waiting in the car."

"I know!" he griped, and took the deli bags to the cooler, but not before he saw her kiss his dad. On the mouth, with tongue, and in public. Gross. They always did that, embarrassing him. But now when Matt thinks back on it, he sees clearly they'd been so in love.

"Storm's coming in tonight. We'll only be out six hours or so." Joel patted her rear.

"Counting on it." One more kiss before she walked back up the dock, waving at friends on a neighboring boat.

Joel looked at his watch. "Time's up, Matt. I have to set off." He ruffled Matt's hair and gave him a high five, and Matt jogged after his mom, never suspecting it would be the last time he'd see his dad.

Gazing out the window at the dark clouds, Matt comes out of the memory feeling like he always does: awful. He can't imagine not feeling this way when he remembers his parents, his mom particularly, which is why he doesn't think about them.

Anytime someone brings them up in conversation, he shuts them down or changes the subject. Elizabeth might have been cold toward him for the eight years he lived with her, but there was one benefit to that. He didn't have to talk about his parents.

But memories of his mom always sneak up when he least expects them and leave him shaken. He can barely picture her face anymore, but he can still hear her laughter. Every once in a while, he'll catch the scents of jasmine and vanilla in the perfect balance that was his mom, and his chest will ache something fierce, overshadowing the constant throb in his head. Those headaches started when the nightmares did.

He had his first bad dream on his second night at his grandmother's. He jolted awake in a dark room that had yet to feel familiar with his heart pounding, gasping for air. In the dream, he'd been searching for his mom underwater. From the corners of his eyes, he'd see her hair, the flash of a pale arm. But each time he turned, there would be nothing. Just cold blackness.

He wiped away his tears with trembling hands, his haunted eyes darting for the sliver of dim light under the closed door. Without thought, he followed that light into the hallway, seeking reassurance as he would have done with his parents. The comfort of their arms chased away his fears.

He found his grandmother's door open a crack but lost his nerve when he saw her reading in bed. She was the last person who'd comfort him. When he arrived two days before and stood mutely shaking his head after she'd asked if he had at least tried to save his mom, she informed him he wasn't to speak to her unless spoken to.

He started to back away from her bedroom door, but the movement caught her attention. She lowered her book and called out. "What do you want?"

He gulped at the reproach in her tone and retreated.

"I asked you a question, Matthew."

"I . . . I had a bad dream." This was where his mom would throw back the covers and invite him into bed. She'd spoon his back and hug him while she hummed a lullaby. He'd feel safe in her arms and fall back to sleep.

"I miss my mom," he said before he could stop himself.

"And whose fault is that?" Her voice added pounds to the unbearable weight of misery he already carried.

"Mine," he mumbled.

"Speak up."

"Mine," he said more firmly, his conviction weaving into his bones.

"Best you remember that. Go back to bed."

"Yes, Grandmother Holloway." Matt fled to his room. He didn't fall back to sleep that night, not even with the light on. And it would be years before he could stomach sleeping in the dark. While the nightmares eventually ceased, the headaches stuck around.

The phone trills loudly, startling Matt. He lunges to answer, pulling himself together. "Matt Gatlin."

"Mr. Gatlin, hello. This is Lenore Pullen with Rosemont Assisted Living and Memory Care. I understand you've been trying to reach me."

Matt paces the room. "Yes. About Elizabeth Holloway, my grandmother. I got the boxes you guys sent. What's going on with her?"

"Have you spoken with Mrs. Holloway?"

"No." Nor does he want to. He'd prefer to coordinate the logistics without involving her. He grips the back of his neck. "I understand she's broke and you're evicting her in a few days. Her power of attorney is missing? What's up with that?"

There's a pause on her end. "How do you know this if you haven't spoken with her?"

His face scrunches up. Way to throw Julia under the bus. After last night's call he was already oh for two with her on first impressions.

He changes the subject. "Why is my grandmother there? Does she have dementia or something?"

"Tell you what, Mr. Gatlin. There's a lot we need to discuss. Mrs. Holloway has you listed as her secondary power of attorney. I have the paperwork right here. Is it possible you can come in and discuss this with your grandmother and me?"

"I'm in New Mexico."

"A video conference, then."

"Let me be frank. I leave for France on Thursday. I'm also on deadline for another project. So, no, I can't come in, and I don't have time to video conference and hash this out with you guys, especially with her. How about I wire money to cover her expenses until I get back, and then we can figure this out?"

"I wish it were that simple. Rosemont has a waiting list. We're at capacity, and we've already signed a contract with another party for her room. I don't have space available for her after the thirtieth. She has to be moved out. Trust me, I'd keep her with us if I could. I don't like evicting residents."

"You just kick them to the curb," he snaps.

"Again, Mr. Gatlin—"

"For Chrissake, call me Matt." Mr. Gatlin was his dad.

"Matt." Her tone implies she's calling on her patience. "I insist you speak with Mrs. Holloway. You have a lot to coordinate within the next few days."

"Fine, put her on," he says in a clipped tone, seeing no way out other than hanging up and abandoning his grandmother to her fate.

"One moment." Lenore puts him on hold only to get back on the line a minute later. "Well, this is an interesting development."

"Now what?"

"She won't speak with you—"

"Knew it."

"—over the phone. She will face-to-face. In person. Apparently, she has something important to discuss with you."

Why that conniving, manipulative . . . "Did she say what about?"

"Only that it has to do with your mother. I suggest you hurry, Matt. You'll want to get here before we 'kick her to the curb.'"

Matt pulls the phone from his ear and rages at the room.

Fuck, fuck, fuck.

What could she possibly have to tell him about his mom that she couldn't have shared with him years ago?

She's using his mom to goad him to California.

Of course she'd stoop that low. Of course he can't turn his back now.

He takes a breath.

He puts the phone back to his ear.

"Give me a sec." He puts Lenore on speaker and searches for flights. He can get a nonstop to Burbank, the only one today, departing in less than three hours. He books the flight as he speaks. "Tell her I'll be there this afternoon." He'll fly in, reserve the first affordable place he can find for her, arrange for someone to move her, and fly home. In and out within twenty-four hours, forty-eight hours tops.

"I'm pleased to hear that. It's good to know someone is looking out for her interests; otherwise I'd have to get the state involved to find her a guardian."

He grunts and goes to end the call when her next words stop him. "One more thing. Since it looks like you're taking over her affairs, you should know that she's been on suicide watch."

"Excuse me?"

"A month ago, she walked into traffic. She swears it was an accident, that she was distracted, but we've taken precautions. Witnesses report she was quite distraught before it happened."

Matt digests this news, seeing flashes of his mom.

"Can I let her know you're coming?" Lenore asks.

Matt blinks away the images. "Yeah . . . okay."

Lenore terminates the call before he can say goodbye.

CHAPTER 9

JULIA

Julia lugs her portable massage table through the halls at Rosemont, rushing to her first appointment. On Saturdays, she's on-site the entire day, and aside from the half-hour lunch break she allows herself, she's booked solid through this evening. Her wrists already ache thinking about the eighty-minute deep tissue ahead with Mr. Garrido, a wily curmudgeon of a man with a propensity for dropping his towel with a dramatic "Oopsies." She's not looking forward to him flashing his shriveled bits.

As much as her wrists need a day off along with a good Epsom salt soak, she doesn't see when she'll have the time today to figure out Mama Rose's living situation. At least not until late tonight. She needs to find an extra income stream fast or her grandmother will run out of funds within the next six months.

She shouldn't have gotten sucked into Mama Rose's diary last night. She was so exhausted she fell asleep on the lumpy couch in the middle of reading an entry when she should have been crunching numbers. Had she not let herself get sidetracked, she might have a better idea this morning on what to do. And she might not feel so stressed about it.

A hand grasps her arm. "Julia."

She swerves around with an annoyed snap. "What?" The table bangs into the wall, and her eyes bug when she sees Lenore. "Yikes. Sorry."

"I was calling for you." Lenore's startled brows dip below her glasses as she takes in Julia's load: folded massage table, overflowing canvas bag, the weight of her worries. Everything hangs on her shoulders.

"Sorry," Julia apologizes again. "My mind was elsewhere."

"I have something to show you. Come with me," she says gently instead and takes the canvas bag from Julia's shoulder.

"I'm late for an appointment." Mentally, physically, and emotionally drained from working twenty-one days straight without even a half day off, Julia doesn't want to tarry. Every minute is a minute where money can be earned. She isn't paid for her time here, but some clients tip her well.

"Who's your first?" Lenore asks.

"Mr. Garrido." She rubs the ache the strap left in her shoulder.

"He won't mind if you miss today. I'll slip him an extra drink ticket for tonight's happy hour," Lenore says with a wink. She turns toward her office, fully expecting Julia to follow, which she does reluctantly.

"Lean your table over there." Lenore points at the far wall and deposits Julia's bag on a chair.

Julia hesitates, wondering how long this will take, then unloads the table with a relieved sigh when Lenore presents her with a cup from Avid Coffee. "Is that a black rose latte?"

"Would I get you anything else?"

"How'd you know I needed one?" The single brewed cup she consumed at home this morning didn't have the quantity of caffeine she needs to get through today.

"I had a feeling. No offense, but you look a wreck."

"I fell asleep on the couch." She greedily sips the charcoal-infused brew.

"What I'm seeing here is more than one poor night's sleep." Lenore circles a hand in front of Julia's face.

"Thanks for the pep talk I didn't ask for." She gives Lenore a thumbs-up.

Lenore takes a sip of her own coffee and grabs a manila folder from her desk. "Let's sit outside. The weather's nice." It's a cloudless June morning. She opens the glass-paned door to the side garden and a private patio. Traffic is light, a gentle hum of white noise on the other side of the vine-covered concrete-block fence. A floral-scented breeze rustles the jacaranda leaves overhead. Lenore sits in a wrought iron chair. She drops the folder on the table.

"What's up?" Julia sits across from her, getting straight to business. Time's a-ticking. She's more anxious this morning than usual.

"How are you holding up?" Lenore starts.

Julia sends her a look that says she's two inches from hitting a wall.

"Have you given thought to what we discussed yesterday? Any plans?"

"No. I fell asleep. Couch, remember?"

"I have an idea, and don't shoot me for suggesting this. Have you considered locating your mom?"

Julia leans back, hands up. "No, not an option."

"Jules—"

"Don't go there, Lenore. You know how I feel about her." Julia considers Lenore a friend, about the only one she has these days. A year ago, after Mama Rose broke her hip and had been bedridden for a month, Lenore took Julia to dinner. Over drinks, Julia opened up about her relationship with Mama Rose, explaining why her grandmother was more of a mother to her than her own mother. Lea Hope gave up her parental rights when Julia was three. Mama Rose raised her on her own since Julia's grandfather Benjie had passed before she was born. Not once during the rest of Julia's childhood or adult life has she had contact with the woman who birthed her.

She pulls the necklace Mama Rose gifted her on her thirteenth birthday out from her shirt and zips the fourteen-karat gold rose charm along its chain.

"Ruby Rose is your mom's mother. People change," Lenore says.

"If she has, she would have reached out by now."

"There might be a viable reason she hasn't, which could change if she knows your grandmother doesn't have much longer."

A fist squeezes Julia's heart. She knows Mama Rose's time is limited. She may have months left, but she could also have years. One never knows. Alzheimer's patients are always surprising their doctors. Their life span can be anywhere from five to twenty-five years after diagnosis.

But she and Mama Rose have never had to rely on anyone but each other, and Julia isn't going to start now, especially with the woman who abandoned her on her grandmother's doorstep.

"I don't know if she's financially able to help, or if she's even alive. She was homeless when she left me with my grandmother."

That's only partly true. Julia has looked her up over the years and hates herself each time. Lea is alive and thriving. She just didn't want Julia. And Julia doesn't want to share what she's learned about her mother with anyone. It only depresses her. Easier and less complicated to pretend she doesn't exist.

"I have another suggestion, then." Lenore pushes the manila folder across the table. "Move your grandmother to a more affordable facility, one where Medicare covers a portion if not all the costs."

Dread tumbles in her stomach. "You're evicting her already?"

"Not yet, no. And I don't want us to get to that point, which is why I put this together for you."

"But this is where Mama Rose wants to be, where I promised to keep her."

"I get that, I do. But you're barely staying afloat, Jules. You've sacrificed everything. What more of yourself can you give up?"

Everything, if it means Mama Rose lives out her remaining days here. She's the only person in Julia's life who's loved her consistently and genuinely, who didn't abandon her. Whether Mama Rose is lucid or not, Julia's not going to disregard her grandmother's wishes in her last hour. Mama Rose might not be aware if Julia breaks her promise, but Julia will be. She couldn't live with herself.

Lenore opens the folder to a stack of brochures and marketing slicks. She fans them across the table. "They're good centers, all with memory care units. They're nearby so you don't have to drive far, and they're more affordable than Rosemont."

Julia doesn't touch the brochures. "I don't want to move her," she says, glum.

"I know. Promise you'll think on it, though. Make some calls. I'm sure you'll find a lovely place for Ruby Rose." Lenore neatly stacks the brochures and hands over the folder.

Julia stands, holding the folder like she wants to burn it. "I should, ah . . . I should go."

"I'm here if you want to talk," Lenore offers.

"Appreciate that." But the thought of even considering moving Mama Rose, let alone discussing it with Lenore or making calls, makes her queasy. It's not right, not for her grandmother.

She turns to leave only to turn right back when she remembers. She snaps her fingers. Liza.

"Matt Gatlin finally called yesterday, Liza's grandson."

Surprise brightens Lenore's face. "How did you know?"

"I covered for Shelly when she was on break. I took his call."

"You're the one he spoke with," she says with a head tilt.

"Briefly." Julia wonders at Lenore's hint of accusation. What did Matt say to her?

Oh dear.

She shouldn't have mentioned Liza was broke. She didn't have a right to share that information. Liza had told her in confidence.

"What did you two discuss?" Lenore collects their empty cups, and Julia follows her back into the office.

"He asked for you first, but when he couldn't reach you, he called back asking for me. I'm sorry I didn't mention it earlier—you'd already left. He wants to cover her fees, at least for the next month until he can get out here."

"I know. I spoke with him this morning." She drops the cups in the trash and sits at her desk. "Unfortunately, Liza's room has already been reassigned. Matt's flying in this afternoon."

"He's moving her?" Julia thinks of what she read in Mama Rose's diary, the questions she wants to ask Liza before she loses the chance.

"That's yet to be seen. Actually . . ." Lenore points a pen at the folder in Julia's hand. "If you're around later, show him those. Since you've already got a dialogue going, perhaps you can look around together, cover more ground. He seems to be in a bit of a rush."

Julia taps the folder against her thigh. "Sure, I'll mention that to him."

Then she remembers the jerk he was on the phone. Better to just give him the folder and let him have at it. She won't be needing it.

CHAPTER 10

MATT

Matt glares at the departures screen as a heavy curtain of rain drenches the airport. Lightning flashes and thunder rumbles, shaking the building. Visibility is shit. All flights have been delayed or canceled, including his. Even if he catches a later flight with a connection in Phoenix or Las Vegas, depending on the delay, he won't get into Burbank until late tonight.

His head pounds furiously at this massive inconvenience.

He searches for flights on his app. He could fly out tomorrow, which would get him to Rosemont after 4:00 p.m., but he loses a day in the process.

Or—he pulls up a map—he could drive. It's twelve hours to Pasadena. Eleven or less given how he drives. He'd arrive by midnight, crash at a hotel, and be at Rosemont first thing in the morning, giving him and Elizabeth the entire day to coordinate her affairs and—he can't believe he's thinking this—talk about his mom. And what's up with appointing him as her secondary? Barring hiccups, he could be back in Santa Fe by midnight Monday. He'd have all Tuesday to work on the Ford assignment.

That's a shit ton of driving and miles he doesn't need to put on his car. A lot of hours he'd be behind the wheel instead of editing photos. But he's impatient and sees only one option.

Matt ditches the airport and heads west on I-40. The wipers chase sheets of rain across the windshield, but if his career as a professional automobile photographer and his frenetic love of road racing have taught him anything, it's how to handle himself behind the wheel in extreme driving conditions. He isn't stupid, but he rarely drives within the speed limit.

As his tires chew up and spit out the miles, Matt searches the backpack in the passenger seat for the edibles that would have been left behind had he flown. He pops one to quell the headache that's been throbbing since yesterday. He then makes a call to Lenore to update her on the change of plans. He'll be at Rosemont first thing tomorrow and wants to meet. But when the call goes to her voicemail, he hangs up and rings Julia instead. He needs to tell someone that he's on the way.

"Matt," Julia answers in a flat tone. She doesn't sound pleased to hear from him. It throws him off.

"Hey, uh, hi. About last night," is all he can get out before she interrupts.

"Worst phrase ever to start a conversation. But if we're hashing this out, so far you've hung up on me and tried to pick a fight. What's next? Are you going to dump me before we get together?" Her voice is soaked in sarcasm. He doesn't know why, but he laughs. "That wasn't meant to be funny," she says, dryly. "And now I feel stupid because you're probably married with kids."

"Not married and no kids. It's just . . ." He laughs some more. "This whole situation is absurd."

"I assume you're talking about Liza and what an inconvenience your grandmother is to you. Well, you aren't the only one responsible for an elderly relative. The world doesn't revolve around you and your dislike for voicemail and filial responsibility."

"Whoa." He clues in that there's more going on than her irritation with him. "Everything okay?"

A long exhale. "It's been a day."

He glances at the dash clock. "It's just after noon."

"That's all?" Her laugh is hollow. "Seems later."

"Want to talk about it? I'm driving. I'm a captive audience." He'd rather focus on her problems than his own.

"With you?" She laughs. "I'm sort of busy right now." A reflective pause or a move to get off the phone, he can't tell. "I hear you're coming here."

"Ah, so you already know I'm on my way." He closes the distance on an eighteen-wheeler, his wipers barely keeping up with the water its rear tires dump on his windshield. He switches lanes to pass.

"Lenore told me this morning. Look—" She sighs. "Sorry I seem short, but if it helps any, I sort of get what you're going through. My grandmother's fees increased. I don't want to move her, but if I can't cover her expenses, I'll have to, even though I promised her I'd never take her out of Rosemont. And why am I telling you this? I don't know you."

"I'm thirty, single, and live alone in Santa Fe. I like photography, fast cars, and southwestern tacos. I identify as a man, prefer to date women, and failed the only marathon I ever ran. Strained my Achilles. I love the water, but you'll never catch me in a boat or swimming in the open ocean."

Why, for the love of God, did he tell her that?

"How's that for starters?" he says, shaking his head at himself.

"Is that your Tinder bio?"

"I don't do dating apps," he says, balking. Relationships should evolve organically. He also prefers solitude to company, and singlehood to coupledom. He's not about to unload his baggage on anyone, let alone a woman looking for love. "What about you?"

"What about me?"

"I don't know you either." Matt chews on his bottom lip, waiting for her to share something. Keeps him from dwelling on who's waiting for him at his destination. "Not much of a talker?" he asks when she doesn't offer up anything.

"What are we doing? What is this?" she asks.

He has no clue. What he does know is she's kind of fun to talk with. He picks a safer subject. "Your grandmother, she's at Rosemont?"

"Yes, three years now. I volunteer here as a massage therapist to keep the cost down. They can't honor that anymore, and I'm not sure what I'm going to do."

"Are you close with her?"

"About as close as I can be with someone who doesn't remember who I am. She has Alzheimer's." She doesn't disguise her love for her grandmother, or her pain. Matt only wishes Elizabeth had forgotten about him.

"That must be tough. I'm assuming you guys were close?"

"You've no idea. She raised me. Tell you what, Matt: You seem to regret how our last two conversations went. I'm going to do you a solid out of the goodness of my heart."

"Is that sarcasm?"

"Take it as you see fit. Lenore gave me brochures to a few assisted living facilities. I guess I should make some calls, plan for a worst-case scenario. If you're interested, I can pass along what I find out. Save you some time when you get here."

"If I'm interested? That—wow. That would be huge, thank you. One problem—" He starts to explain he won't be able to meet until tomorrow morning since he's driving instead of flying, but a wave of dizziness tilts the horizon sideways. He eases his foot off the accelerator and slows the Porsche to the speed limit. He blinks hard to regain focus. "Whoa, that was weird."

"What was?"

"Nothing." He frowns. Whatever just happened passed. "Julia, the weather here is crap. My flight was canceled. I'm driving instead."

"From New Mexico?"

"Yeah."

"That's a long drive."

"I don't expect to be in Pasadena until midnight. Can we meet tomorrow? Can I buy you lunch, or breakfast? I like coffee. You like coffee?" He realizes as he asks that he doesn't know what she looks like. He hasn't even tried to picture her or google her. She could be decades older than him, or much younger. And why the hell is his brain taking him on this trip? Why does he care?

"I like coffee. And I'm here all day tomorrow. I'll make some calls today. Not sure I can set up tours. Tomorrow's Sunday. But I'll try."

Like hell he's going to spend time touring facilities. He'll go with whichever one Julia recommends. Buoyant with gratitude, he grins. She just saved him a fuckload of time and hassle.

"Thank you, Julia. I really appreciate it."

The rain lets up to a drizzle. He guns the car to make up time.

"Can I share something with you? Do you have a moment?" she asks.

"Shoot." He's driving across three states. He's got nothing but time.

"Did you know our grandmothers knew each other when they were younger? They met in seventy-two, and I think they were friends."

"Really?" He's about to ask why anyone would want to be friends with Elizabeth when his vision fuzzes along the edges. He squeezes his eyes shut and opens them. The sky is now utterly blue, not a cloud in sight. As if the storm evaporated in a snap. Poof. Gone. Everything is dry: the road, the dirt, his car. He leans over the steering wheel and peers upward. It's so bright outside it burns. "Weird," he murmurs to himself.

"Right? Small world. Liza's been here for a year and she never mentioned anything. I mean, I suspected, and there were signs when I think back on it, but it wasn't until I read Mama Rose's diary—oh, gosh. You didn't hear that from me. Don't mention it to either of them when you get here. I feel guilty enough for reading it."

"No worries. I've got you covered." He takes a right off the freeway and coasts a quarter mile until the shoulder's wide enough to pull off. He eases to a stop.

"I plan to tell her. I have so many questions for her and Liza. But I worry Mama Rose won't remember she asked for the diary. And Liza, I doubt she'll even talk to me. She's never been forthcoming about anything unless she's pressed. It took forever to get her to admit you're her grandson when I asked her. Maybe that's why I'm telling you. I'm worried they won't talk about it, and I need to discuss it."

"Then tell me everything. Where did they meet?" He puts the car in Park, not particularly interested in anything that has to do with Elizabeth. He just wants to keep Julia talking. Resting his forehead on the steering wheel, he breathes through the rising nausea. What's going on with him?

Keep talking, he silently begs. He doesn't know what's come over him, but her voice is calming. He decides he'll wait here and let this run its course and then get back on the road.

"Hollywood, in a Ralph's parking lot of all places." She tells him an outlandish story about a young Elizabeth inviting Ruby Rose, a fresh-off-the-commune early twentysomething-or-other, to her home after a chance meeting over a torn bag of groceries.

All the while, Matt is tripping. She's talking about his grandmother, but the woman Julia is describing doesn't match up with the woman he knew. That woman hadn't been generous or inviting, not with him.

Julia's voice lulls him into a near trance. He recalls she mentioned she's a massage therapist, and his mind drifts in an inappropriate direction. He pictures Julia's hands, and then he pictures her hands on him, as appeasing as her voice. They release taut muscles, harden other parts. A delicious ache forms below his belt, and a groan builds in his throat.

Then he remembers where he is and who he's speaking with. A practical stranger.

Get a hold of yourself, man.

He lifts his head and startles at the sight before him. There's a woman outside sitting on a large hard-sided suitcase, the old kind without wheels. A smaller case covered in peeling bumper stickers rests at her feet. Her sheer paisley blouse flutters on her arms. Her face is tilted toward the sun, soaking up its warmth. Long wheat tresses of the silkiest hair he's seen reach her waist.

Who is she and where did she come from?

Aside from the highway, the area is desolate, nothing but barren land for miles.

Slowly, she turns her head and looks at him. Then she smiles. Holy—

Matt sucks in a sharp breath. She's gorgeous. Like drop dead. Flowing hair and pixie eyes. All the feels hit him with force, and his chest hollows on a powerful exhale.

Gaze locked with his, she approaches the car. Through her shirt, Matt can make out her dark areolae. Her tongue glides along her bottom lip suggestively and sends an arrow of heat to his groin.

He tracks her to the passenger side. He feels compelled to open the door, invite her along for a ride. Uncover her secrets. Undress her.

What is his problem?

The logical side of him tells him she's an illusion. She's not real.

But his curious side? The photographer who wants to lay bare his subjects? That guy opens the window.

She folds her arms on the door and offers a ravishing smile, revealing a small gap between her two front teeth. Through the opening of her shirt, he sees the sharp peaks of her breasts, the flat plane of her stomach.

"Hey, stranger." Her voice is buttery soft.

"Hey." He frowns. "Do I know you?" He feels like he does.

Skin puckers between her brows. "You don't remember me?"

He wants to say yes. He has a feeling this isn't the first time he's seen her. He knows this woman. But the origins of his feelings are elusive when he attempts to grasp them.

"I'm sorry. I don't remember your name."

She clicks her tongue on the roof of her mouth. Then her smile turns full wattage.

"Baby, it's Magnolia Blu."

CHAPTER 11

MAGNOLIA BLU

June 18, 1972 (continued)

Elizabeth Holloway drove fast. She peppered me with questions, yelling over the roar of the wind as we shot through traffic. She wanted to know my story and knew without asking that I had run away. She just didn't know if I ran away from home or the law. Her finger was on my family. She didn't think I'd be busking with a flute if I were hiding from the authorities. I'd just steal what I needed and continue to run.

Her high ponytail whipped in circles, and my eyes watered as I clung on. I'd never been in a convertible, and certainly never ridden in one while driving that fast within city limits. My father obeyed every traffic law because it was the law. Sam stuck to the speed limits because he didn't have a license and didn't want to risk getting pulled over.

I gasped when she cut off a Buick and took a sharp right. "Do you always drive like this?"

We flew up into the hills, winding through neighborhoods with grand homes and towering security gates. She pushed again for me to answer her question, refusing to answer mine. Then she laughed, telling me she got me. "You're here because of a man. Fucking men, they all suck."

I asked if that included her husband. It was impossible not to notice the enormous diamond on her left ring finger.

With a dry laugh, she said her husband was definitely included. "Ask me again tomorrow, and I'll tell you all's forgiven and I'm head over heels again." That was the thing about Matty, she explained. You couldn't help but love him. She warned me not to believe a word of what I'd read about him in the tabloids.

I told her I didn't read tabloids. They're trash. Nothing in them is true.

"There's always a little truth in everything." The smile that touched her pink-stained lips when she said that didn't reach her eyes. Unwittingly, I felt sorry for her. The feeling sort of crept up on me. I found myself wanting to know more. What was her story? I decided to volunteer a little of mine. I told her I'd run away for three reasons—family, men, and the law. I was driving a stolen vehicle. But I doubted Sam had reported it missing given his aversion to authority.

Liza told me I was radical and swerved into a circular drive. The sleek convertible came to an abrupt stop in front of a sprawling two-story split-level house.

"Where are we?" It was not a coffee shop.

"Home." With the grace of a ballerina, she swung her legs from the car and slammed the door. I asked about coffee, to which she replied that there was coffee inside. "Trust me, darling. You'll want to see this." Adam would take care of the groceries if I would just come along with her, she told me.

She led me across polished marble floors and plush cream carpeting, past walls covered in soft blue damask, and under crystal chandeliers that shimmered in the afternoon sunlight. We reached a wall of sliding glass that opened to the backyard and the most luscious private garden I'd ever seen. It burst with flora and fauna.

Compared to the abundant greenery in this yard, the commune's gardens were haphazard plots of weeds and wildflowers. Liza's covered at least an acre. Numerous rose varietals, pruned hedges, and vines edged a lawn that plunged down a slope, where I barely made out a small white structure hidden under a blanket of pink climbing roses. The yard was overgrown, and parts appeared neglected, but that didn't detract from its stunning beauty.

"This is yours?"

"Down to every last petal." The garden had belonged to her mother. She'd passed when Liza was young, and her father didn't have a green thumb. Liza had taken it upon herself when she was a teenager to bring the garden back to its former glory, even expanding upon it until she had to hire a full-time gardener. "Reuben, unfortunately, has retired."

"Your husband? I thought his name was Matty."

"Reuben was my gardener, silly."

"Then who's Adam?"

"My butler. I'll introduce you. You'll adore him as much as I do."

Adam isn't the only staff on-site. He works during the days, and Liza's housekeeper, Sally, lives here full time. Her room is on the far side of the house off the kitchen.

"Don't look so confused." Liza tittered. "You'll get them straight soon enough. Now tell me about that van of yours, the one in the parking lot."

She could tell that was mine?

"You've been living in it, haven't you?"

My teeth scraped over my bottom lip. I nodded, looking at my shoes. It shamed me I couldn't afford my own place. I hadn't thought that far ahead when I'd left Sam.

Liza clapped once. "Goodness, this is perfect. Come." She grasped my hand and drew me with her down the sloped lawn to a gravel path. Trellises heavy with blooms arched overhead. The garden breathed with the hum of bees. She took me to the little house in the far corner of the yard and announced that at back I'd find a shed with Reuben's tools. It was well stocked, but if I needed anything, I was to let Adam know first thing. He'd call in an order at the nursery and I would have it in a jiff.

"And this side . . ." She led me around to the front, which faced the big house. There was a large square window and red dutch door. The tiny flagstone patio had a small teak table with two accompanying chairs. A large clay pot overflowing with bluebonnets squatted proudly beside the doormat. She told me that inside was a studio. It got the best morning light and had a lovely garden view. I would love it.

Then she opened the dutch door with a flourish and stopped. The color leaked from her cheeks.

"Liza?" I peered inside the studio. It was small, with a double bed along one wall, a closet on the other, the door removed and replaced with a curtain of yellow and orange beads. The only other pieces of furniture were a dresser and table, their tops crowded with infant supplies. Clothes with their tags still on, shoes in their boxes, unused bottles, and unboxed toys. The parts to an unassembled crib leaned against a chair.

Liza zipped her *L* charm along its chain. "I forgot these were here."

"Reuben didn't live here?"

She shook her head.

My breath left me as the meaning of what I saw sank in. I told her we didn't have to go inside. Whatever she wanted to show me could wait. But she flapped her hands, marching into the studio with purpose, and announced that she would have the room cleaned up in no time. Adam would have it done before he left for the day.

By this point, I was thoroughly confused. I didn't understand why she was showing me all this. "What does this have to do with me?"

"You know plants, and my gardener quit on me."

"I'm sorry . . . I still don't understand."

"Catch up, Magnolia." She snapped her fingers twice near my face. "I need a gardener and you need a job. You also need a place to live. I'm giving you both. Keep my yard in better shape than Mrs. Tillman's down the road and I'll let you stay rent-free."

I was speechless. Her offer was too good to be true. It eliminated so many hurdles I faced in LA. But she tucked a hand on her hip and warned me it wasn't a small job I'd be taking on. I'd have to work hard and full time, even some weekends. That didn't worry me. I'm no stranger to hard work. Still, I was reluctant. How could she trust me? We'd just met. Was her husband all right with this arrangement? This had to be his house too.

"Bosh." She waved a hand. "After what Matty's been up to, that man will have to grovel at my feet to get back into my good graces. He'll be fine with this. He probably won't even notice you." Her eyes dimmed, and her mind seemed to wander toward the big house. Then she blinked, and she was back in the room with me. "Besides, he's on location until next week. We'll worry about him later."

"On location?"

"Filming."

Now I blinked, the dots connecting between her remark about her husband being in the tabloids and for me not to believe what I'd read. "He's a movie star."

"Where have you been, darling? My husband's Matthew Holloway. Why do you think we were speeding? The paparazzi love him and, in turn, love to harass me. We were being followed."

"I didn't know."

"That's why I adore you. You're a breath of fresh air, and you're my little discovery. What do you say? Come work for me?"

Usually, my curiosity gets me into trouble, and acting impulsively never ends well for me. Liza offered me a job, a place to live, and her friendship. I would be insane not to accept, and I can't see what could possibly go wrong.

I can only see bright horizons ahead. A future that might make my parents proud.

I accepted Liza's offer.

CHAPTER 12

JULIA

Julia spent almost the entirety of her lunch break on the phone with Matt. Shocking given how rude he was on their previous calls. But the empath in her couldn't turn her back on him any more than she could disregard a client's inflamed tendon. If she were to hazard a guess, Matt doesn't like talking about his relationship with Liza, given he always turned the conversation back on her. But once they got to talking about their grandmothers' relationship and guessing at what could have happened between them, conversation flowed. She was reluctant to end their chat, caught up as she was telling the story of how their grandmothers had met. Mama Rose never told her she'd once gone by the name of Magnolia Blu. Julia always believed that was just the name of her business, not that she'd named the business after herself.

Of course, Julia didn't leave herself time to call the facilities in Lenore's folder. Not that she wants to. She doesn't intend to move Mama Rose. She shouldn't have offered to pass along the information to Matt. Now she feels obligated to do the research.

Julia glances at her phone. She has just enough time to swing by Mama Rose's room before her next appointment.

She lugs the unwieldy massage table and clunky shoulder bag through Rosemont's halls. She leaves both outside her grandmother's door, tucking the Magnolia Blu diary into her scrub top, the journal just slim enough to fit in the front pocket.

Dressed in a powder-blue velour tracksuit and slippers, Mama Rose shuffles toward Julia as soon as she enters the room.

"Thank goodness you came. Have you seen my hand trowel? I've looked everywhere."

"Your trowel?" Julia frowns, taking in the room. It's a scattered mess. The blankets are back on the floor and the sheets torn off her bed. She's even emptied the drawers. Julia will have to buzz the staff. She doesn't have time to help straighten.

"Yes, my trowel and gardening gloves. Hurry, please find them. They're doing it wrong." Mama Rose wrings her weathered hands, glancing toward the window.

"Who's doing what wrong?" Julia can't tell if something in the present is bothering her or if her grandmother is stuck in an old memory, which has been happening more frequently. Mama Rose often relives moments from her past, getting lost in time.

The first time Julia recalls this happening was right before she and Lenore had a serious discussion about moving her grandmother from the assisted living side of the facility to the memory care unit. Mama Rose had woken thinking it was 1978 and wandered through Rosemont's parking lot searching for the truck she used for her landscaping jobs. When she couldn't find it, she trekked through a nearby neighborhood. A kind soul noticed her confusion, luckily guessed where Mama Rose had ventured from, and walked Julia's grandmother back to Rosemont.

"Out there, look." Mama Rose grasps Julia's hand and leads her to the window. She points outside. Two men in khaki pants and olive polo shirts tend to Rosemont's gardens, planting shrubs, doing their jobs.

"Everything looks fine to me," Julia says.

"They aren't loosening the root balls," Mama Rose argues. "They aren't adding enough fertilized soil in the holes. The holes are too small. Those plants won't survive one season." Agitated, her voice pitches higher. "Take me outside. I'll show them the right way."

"I don't have time, Mama Rose. I have an appointment in a few minutes. Can we visit the garden later?"

"It'll be too late," she cries. She erratically rubs her sweatshirt collar, her gaze bouncing around the room, landing on the wall with the door to the hallway.

She zips across the room toward the door that blends into the wall, but Julia beats her to it. Even though a code is needed to exit the room, Julia blocks the door. "I'll tell one of the staff to talk with the gardeners; is that all right?"

"I guess." Mama Rose's faded eyes swing back to the window.

"Mama Rose," Julia begins. She feels pressed for time but doesn't want to leave her grandmother while she's flustered, or with her room in disarray. Her grandmother could trip and injure herself. She buzzes for an attendant. Meanwhile, Julia shows her the diary. "Look what I found."

Mama Rose barely glances at the journal, too fixated on the men working outside. "That's not mine."

Julia doesn't bother trying to convince her grandmother otherwise. It's pointless with her memory lapses. To keep her distracted until assistance arrives, she talks about the journal instead. "I hope you don't mind, but I read some of it. I wanted to be sure this is what you were looking for."

"I wasn't looking for anything. Except my trowel." She harrumphs and limps back to the window. "And my gloves. Why aren't you looking for them?"

"I don't think you'll find them here. But this . . ." Julia opens the journal to the first entry. "Is the Liza Holloway you mention here the same one who lives here?" Of all the assisted living facilities in the Los Angeles area, it can't be a coincidence Liza ended up at Rosemont. Wouldn't she have found a place near her Beverly Hills neighborhood?

After spending the morning thinking about what she'd read, and again after sharing that with Matt, Julia had an epiphany of sorts. Has Mama Rose finally realized who the woman badgering her in the common room is? Is Liza the reason her grandmother asked for the diary?

"Liza Holloway," Mama Rose repeats in a distracted mumble. Her mouth continues moving without sound, chewing on the name. She shakes her head. "I don't know a Liza."

"But you do. You see her every day when we visit the garden."

"I'm pretty sure I don't. Now . . . now . . . m-m-miss." She struggles to remember Julia's name, which only aggravates the ache in Julia's chest and Mama Rose's impatience.

"Please go talk to someone who can help me." Mama Rose shoos her away. "They just planted another shrub, and they did it wrong. They have to fix it or the plants will die. Go on, get. Bring back someone who'll do something other than just stand there like you are. They should fire you."

Julia backs up toward the door, her chest tight and eyes burning. Why does she subject herself to her grandmother's torment?

Because one day soon, Mama Rose will be gone, and you'll be alone, without any family.

She reminds herself why she must treasure every moment with her grandmother. The good moments, and the ugly.

A knock comes at the door, and the assistant caretaker pokes her head in. "Oh dear." Kellie takes in Mama Rose's room with wide eyes. "Ruby Rose, what happened here?"

"She's looking for a trowel and gloves," Julia says.

"That's new."

"Thanks for coming. I have to get to an appointment. Watch out, she's a little agitated."

"You go. I'll take care of her." Kellie enters the room with a sweet smile. "Ruby, help me clean up. Maybe we'll find your gloves and trowel when we pick up this mess."

"All right." Mama Rose moves a book from her bed to the nightstand.

Julia slips out unnoticed. She returns the diary to her bag and hefts the massage table onto her shoulder. Lenore's program director rushes down the hallway. Julia stops him. "If you go outside, tell the gardeners they need to dig larger holes for the shrubs they're planting."

"Okayyyyy," Paul says, walking backward with a frown at her odd request before he hurries off.

Julia heads in the opposite direction for her appointment with Mrs. Blumstein.

CHAPTER 13

MATT

Magnolia Blu.

"That's an interesting name," Matt says to the mysterious woman leaning into his car. "I think I would have remembered you." Maybe they met overseas on one of his assignments. Maybe she's posed for him before. He's worked with some incredibly beautiful models on his shoots. She's certainly gorgeous enough with her fresh-faced, nostalgic beauty: trimmed eyebrows brushed and tamed, naked lashes, and just a hint of pigment on her lips.

He has the urge to kiss those lips.

He clears his throat, looking anywhere but her mouth or down her shirt. "Sorry. Can't place you."

Those full pink lips turn downward into a pout before they hug the end of a joint. Her cheeks hollow as she draws in the spicy smoke and slowly exhales into his car. The smoke idly reaches him. She notices him eyeballing the joint. "Want a hit?"

He doesn't have to think on his answer. "Yeah."

He cuts the engine and joins her outside. She leans on his car, smiling as he takes the hand-rolled cigarette and inhales a long drag. Smoke fills his lungs, curls into his nose. He admires her through the haze. Teeth scrape over her bottom lip as she watches him.

She's a tease. If she offers, he might—just might—be all in.

He holds on to the smoke for a couple of beats. It's good, damn good. With a steady exhale, he leans a hip against his car. Taut muscles loosen as the pot works through his system. He's already feeling the effects. He doesn't give a fuck they're both leaning on his Porsche.

"This is some good shit. Where'd you get it?" He passes her the roll.

"A friend." She inches closer until he can feel the warmth of her, smell the earthy notes on her breath.

"Your friend nearby?" He wants to know where he can pick up a few buds like this of his own. The weed's doing wonders for his migraine. He barely feels it now. He's hardly feeling anything but the desire to unravel this mystery woman.

Magnolia takes a hit. "Not sure where Sam is. Haven't seen him in some time."

"Who's Sam?"

"Somebody I used to know."

They pass the joint back and forth. He remarks on the weird weather pattern, the lack of cars. She asks him where he's headed.

"California."

"What's in California?"

"Nothing of import." His mouth pulls to the side. He toes the gravel. "That's not true. My grandmother. I need to move her into a new home."

"That sounds important."

"Yeah, well, she somehow ended up broke with me listed as the secondary power of attorney," he says, then surprises himself when he goes on to explain, "Thing is, we're not tight. Never been. She doesn't like me." He takes one long drag and lifts his gaze to the horizon. "Doesn't make sense why she'd want my help or think I'd give it," he muses, recalling what Lenore told him. Elizabeth has something important to share about his mom. She knew how to get him to come. *Rabbit, meet carrot.*

"Maybe she's sorry you two aren't close. Maybe she wants to change that."

Matt scoffs. "What she wants is to make me miserable," he gathers, because she's dredging up a past he's avoided. She has to know the mere mention of his mom just reminds him that he failed her.

"I wouldn't jump to conclusions if I were you. Give her a chance, hear her out."

Matt grunts. Easier said than done.

Magnolia snuffs out the butt with the heel of her Birkenstock slides. She takes his hand and traces a line on his palm. A jolt of heat runs up his arm.

"Whoa." That was something.

"You feel it too?" Her fingernail traces a vein along his forearm, inside his elbow, and over his bicep to his shirt sleeve. She grazes her lips over his knuckles. Desire washes over him at the damp press of her mouth.

"You're friendly." He watches her like a pivotal scene in a movie, unmoving, breath held, unable to look away. He's bewitched and transfixed.

"You know me, Matty."

"How do you know my name?" He removes his hand and steps back, a little creeped out. Aside from the fact he didn't tell her his name, the only person to ever call him Matty was his mom.

But he can't convince himself to abandon her on this road, and he's feeling chill, in no rush to leave. He goes along with Magnolia's charade, curiosity leading him like a dog on a leash.

He nods in the direction of her vintage luggage. "Where'd you come from?"

"Everywhere and nowhere."

That, he understands. There were a few years after he left Elizabeth that he drifted from state to state before he landed in New York and met Dave.

"Where are you headed?"

"Home."

She's back to touching him. Her fingertips draw invisible circles on his chest, inching downward to his abs with each loop. Skin and muscle tighten under his tee. He exhales roughly, his body responding. What is she doing to him?

He retreats another step. Though he can't stop looking at her mouth, the silhouette of her breasts through the blouse, and he hears himself asking, "Can I give you a lift?"

If she tells him home is in Canada, he knows he'll drive her there.

"Yes." Her agreement is the sweet taste of sugar to his ears.

Matt puts aside his promise to Lenore and his responsibility toward Elizabeth. He pushes tomorrow morning's coffee date with Julia to the back of his mind. Grinning widely, stupidly, he retrieves Magnolia's luggage with an enthusiasm he doesn't recognize.

Magnolia settles comfortably into the passenger seat with a giggle when he opens the door for her, and she purrs with delight at the leather seats and dash. Her face is a mixture of wonder and innocent bemusement that has him smiling even more.

"Where to?" He settles beside her.

"You don't mind?" she asks. "It's a bit of a drive."

"No prob. Wherever you need to go."

"All right." She points southwest. "That way."

He starts the engine and everything lights up: the dash, the music, her face.

She pushes back into the seat. "Far out."

"You are so . . . unique." He laughs and revs the engine.

Her eyes go moon size. "What is that?" she asks of the noise.

"Five hundred and two horsepower and three hundred forty-six pounds per feet of torque."

She stares at him as if he's speaking a foreign language.

"She's really fast and her engine's magical."

"I've never heard anything like it." Magnolia admires the components on the dash. "I've never seen anything like this. It's like a spaceship." She strokes the leather seat.

He just shakes his head, amused. She's more stoned than he realized. "Fasten your belt."

"My what?" She looks at her waist.

"Seat belt." He buckles himself, and when she only stares at him, he leans across the console and fastens her belt.

"Oh." Her finger coasts over the strap. "I never wear mine."

"We do in my car. I drive fast."

She tugs at the strap between the valley of her breasts. "This is different."

"You are odd."

"Is that bad?"

"Not at all." He laughs, bemused. "I appreciate the company."

He makes a U-turn and guns the engine. They fly up the on-ramp, and she throws her head back with a booming laugh.

"Tell me, Magnolia, what do you do?"

"What do you mean?" She's lit up like a disco ball, grinning ear to ear.

"Do you work, are you in school? Stay at home?"

She scoffs. "My parents would love that for me, staying at home. The happy housewife. That's why I left."

"They feel that way?" He glances at her. "What, were they born in the fifties?"

"Twenties."

"You're joking?" She's being facetious. But she stares at him, unblinking, and an uneasy laugh escapes him. "Why are you going back if they're like that?"

"Been away too long. Don't have anywhere else to go."

"There's always someplace to go."

"Not when you're lost."

He frowns at that. "Where were you before this?"

"California. And before that, Colorado. I lived in a commune."

"A what?"

"A commune. You know, we shared food, shelter, resources. Beds."

"Yeah, I know what a commune is." He takes a hard look at her, wondering what else she's been smoking. "Those still exist?"

"Of course, silly. They're all over the place."

"Never would have thought that."

She's a strange one. Far out. It's the most accurate description he can think of to describe her vibe.

She points at the phone propped in a cup holder. "What's that?"

"My phone."

"Get out. That's not a phone."

"No joke. Want to call your parents?"

Her face loses some of its color. "I haven't spoken with them in over five years."

"Do they know you're coming?"

She chews on her bottom lip.

"I'm sure they'll be happy to see you."

"I doubt it." She wraps and unwraps her hair around a finger. "What about your parents? Are you close with them?"

His jaw tenses. He shakes his head.

"Where are they?"

"Dead."

She touches his arm. "I'm sorry."

"Happened a long time ago."

"Talking helps."

"No, it doesn't." Talking forces him to remember.

She goes quiet, watching him. He glances at her. "What?"

"Is your grandmother your only living relative?"

"Yup." He adjusts in his seat and switches topics. "So, who's this Sam guy?"

She peers at him for a cool second before she sighs. "The man my parents didn't want me to marry."

"Did you marry him?" He doesn't see a ring on her finger.

"No."

"Who did they want you to marry, then?"

"Benjamin Stromski, the kid next door." She picks up his phone and nearly drops it when the screen lights up. She puts it back and rubs her fingertips as if the device made them tingle.

"What about Benjamin? Did he want to marry you?"

"I'd say so. He proposed. We were engaged almost three months." Magnolia points out their exit, and he pulls off the highway. "Benjie's a good guy. I do love him. But he isn't exciting. That sounds terrible, I know, but I wanted more out of life than a picket fence, meat loaf on Sundays, and vanilla sex on Saturdays."

"Don't we all?" he scoffs.

"I flipped out the night before our wedding and went to this dive bar where nobody I knew would look for me. I met Sam, and we started doing shots. Keep going straight," she tells him when they reach an intersection. She angles her body toward him, tucking one leg under the other. She traces circles on his thigh. "Sam was everything my parents didn't want in a husband for me. They see sex, love, and marriage as a package deal. Not Sam. He's all about free love and living life in the moment, and I feel exactly the same. Sam understood me. He didn't judge. He accepted me as me. We fucked in his van. Best sex I'd ever had. The things he did with his tongue." She displays some tongue acrobatics and laughs deeply at Matt's mortification.

"Whoa. TMI." Matt gently nudges her hand off his thigh, shifting uncomfortably in his jeans.

"Long story short, Sam crashed my wedding. He pulled up in his van, threw open the door, and I was out of there. Haven't looked back since. Your turn."

"My turn, what?"

"Your parents. What were they like?"

"Already told you. Don't want to talk about them." Especially not with a woman he just met. Come to think of it—this woman, the overall strangeness of this situation . . . He looks out the windows, not recognizing the landscape. "How much farther?" he asks.

"Almost there. Hey, I know this song." Magnolia turns up the music, a Bob Dylan tune, and hums along.

It doesn't take long for Matt to get caught up in the lyrics. His thumbs tap along to the beat.

CHAPTER 14

MAGNOLIA BLU

July 6, 1972

Two weeks have gone by and I still haven't met Liza's husband, Matty, but Liza's staff, Sally and Adam, already treat me like family. Liza and I have fallen into a comfortable friendship and routine. We meet on the patio for breakfast each morning and discuss the day's projects, what section of the yard I'll work on, what flowers to plant or bushes to trim. By 10:00 a.m., when I'm well into my day, Liza leaves to do whatever it is she does. Tennis at the club. A luncheon at the Beverly Hills Hotel. Or a meeting to plan a charity function.

Adam brings me lunch around noon, and I have a couple of hours of personal time before I cook dinner for myself in my studio. I visit the beach or go to the library. I walk the neighborhood and study the landscaping, collect ideas. My notebook is already bursting with sketches and plant lists. I imagine pairing rosebushes and hedges like pairing fine wine with cheese. I treasure these hours, as well as the quiet ones before bed. There isn't anyone around to interrupt me or invade my personal space. No one to demand my time to ease their minds or needs. I can sit quietly, play my flute, and just be me.

But today was interesting. I was kneeling in the dirt, digging out a particularly aggressive ground cover that was choking a gardenia when a man I hadn't seen before threw open the glass sliding door and stalked onto the patio in a rant. An amber liquid sloshed in his glass tumbler, and he shoveled the hair draping his forehead back over his head. His shirt was fully unbuttoned and wrinkled, his jeans low waisted, hanging on narrow hips, so that I could see the full expanse of his chest and abdomen. He was barefoot and intoxicated, but he was gorgeous. I couldn't look away from him.

Liza followed him outside and dogged him around the patio, arguing about something. I wasn't comfortable witnessing their fight, so I collected my tools and got up to leave.

"Who the fuck are you?" the man yelled.

I almost dropped the spade on my foot.

I started to explain that I was the new gardener and to just ignore me, but Liza beat me to it. Hand on her hip and looking utterly exasperated with him, she said, "Magnolia's our new gardener. I told you about her."

"You never told me anything."

"I did. But you don't listen to me."

He glared at Liza. "I don't want some stooge snooping around here."

Liza rolled her eyes. "Magnolia wouldn't dream of it."

I told him that I didn't hear what they'd been arguing about and that I was going to the shed to give them privacy.

"Just leave. I don't want you here when I'm around."

"She lives here, Matty." Liza sent an apologetic look my way to soften the blow of his dismissal before doing a quick round of introductions. "Magnolia, this is Matty, my husband. Matty, say hi."

"I didn't agree to this."

"I don't need your approval to hire staff."

He tossed back his drink and waved his hand at me. "Come here."

I hesitated, glancing to Liza.

"Are you deaf?" he snapped.

Fed up with his orders and attitude—he reminded me of my father—I removed my gardening gloves. "No, I can hear you quite clearly. I'm sure your neighbors can too."

Liza's mouth twitched. She ducked her head and took interest in her satin house slippers.

"Wiseass, aren't you?" He cracked a piece of ice in his mouth.

"I've been called worse."

He glared at me as I made my way over to them. He then said I looked like a vagrant.

"She works with dirt, Matty." Liza crossed her arms.

I'm fed up with men like him, but as much as I wanted to give Liza's husband a piece of my mind, I held my tongue. Liza might be a friend, but she's also my employer. I have free room and board in the safety and comfort of her expansive backyard, and I didn't want to lose it. I also didn't want to upset Liza's husband further. I can tell there is trouble brewing between them, something I haven't been privy to until now.

She explained to him—and not for the first time, apparently—that she'd met me at Ralph's, that I'd helped her pick up her dropped groceries and we'd gotten to talking.

"Wait, wait, wait." He covered his eyes, then gaped at his wife like she'd done the stupidest thing he'd ever heard. "You picked up a random? You've given her access to our home, to us? What were you thinking? She could be feeding dirt to the paps. What if she's selling us out?"

Liza flinched, and I knew his words hurt even if she wouldn't show it, because her expression quickly became bored. Even her posture alluded to the fact that she'd heard this story from him before.

I flipped a hand to dismiss his concern and reassure Liza she didn't have to worry about me. "Don't read those mags."

He scowled at me like he was disappointed, and Liza's chest quaked with a dry laugh. She happily told Matty that I was probably the only person on the planet who didn't know who he was. Of course, he didn't believe that. Apparently, *everyone* knew who Matty Holloway was. He couldn't believe his wife would buy that. He scoffed at her gullibility.

"She lived on a commune for five years," Liza said, refusing to show her dismay over his lack of faith in her hiring decision. Matty looked at his wife, and his eyes flashed with what seemed like admiration, and their defensive posture turned into something else entirely. There was some sort of silent communication happening between them, because their anger diffused. Liza's teeth scraped over her bottom lip, a smile toying at the corner.

"No shit." He studied me with wary fascination, as if I'd been living under a rock, and in a way I have. I haven't been to movie theaters, and I hardly watched television at the commune. I hadn't been interested, and there really hadn't been time. There was always so much to do to keep the commune running. Our heated discussions on politics and corruption and war that ran late into the night were more enlightening and invigorating than watching car chases and love stories on a big screen or television.

Liza took his empty glass, handing it off to Adam, who always seemed to be nearby, and remarked that my companionship has been refreshing.

"You one of those hippies?" Matty asked.

"I'm just me." I tucked my hands into my overall bib. "If it helps any, I have lots of experience with landscaping. Liza closely oversees my work, and Adam doesn't purchase any of my requests without consulting with her first. I promise by the end of the season, you'll have one of the best-looking yards in the neighborhood."

"I don't give a shit what you can do. That's on Liza. What I care about is that what you see around here doesn't end up in the papers."

"I wouldn't dream of it." I echo Liza's words. If there is one thing I value, it's privacy. That, and for people to mind their own business. My parents always had their noses in mine and it drove me away.

Liza winked at me before smirking at her husband. "She hasn't seen even one of your movies."

"You'll have to remedy that," he said to Liza and grinned at me. She rolled her eyes. But then she got him to agree that I could stay on with them. As for living on their property . . . as long as I keep myself scarce and away from the house when he's around, he can tolerate my presence.

"Where's my drink?" He looked around the patio, forgetting Liza had handed the glass off to Adam. "I need a refill."

Before he could go, Liza snatched his hand. He stalled, briefly lacing his fingers with hers, but his eyes swung to mine as if noticing me for the first time underneath the layer of dirt. A warm feeling spread out from my stomach, and I dodged his gaze, embarrassed he could tell how shamefully attracted to him I was despite his gruff first impression.

"I'm so sorry." Liza gushed with apology when Matty returned to the house.

I tore my gaze from his back and hoped I didn't look as flushed as I felt. I also don't want to be the cause of any friction between Liza and her husband and told her so. Nor do I want to make Matty uncomfortable in his own home. As much as the idea of walking away from this golden opportunity pained me, I told Liza that leaving seemed like the best option.

"Nonsense." Liza grasped my hand and insisted that I stay. She didn't want to lose me. She said I was the best gardener she'd had and was becoming a dear friend. She also confessed that things were tense between her and Matty long before I showed up. What I'd witnessed was nothing new.

"I'll always love him no matter what; I can't help myself. He really is an adoring husband when he isn't in a foul mood. He's been working ungodly hours and is unusually tired."

I must not have looked convinced, for she slipped her arm through mine and walked with me to the ground cover I'd been removing. "Matty will come around, trust me. With time, he'll adore you as much as I do. You know what I love about you, Magnolia?"

"What is that?"

"Everyone here is caught up in the scene. They want what I can give them: connections. Matty's popularity definitely helps in that regard, but I've been in this industry since birth, and I know a lot of people too. It's what I'm good at; it's what I do. Introduce the right people to each other. Many stars are famous thanks to me, whether they met their agent through me, or auditioned for a role because I introduced them to a director. But I'm never sure if people love me for me or love me for what I can get them. It's easy to feel taken advantage of."

"I'd never."

"That's why I like you." Liza squeezed my hands, not minding the dirt under my fingernails. "It's why I trust you. You didn't grow up here. You don't *need* anything from me. You'll never take advantage of me."

I smiled at her. It was the only thing I could do because I was tongue tied with guilt. I couldn't stop thinking about when I'd see Matty again.

CHAPTER 15

MATT

Matt looks up at the darkening sky as Magnolia knocks on her parents' door. She waits for them to answer, nervously fidgeting with her hair.

When they arrived, Magnolia didn't immediately get out of the car. She scratched at her denim thigh.

He leaned forward to get her attention, wondering at her hesitation. He needed to get back on the road. "You okay?"

"Yeah." She opened the door and glanced back at him. "Will you come with?"

"Uh . . . Sure." What was a few more minutes?

Magnolia knocks.

Matt hooks his thumbs in his front pockets. "I don't think they're home."

She walks backward off the porch, looking up at the second-story windows. One of them, the small tinted bathroom window, is cracked open. She cups her mouth. "Mom? Dad? It's Ruby Rose!"

Matt drops his head and smirks. He had the feeling Magnolia Blu wasn't her real name.

"I'm home," she yells, then watches the door.

"Magnolia—"

"They're here. They have to be," she cuts him off.

He holds up his hands and backs off. Not his business.

She returns to the porch and shoves her hand into the mailbox next to the front door. "It's not here." She slams the lid.

"What's not?"

"The house key." She strides across the lawn to the sidewalk, looks up and down the street, then fixes her attention on the house across from them.

"Whose house is that?" he asks of the ranch-style house with a well-tended yard.

"Benjie's." She hugs her ribs. "It's different from what I remember."

"The light's on. He might know when your parents are expected back."

She steps off, then back on the sidewalk. Her fingers twist in her hair. She's got to be nervous. She left Benjie at the altar when she ran off with the guy she'd met and hooked up with the night before the wedding.

"I can go ask if you don't want to go over," he offers.

"He's probably not home. He was going to go to Yale. He might not even live here anymore. It should be okay." She smiles weakly at him and jogs across the street.

Matt follows at a slower pace. He stops at his car and waits in case she needs him. She knocks, and a middle-aged man of average build answers. He's wearing joggers and a worn shirt. She asks for Mrs. Stromski. The man tells her nobody by that name lives there. She asks after her parents. He says no one with the last name of Hope lives in the house across the street.

Magnolia looks back at Matt, troubled. She tells the man he's lying. Matt's about to go over and help when the man shuts the door in her face. She gapes in shock, then returns to Matt.

"He said the strangest things." Magnolia rubs her hands. "He accused *me* of lying. But I grew up in that house." She points at her parents' place.

"Is it possible they've moved?"

"They'd never leave without telling me." Her face shadows with doubt. Matt refrains from saying the obvious: Her parents probably didn't know how to reach her. They might not have wanted to. "I don't know what to do. I can't go back."

He assumes she means going back to Sam, or to whomever she was with in California. "Is there someplace else I can take you? A hotel? Starbucks?"

Her brows pull together at the center. "What's Starbucks?"

A bark of laughter. "Seriously?" She's pulling his leg. Who doesn't know what Starbucks is? "It's a coffee shop. They're all over the place."

She shakes her head, nervously rubbing her hands. "No, I'll wait here."

"I'm not sure . . ." He looks back at the neighbor's house. A curtain flutters closed.

"Don't worry about him. He doesn't know what he's talking about. My parents will be back. They're probably just out to dinner or something. Help me with my suitcases?" She gets the small case, and Matt grabs the larger one. He leaves it on the sidewalk when she declines his offer to carry her luggage to the porch.

He doesn't feel right leaving her without access to a car or a phone. He scribbles his number on the airport parking receipt. "In case you need to reach me." She can borrow a phone from another neighbor or use her parents' once she gets inside the house.

"I'll be fine." She refuses the slip of paper and shoos him away. "Go see your grandmother."

He grimaces, opening the car door.

"Matty."

"Don't call me that."

She gives her hand a dismissive flip. "Word of advice? Make peace with your past or you'll be lonely for the rest of your life. Nobody wants that."

He just smiles, shaking his head at her strangeness, and gets in his car. He heads straight for the highway to make up for lost time.

CHAPTER 16

JULIA

Julia hurries as fast as one can go lugging a folded massage table through Rosemont's wide hallways toward her last appointment. She passes the common room and notices Liza sitting in her usual chair facing one of the garden windows. Mama Rose's diary is a weight in Julia's bag.

She veers in the elderly woman's direction, her rubber-soled shoes whisper light across the luxury vinyl planks. Liza jerks when Julia appears beside her, and she drops the book she's reading in her lap.

"I'm sorry," Julia apologizes. "I didn't mean to startle you."

"But you did." Liza picks up the book and searches for the page she was on.

Julia sets down her bag and table and rolls her shoulders to soothe the ache.

Dressed in pressed wool slacks and a dusty-rose blouse, Liza peers up at her over her wire-framed readers. "I didn't book a massage today." As if triggered by the thought of one, she rubs her arthritic hands.

"I know." Julia looks around for an empty chair, spotting one at the table behind them. She drags it over. "May I sit?"

"Will you leave if I say no?"

"I just need a moment." Julia smiles pleasantly and drops into the chair, exhausted from being on her feet all day. Sitting down is probably a bad decision. She might not be able to get back up. She certainly doesn't want to.

Liza lifts her nose. "Why are you bothering me?"

"I don't mean to."

"But you do." Her gaze narrows.

Julia sighs and gets to the point. "Why haven't you told me you and Mama Rose were friends?" Not that it would make a difference. Julia suspects Liza would have still been rude toward her and Mama Rose like she is with everyone else.

"You found the diary."

"Yes."

The flush from the room's warmth drains from Liza's face. Pink-tinted lips press to a straight line. The creases around her mouth all but disappear. She looks away and stares out the window.

"What happened between you?" Julia gently asks. Liza's friendship meant something to Mama Rose at one time, enough for her grandmother to write about it in a diary and then remember it out of the blue a half century later. Surely, Liza must have felt the same.

Liza's nostrils flare. "You have the diary. Read it."

"I am, but—"

Liza reaches for the cane leaning against her chair and grasps the polished silver handle until her knuckles strain. The bluish veins on her hand expand with the force of her grip.

Sensing Liza's desire to leave is as great as her unwillingness to discuss their history, Julia plucks the diary from her bag. "She wrote something here . . ."

Liza gasps at the sight of it. She stares pointedly at the powder-blue journal with the gold embossed title, her face pinched.

"Have you read it?" Julia drags her thumbnail along the edge, flipping the pages.

Liza's gaze flits away.

"Of course you have." Julia answers her own question. "You mentioned secrets." She presses back in her chair. "You gave Mama Rose a place to stay. You gave her a job. Why aren't you talking with her? Why do you ignore her?" As far as she knows, they've never eaten a meal together since Liza moved in. They've never played cards together. Mama Rose loves gin rummy, but Liza prefers to play alone with games like solitaire and pyramid.

Liza glances erratically around the room.

"From what I've read, she really liked you."

Liza's head swivels to Julia. She glares at her. "You're a fool if you believe that."

"But you're the one who told her you'd be great friends. The day you met, you wanted to be friends with her. In here"—Julia taps the book—"you are."

"What has she told you?"

"Nothing, not even before she lost her memory. She never mentioned you, and you never mentioned knowing her. I feel like you're both keeping secrets."

"How dare you." Liza bangs her cane, and Julia lurches at the noise. Liza waves to one of the staff, agitated.

"Forgive me, I didn't mean to upset you. But I can't figure out why my grandmother suddenly wants this diary I never knew she kept." Julia rushes the apology, wanting Liza to understand why her history with Mama Rose is important to her. Mama Rose was always candid with Julia, sharing stories from her wild past. But she never told her about Liza.

The fact Mama Rose kept her friendship with Liza a secret and that Liza chose Rosemont over all the assisted living facilities in the area, plus Julia's sworn promise to Mama Rose never to move her from Rosemont, makes Julia believe it's all connected. That her grandmother expected Liza's arrival. That this was planned beforehand, perhaps years ago. They might have unfinished business.

Julia could also be reading too much into this. Maybe the entire situation is coincidental.

But if her grandmother has a last wish she never shared with Julia, one she couldn't remember except for that brief lucid moment she requested Julia to locate the diary, Julia is determined to find out what it is.

Liza struggles to her feet. Her book drops onto the floor, followed by Mama Rose's diary when Julia leans forward to assist.

"Don't touch me," Liza seethes.

Julia lurches back. "Sorry."

Then because she can't help herself, Julia asks, "Did you know Mama Rose lived here before you'd moved in? Is that why you chose Rosemont? Was it because of her?"

Liza wails for assistance.

"Oh, jeez. Let me help." Julia reaches for Liza's elbow. Liza pivots to avoid her and loses her balance. She grabs at the chair in a weak attempt to keep from falling, and misses. Suddenly, Trevor is there like a guardian angel. Liza lands against his chest. Her cane swings out, knocking Julia's wrist. Pain flares up her arm. She cries out at the sting, but also with relief that Trevor saved Liza. She could have fractured a hip or shattered a wrist, and it would have been Julia's fault.

"Thank goodness you're here." Liza grasps Trevor's forearm and points her cane at Julia. "This woman is harassing me."

"I didn't mean to upset you." She rubs the tender spot the cane left, her wrist already aching from her job.

Trevor shoots Julia a look of confused disbelief, clearly thinking Julia wouldn't dare do such a thing. Mrs. Holloway must be mistaken. Rosemont's residents adore Julia. She's the one who occasionally tolerates their abuse. They aren't always kind and don't always treat her with respect during their massage sessions. Julia is a volunteer and doesn't feel she has the right to complain. Instead, she and Trevor share war stories over custard and apple juice during their breaks.

Julia mouths "Sorry" to him.

"I want to leave," Liza announces.

"Yes, Mrs. Holloway."

Liza grips Trevor's hand. "Take me back to my room."

"Of course, Mrs. Holloway."

"My book!" Liza glances back at the chair.

"I got it." Julia grabs the hardback, a self-help book about appreciating life that she recognizes as one of Rosemont's therapist's favorites to share with her patients. "I think you're the reason Ruby Rose wants the diary." She gives Liza her book. "It has to do with you."

"She's still harassing me." Liza walks alongside Trevor.

"I'm not harass—"

Trevor sends Julia a warning glare. He'll have to report this.

She forcefully exhales through her nose, frustrated at how quickly this spiraled out of control until she thinks back on their conversation and Liza's reaction. Whatever happened between her and Mama Rose left deep scars.

What did Mama Rose do to her?

CHAPTER 17

MAGNOLIA BLU

July 14, 1972

I haven't seen Matty in a week, but it hasn't stopped me from thinking about him. I should, though; I feel guilty each time because Liza is my friend. Nothing will happen between Matty and me. It can't, and I won't let it, and I doubt I'm anything but a passing thought to him. Plain compared to the resplendent celebrities clamoring to be photographed on his arm. But he invades my dreams, and my mind wanders toward him while I'm toiling in the soil. Shamefully, I was having an intense fantasy about the two of us on the beach when Liza surprised me with a visit this evening as I was getting ready for bed. Earlier in the day, when she didn't join me for breakfast, Adam told me that she was at a fundraiser planning meeting with the arts council. He said she had a very busy month ahead and wouldn't be home much. But I found her inside my studio when I came out of the bathroom towel drying my hair and wearing nothing but a short, thin robe. She looked like a specter. Her complexion was as white as the sheets she'd purchased for me during our shopping spree when she helped decorate the studio.

She told me that she'd knocked and was worried when I didn't answer. She stared at my bed with an empty gaze, rubbing her palms.

I hung the damp towel on the bathroom doorknob and asked if she wanted to sit down. She looked around the room and settled on the armchair under the front window. I offered her a drink.

"Got anything strong?"

"Vodka on the rocks?"

"Perfect." She smiled, still rubbing her hands.

I fixed us a couple of tumblers and asked about her meeting, wondering if that's what was worrying her. But her gala planning was moving along fine. The event would be lovely at $500 a head. She said that she'd invite me, but she knew I couldn't afford it, and they needed to sell every seat to meet their goal.

"It isn't my sort of thing," I said. I wouldn't know the first thing to say to her people, most of whom were studio executives and their wives, or actors and producers and other important people I couldn't even start to name. Everyone I'd met at her impromptu garden parties was larger than life. Their auras made them magnetic on-screen, and I felt intimidated in their presence. I only attended the parties because Liza asked me to. I suspected she liked showing me off. I'd already collected a stack of business cards and phone numbers penciled on cocktail napkins, neighbors begging me to come work for them after seeing what I'd done for the Holloways' garden.

I took Liza her drink and sat on the edge of the bed with mine in hand. "Cheers." We clicked our glasses and she took a deep drink from hers. She crossed and uncrossed her legs. I asked if everything was all right.

"I don't like it in here."

"Oh." I'd nearly forgotten what the studio reminded her of—the place had changed a lot since I arrived. I'd painted over the 1950s floral wallpaper with a vibrant, cheery yellow to match my bedspread. Plants filled the windowsills in the main room and bathroom. And I'd hung the psychedelic prints my friend June had painted a couple of years back above my bed.

"It's groovy. I love what you've done to the place. Honestly, it's never looked better. It's just—Not good memories . . . for me . . . in here." The words seemed difficult for her to express. She gulped the vodka and set down the tumbler.

"Let's sit on the patio," I suggested.

Relief flooded her face. "That would be lovely." She darted from the studio, and I replenished our drinks before joining her outside. I sat across the square teak table from her and folded my legs.

"Matty's left." Liza sipped at her drink, her attention on the expansive yard. A light breeze teased the hair around her face.

"On location again?"

She nodded and explained that he was in Bakersfield all week for night shoots. She expected he'd be a bear when he returned and wasn't looking forward to his mood. I asked if she missed him when he was gone.

"Yes and no." She turned to me. "Do you see yourself ever getting married?"

I debated what to share. I wasn't too proud of what I'd done to Benjie. But I wanted a friend in Liza. "I was engaged once. I left him at the altar."

Her eyes widened. "Do tell." She leaned back in her chair and casually crossed her legs as I told her about Benjie. He lived across the street, and we'd grown up together. My parents adored him, as did I. He was my friend. Our parents had planned out our whole lives. Marriage, kids, Christmases with our families. Summers at his parents' lake house. Benjie liked the picture they'd painted, and for a while, I had liked it too. Life would have been easy with Benjie. We were happy together. But while he was in love with me and I loved him back, I wasn't *in* love with him. Toward the end of high school, I grew restless.

"You grew bored," Liza deadpanned.

"Am I that transparent?"

"It's refreshing."

Yes, I'd been bored. I lived in a small town with nothing to do. There was a big world out there that I wanted to explore.

"You were a teenager," she also remarked.

I was, and I hadn't been getting along with my parents. So, the night before the wedding, I skipped out on the rehearsal dinner. I was eighteen, legally an adult, but still emotionally young and very unsure about being tied down in marriage. I went to a dive bar where I knew nobody would look for me and the bartender didn't check IDs. I started taking shots with a guy at the bar. His name was Sam, and he was a drifter. We talked through the night. We did other stuff too, but mostly we talked. I spent the night in his van.

"Look at you." Liza shook her head, impressed at my rebellious streak.

My parents were conservative, their ideals stuck in the forties. Sometimes I felt like Benjie was stuck there too. Sam believed in women's equality—at least until it was time to do his laundry, which I found out later. But after that first night with him, I'd been high on Sam and our conversations, and went home prepared to tell Benjie that it was over between us. I'd cheated on him.

He'd been waiting for me outside my parents' house. He knew I'd been having second thoughts and offered to postpone the wedding so I could think about it. He wasn't ready to give up on us. I let him talk me into sticking around. But I knew that if we didn't marry that day, I'd never marry him. My parents were outraged at my behavior, but when were they not? Still, Benjie and I talked, and we agreed to keep the wedding on. I went upstairs and got ready. Then I came downstairs in my gown. The wedding was taking place in my parents' backyard. All the guests were waiting for the ceremony to begin. But through the front window as my mother preened around me, adjusting my dress, I saw Sam drive up in his van. He pushed the side door open and waited.

"For what?" Liza leaned forward, fully invested in my story.

"He'd told me the night before that he was leaving that day for the commune. He also told me not to get married. Said it would never work between Benjie and me, and that I was wasting my life by doing what Benjie and my parents wanted of me. He said it was my life, my one chance to thrive on this big blue marble of ours, and I needed to live it the way I wanted to."

I don't recall making the decision not to go through with the wedding. I don't even recall opening the front door. I just remember running, and that first taste of glorious freedom bursting like a firework inside me. Sam whooped with excitement when I flew out the front door. I threw myself into his van. He slammed the door and gunned the gas. We drove straight to Colorado. It was the most spontaneous thing I'd ever done.

"Do you regret it?" Liza asked.

"Leaving? No." I only regret hurting Benjie. He hadn't done anything to deserve me leaving him the way I had.

"Good. And you shouldn't. Never settle."

"Would you marry Matty again?"

"In a heartbeat. I love him as much as I hate him. Well, not him, just his profession. And some of the industry people he brings home. But he loves being an actor. The attention, the off-screen drama, the glamour and the money. Who wouldn't love that, and who am I to take that from him? He came from nothing. I can't ask him to stop acting just because I don't like the mess that comes along with it."

"You should talk to him about it, let him know you're unhappy."

"Oh, he knows." She sighed. "Matty doesn't belong to me. He belongs to the world. Eight years married and I'm still getting used to sharing him. And I grew up in this industry. He didn't. I don't think I could ever leave him either. He could flaunt his starlets in front of me and I'd look the other way," she reflects with a faraway look. "If I ever did walk away from him, it would only be because I'd want him to come after me, for him to prove he loved me just as much."

"Do you think he'd follow you?"

She didn't answer, and my heart pinched for her, for them, for surely she must not believe he would or she would have said something.

"Why are you unhappy, Liza?"

She finished her liquor but held on to the glass, staring up at the house. Lights blazed in nearly every room. One went off, then another. Sally was making her final round before bed.

"Is it because of the baby?" I dared to ask.

"There's never been a baby. What there's been are six miscarriages and a stillborn."

"Liza."

She dismissed my shock with a wave, explaining she took full responsibility. She and Matty were both fertile. In theory, everything should work. She just couldn't carry.

"You can't blame yourself."

"It's all right. Matty really wanted a baby. We both did, so much. I've accepted that one isn't in the cards for me."

"And Matty?"

She lifts a delicate shoulder.

"Why haven't you adopted?"

Liza vehemently shook her head. "Can you imagine what the press would say? Matty's a sex symbol. He's the hottest male commodity right now. His publicist hates that he's married. In fact, Matty's team downplays our marriage so that he can keep attending parties at the Playboy mansion for photo ops. The more he's photographed partying and boozing, the more scripts he's offered and the more negotiating power his agent has. He brings the studios a lot of money. Yes, we both benefit from his fame. We get to keep this grand lifestyle." She flagged an arm over the yard. "I can't blame him for being so possessive of his privacy when he's home."

I almost offered again to leave when she sighed heavily and continued on. "We stopped trying for a baby over a year ago. But I still feel the urge to talk about it every once in a while. I still get emotional about it. Little things, like being in this studio, set me off. Sorry. It's where I lost the one baby I carried to term." She swiped a finger under an eye.

"It's got to hurt when Matty goes to . . . when he parties." Even I knew of those Playboy mansion parties. My father had a subscription to the magazine. I'd accidentally found issues hidden under his socks.

"Thank God for Adam. He's so supportive. Always by my side. And for you." She squeezed my fingers. "Adam's wonderful in so many ways, but he doesn't make up for real girl talk." She smiled and looked into her empty glass. "That went down fast."

"I think you needed it."

"I did. And now I need to go to bed before I get too tipsy to make it back. Good night, darling."

I stood with her and wished her a good night when she kissed my cheek.

"Oh, it will be." She waved without looking back and walked up to the house, weaving slightly up the gently sloped lawn. That's when I noticed she was barefoot and wearing her nightgown.

It was also when I realized how lonely she truly is, and it made me wonder if that's why she's unhappy.

Liza surrounds herself with people and is married to a man any woman would die to have a piece of. You peel all that back, remove the glitz and glam, take away the money and connections, and who is she? Who is there for her? No wonder she's drawn to me, another broken soul just looking to be loved.

CHAPTER 18

JULIA

Julia finds Lenore waiting for her outside Mrs. Eaton's room when she finishes the elderly woman's evening massage. She's exhausted, her entire body aches, and she just wants to go home, pour a glass of wine, and read the rest of Mama Rose's diary. She hopes she'll find the answer to what happened between her and Liza. She also hopes what's on the pages will help her pinpoint why Mama Rose wanted the diary so badly.

"Trevor told me what happened with Liza," Lenore greets her. Julia exhales loudly and starts walking toward the exit. Lenore joins her.

"He went straight to you." She thought he'd give her a chance to go to Lenore first, explain her side.

"Don't blame him. He's only looking out for our residents."

"Basically doing his job. I know. It's just—" Julia stops midthought. She stops walking too.

Lenore turns to her. She takes the bag off Julia's shoulder.

Julia mumbles her thanks and rubs the taut tendon at the base of her right thumb. "I know for sure now that Liza and Mama Rose were once friends."

Lenore's chin pulls in. "Before Rosemont?"

"Back in the seventies when Mama Rose first moved to California. I asked Liza about it and she got agitated."

"Judging from what Trevor told me about Liza's reaction, I take it the friendship didn't end well."

"Liza was not happy I'd brought it up." Julia presses a knuckle into her palm, trying to release the locked tendon. "But I have questions."

"And Ruby Rose can't answer them," Lenore says, putting two and two together.

Julia's mouth presses into a thin line. She switches hands, rubbing the ache at the base of her other thumb.

Lenore's gaze drops to Julia's hands. "How'd you find out they were friends?"

"In a moment of lucidity, Mama Rose asked me to find her diary. No idea what triggered the request. But I found it last night and read some of it, which got me to thinking. Before Mama Rose arrived, she made me swear not to move her from here. Now that I know about her and Liza, I wonder if Mama Rose was waiting for her."

Lenore nudges her glasses up her nose. "Are you sure it isn't just coincidence?"

"I'm thinking it's something more."

"Like what?"

"Like unfinished business. If so, I need to figure out what. I was hoping Liza might know."

Behind her glasses, Lenore's eyes soften just as a shout down the hallway draws both their attention. Lenore lets out a weary sigh. Whatever is happening, she'll have to deal with it, which means whatever she was going to say to Julia when Julia saw that flash of empathy gets pushed aside. Lenore instead tells her something more practical. And disappointing.

"I understand your need to help your grandmother," Lenore says, turning back to Julia. "But I have to ask that you leave Liza out of this. You're not to bother her."

"Lenore."

"Liza is under a lot of stress. Between the upcoming move and last month's near accident . . ." Her voice drops to a level only Julia can hear.

Lenore and Trevor are still taking precautions with Liza as if she intentionally stepped into traffic. "I can't have you upsetting her further."

"I didn't mean to upset her," Julia says. "I didn't know bringing up their friendship would."

"I understand, but keep your distance. When Matt arrives, you can ask him about it. Liza might handle it better with him around."

Julia doubts that. Matt doesn't have much of a relationship with his grandmother. They aren't on speaking terms. But it's none of her business, so Julia just nods and rubs her eyes. She's so exhausted, they burn.

Lenore angles her head and frowns. "It just occurred to me that you're still here. Why?"

"What do you mean?"

"We don't have an arrangement anymore. You don't need to be here unless you're visiting."

"I didn't want to cancel my appointments." She also didn't want to do what she knows she needs to do. Find a new income source so Mama Rose can stay at Rosemont.

"You're exhausted and overworked." Lenore grabs her hands. "And you haven't stopped rubbing your hands since we started talking. You are literally in pain from relieving everyone else's pain."

Julia glances away. Up until yesterday afternoon, volunteering was the only option she had. She could find a second job, but doing what? Massage therapy is her only skill. But if she worked those hours at another spa rather than at Rosemont, she'd lose flexibility with her time. She wouldn't be able to visit her grandmother when she wanted or as often. That isn't an option Julia will consider. Who knows how long Mama Rose has left.

"Go home and rest, Julia. Research the brochures I gave you. In fact, unless it's to visit, don't come back until you've taken care of your grandmother's living arrangements and your hands. You can keep the clients you have here, but only if you charge them. You need the money."

Guilt winds through her. "I can't charge them. Their incomes are limited. Look at Liza. She's broke."

"And she's moving out. Let Matt worry about her. You worry about yourself. I'll walk with you to your car."

Before Julia can object, Lenore takes the massage table off Julia's shoulder and heads for the front exit. Julia doggedly follows.

CHAPTER 19

———

MATT

The farther Matt drives from Magnolia's house, the more aware of himself and his surroundings he becomes. He's in no condition to be behind the wheel.

He's famished. His migraine is back. He's coming off a high. And he needs gas.

He pulls into a station near the freeway on-ramp. While the car fills up, he enters the convenience market and wanders up one aisle and down the next. He grabs whatever looks tasty. Cheetos, pork rinds, beef jerky. He drops two bags of Lay's barbecue chips along with a box of Oreo cookies and several Twinkies in the basket.

On his way to the checkout counter, he adds a liter of Coke, a six-pack of Heineken, and a bottle of Jack Daniel's. And when the pimply-faced twentysomething behind the counter rings him up, he asks the guy to toss in a pack of Camels. Matt hasn't smoked a cigarette in over ten years. He normally doesn't eat the crap he's buying either. But he's also never gone miles out of his way to drop off a stranger he got stoned with. Nor has he ever abandoned everything to help Elizabeth. He second-guesses why he's doing so now. What, if anything, could Elizabeth share about his mom that would warrant a face-to-face?

Old bitter feelings resurface as he stands beside his car with the door open. So do the memories as he stares off into space. Two months after he moved into his grandmother's house, he turned eleven. His birthday came and went without cards or cake. Kids didn't have cell phones then, so he hadn't heard from his Florida friends. They probably didn't know where he'd moved to. He ended up spending his birthday the same way he'd spent every day since he'd moved there. Alone.

But something changed the following day. Nothing major. Just a slight shift that made living in his grandmother's house more bearable.

On that day, he sat on the edge of Elizabeth's kidney-shaped pool, his feet dangling in the water. The pool overlooked the most vibrant flower garden he'd seen, but he didn't care. He'd never felt so alone. Nobody cared for him. He was unloved and unlovable.

It was summer break. He hadn't made any friends yet. His grandmother rarely acknowledged him. And he wasn't allowed to leave the house by himself. He also wasn't allowed to swim without adult supervision, even though he was probably more experienced than anyone in the house since he'd grown up on the water.

Occasionally, Adam would watch him from the patio during his breaks because Matt's grandmother couldn't be bothered with the inconvenience of supervising him. But on that particular day it was Elizabeth who appeared on the patio in a silk robe and designer one-piece with side cutouts.

Matt straightened, hope lightening his chest at the thought his grandmother wanted to spend time with him. She'd forgive him for not saving his mom.

But she took one look at him, lifted her nose in disdain, and retreated inside the house.

Matt's back buckled. His grandmother, his only living relative, despised him. He kicked the water.

A moment later, Adam appeared.

He circled the pool in his polished wing tips until he reached Matt. He cleared his throat, beckoning Matt to look up at him.

Matt lifted a hand against the sun's glare and squinted at the tall man.

"Your grandmother has requested you remove yourself from the patio."

"And go where?"

"Your room?" He sounded just as befuddled.

"I can't swim?"

"No, not today."

Matt's heart sank to the bottom of the pool. For a brief second, he considered plunging into the water. He could hold his breath for over a minute. He'd sit on the bottom of the deep end until his grandmother was forced to jump in to rescue him. He craved attention so much that he'd risk drowning himself. He wanted to yell and push and break something. He'd been broken when he arrived, but her neglect was killing him.

Which was why he pushed to his feet. He didn't believe his grandmother would jump in to save him, just like he hadn't saved his mom.

Matt shuffled into the house with Adam following. The butler tapped him on the shoulder and pointed to the kitchen, where Matt melted onto a chair at the table. He stared at nothing.

"Why so glum?" the old man asked.

Matt lifted his shoulder.

"Missing your mom?"

Matt didn't give him the dignity of a reply. He didn't want to talk about his mom.

"What is it, then?"

Matt shrugged again. He didn't want to sit there. He didn't want to be anywhere around there. He wanted to go home. He wanted everything to go back to the way it was.

He wanted his mom and dad.

"Use words, Matthew."

He groaned. "Yesterday was my birthday." He pouted, looking up at the butler when Adam didn't say anything. Matt didn't like whining or complaining because it gave his grandmother more reason to be annoyed with him. But he'd been feeling especially low.

Adam stared at him. Then he pivoted and opened the refrigerator. He took out a half-eaten cake Matt figured was left over from the previous Saturday's garden party.

"You should have told us," Adam said.

"Like you care." Matt stared at his hands on the table.

"How old are you?"

"Eleven."

A moment later, Adam set two slices of cake on the table and sat beside Matt. He gave Matt a fork, which Matt reluctantly took as he warily eyed Adam.

Adam nudged Matt's plate closer. "Happy birthday, young Matt."

Matt didn't know what to say. He watched Adam take a bite of his cake, and when the older man nodded, Matt dug into his. Adam asked what he missed most from his life in Florida, aside from his parents, of course, and Matt told him he missed his friends. He missed crabbing with them, hanging out at the shake stand where his dad docked his boat, and Saturday morning baseball games.

The next day, he found a wrapped gift waiting for him on his bed. Inside were a baseball and glove. He'd left his glove behind in Florida. There wasn't a card, but he didn't need one to know it hadn't come from his grandmother.

A horn goes off, jolting Matt back to the present. He's holding an open beer can. He stares at it with no idea how it got there. But he doesn't hesitate to tip it back and guzzle half. As if he's looking for an excuse to procrastinate.

Across the road he sees a motel with a fenced pool out front and a neon sign flashing VACANCY. Exhaustion pours into him, and he makes a decision. Today is shot. Julia's doing research on his behalf. He can afford the time. He'll crash for a few hours, sleep off this funk, and leave before dawn. He estimates another eight hours. He'll make it to Pasadena around noon.

Matt drives to the motel and checks into a room on the second floor above the pool. It's the size of a shoebox and smells like stale cigarettes and sex. But it has a queen bed, functioning shower, small couch and table, and square minifridge. He doesn't need much else.

He leaves the grocery bag on the table, drops his duffel on the bed, and opens the window to air out the room. He then finishes off his beer and drops onto the couch with a bag of Lay's barbecue chips. He eats by the handful, eyeing his phone. He picks it up to call Julia to tell her that he's arriving later than planned.

"Hey, it's Matt," he says when she answers.

"Hi. You here already?"

"Not yet." He glances out the window. Some guy walks past his room pulling a piece of luggage. The wheels rumble loudly across the concrete balcony. "Not exactly sure where I am." He can't remember specifically from the map. Only that he's over a hundred miles farther south than he should be.

"Are you okay?"

He thinks on that a moment. "Not sure. Ran into a couple snags." They go by the names of Magnolia Blu and Jack Daniel's.

His gaze levels on the bottle, and he debates opening the hard stuff. This Liza debacle is making him remember things he prefers to forget. Events he's neglected to process as expertly as his grandmother neglected him. He isn't prepared to deal with them now.

Hence, Jack. He'll help him get through the night.

"Were you in an accident?" Her voice warbles with concern.

A short laugh escapes. Picking up a stranger and driving her to God knows where was the accident. He should have stuck to the course. Now that he's veered off, he's tempted to go home.

He would if he weren't curious. He's hoping Elizabeth wants to share a family secret that changes the course of his life. Wouldn't that be something? He'd love for her to tell him they aren't related.

"Nah. Just . . ." He cracks open another beer. "Tired."

"Are you drinking?"

"Yes, but I'm not driving. I checked into a motel, so don't worry about me. I won't get pulled over for a DUI."

"Matt, Liza only has a few more days here. You're not leaving yourself much time to help her."

"You don't think I know that?" He guzzles the beer and grimaces. It doesn't taste as good on a guilty stomach.

There's a long pause. "You're obviously in a mood. I don't need to put up with this. I'm hanging—"

"No, don't," he blurts. *Please don't hang up.* "Don't go." If she does, he'll get stuck in his head, his least favorite place to be.

"Can I ask what's going on with you? Does helping your grandmother bother you that much?"

"I don't want to talk about it. It won't help."

"Talking usually does the opposite."

He lets out a helpless chuckle. "Is this where you give me some BS that I'm storing it if I'm not speaking it?"

"Why'd you check into a motel?"

"Why do you care?"

"I'm worried for Liza. Tell me, what's really going on with you? Is this just about Liza? Or does this have something to do with your parents too?"

He glares at the wall in front of him. How does she know about his parents?

"Matt?"

"Yes?" he says, bitterly.

"What happened between you and your grandmother? I imagine coming to see her isn't easy."

He's flattered she cares enough to ask. But he's never trusted anyone aside from his mom with his feelings. He isn't going to start today.

"You've no idea, and I'm not going to begin to explain." If he weren't stoned and hadn't started drinking, they wouldn't be having this conversation. He'd still be driving.

A pause. "All right. Let's talk about something else, then. What do you do?"

"What do I do?"

"Your job. What do you do?"

His job. He'll happily talk about his career all day. "I'm an automobile photographer. That's why I should be in my car driving to you and not sitting here on my ass. I'm on contract with Ford. I have to be in France at the end of the week for the Twenty-Four Hours of Le Mans race."

"That's exciting. So why *are* you sitting on your ass? Aside from the fact you're drinking?"

"Why'd you read your grandmother's diary?"

"I was curious."

"Did you tell her you read it?"

Her end of the line is quiet.

"Julia?"

"She didn't remember asking for it. She said the diary wasn't hers when I showed her." Sadness dampens her voice. Dementia is a bitch because it's the afflicted person's loved ones who suffer. He can't fathom what Julia deals with on a daily basis.

"Do you have it with you?" he asks.

"Yes. I brought it home."

"Are you going to finish reading it?"

"I might. Yeah, probably. She used to tell me stories about her past, but she never told me about meeting your grandparents. I feel like I'm learning a whole new side of her."

"What was she like?" he asks to get her talking. She seems happier when she's reminiscing.

"Young." She laughs lightly. "Provocative, bold, daring. Very bohemian. She didn't care about rules, and she loved big. I envy those qualities about her."

"She's your grandmother. Those qualities must be in you too." That's why being an asshole comes naturally to him. He gets it from Liza.

116

She hums, unconvinced. "I don't have the freedom she did."

Because she's solely responsible for her grandmother's well-being.

Will that happen to him? Will he lose his freedom if he assumes Elizabeth's financial obligations? He earns a decent income that allows him to save and invest with some to spare for travel and play. How much of his life will he have to give up to keep a roof over that woman's head?

"Don't you find it odd both of our grandmothers ended up at Rosemont?" she asks. "Liza never once mentioned she knew my grandmother. Oh, Matt, I am so sorry. I asked Liza about what I'd read, and she got upset."

"She'll get over it."

"No . . . I *really* upset her. Lenore will tell you about it when you get here. I wanted you to hear it from me first. I'm sorry."

"Trust me, it's not a big deal. Everything sets her off." Then curiosity gets the better of him. "What exactly did you say to her?"

"I asked why she never told me she knew my grandmother. That's all."

"Well, she can piss off."

"Anyway, I'm sorry. It's getting late. I should let you go."

"Yeah." He glances at the clock. "I should get some sleep. Finish the diary, Jules. You can tell me about it tomorrow."

"I'd like that. You'll be here then?"

"I should be."

"I hope so. Good night, Matt."

"Night, Jules."

He ends the call and sets the alarm on his phone for 4:00 a.m.

Outside, water splashes and kids shriek. He goes to the window. Five teens are hanging around the pool. He closes the window and presses his back to the wall, thinking about what's in store for him tomorrow.

He reaches for Jack and unscrews the cap.

CHAPTER 20

JULIA

Julia ends her call with Matt, but her mind doesn't wander far from him. From what little she could gather, and considering he's drinking at a motel when he should be driving to California, Liza troubles him, and not because she's broke and her days at Rosemont are numbered. The massage therapist inside her wants to ease the tension between them and get to the heart of the matter. But emotions aren't sore muscles that unwind with a few strokes of a thumb.

Should she be worried about him? Maybe she should mention something to Lenore or Liza.

No, she better not. Lenore specifically warned her away from Liza. She was also clear that Julia needed to focus on her own problems and not everyone else's. Matt will take care of Matt.

That settled, Julia gives her laptop a withering glare. She's sitting cross legged on her bed with more browser windows open than she cares to count. Before Matt's call, she was running numbers and had finally accepted her reality. She can't see how she can afford to keep Mama Rose at Rosemont.

She'll have to break her promise to her grandmother.

Discouraged, she closes the window to Mama Rose's bank account and clicks on a browser window where she's already typed

Lea+Hope+Los Angeles in the search bar. She stares at the name and zips her rose charm back and forth along its chain.

What are the chances her mother can assist financially? Would she want to?

Julia was three months shy of turning four the first time she met her grandmother Ruby Rose. It was also the last time she saw her mother.

Despite her young age, Julia recalls that day vividly. It's one of the most poignant memory markers from her life. And her mind always rewinds to that moment whenever Lea crosses her thoughts. A good reminder of the type of woman she is, what she's capable of.

On that day, Julia stood beside her grandmother on the porch, hugging the filthy rag doll her mother had found in someone's trash. A single piece of worn luggage squatted at her feet like a neglected puppy.

Mama Rose was screaming at Julia's mother. "This is it, Lea. The final straw. You can't have her back if you leave."

"She's all yours," Lea tossed as she strode to the beat-up car that Julia had called home since birth.

Julia trembled at the finality of those three words.

Mama Rose's cheeks flushed deep red. "You're never to come back here."

"No worries there." Lea splayed her arms. "You'll never see me again."

High as a kite, Lea had told Mama Rose that she didn't want Julia anymore. She wasn't cut out to be a mother. She deserved more from life than to be saddled with a demanding toddler.

She said she had her car and the man who kept her supplied, Mama Rose had once told Julia. Lea hadn't wanted anything else.

Julia's young mind refused to believe her mom. She ran after her only to be yanked back by Mama Rose. Her grandmother hugged Julia as the girl screamed for her mom. She swore to Julia that she was loved and would always be loved. That she was safe with her. She'd never be left to face another dark night alone.

Lea's rejection wounded Julia emotionally, and it still stings whenever Julia thinks about that day. Because here's the thing about wounds: they leave scars. Scars diminish over time, and they become less raw. But they never go away. They're carried for life. They're tender when poked.

Or in Julia's case, when her emotional wound, her fear of abandonment, is triggered.

Like when her ex, Nolan, left her.

She met Nolan at the gym her first year in college. She was studying kinesiology. He was prelaw. Initially friends, they'd started dating her third year, remaining together when she had to drop out her fourth year and return home after Mama Rose was diagnosed with Alzheimer's.

Nolan moved in with them after he graduated. He spent his days at law school and nights studying. Julia divided her time between her shifts at the spa and tending to Mama Rose. She took her to her doctor appointments and helped around the house. They spent weekends tending Mama Rose's garden. Then Mama Rose fell down the stairs, spraining both ankles.

While her grandmother was bedridden for two weeks, Julia used her paid time off to nurse Mama Rose back onto her feet. But even after she was walking again, Mama Rose's cane never left her side. It helped her get around. It even became a weapon.

One evening Nolan came home later than usual, exhausted from studying for his exams. Mama Rose didn't recognize him when he entered the house and went after him with her cane. Nolan was able to yank it from her but only after he'd taken quite a few wallops. Angry welts formed on his arms and back. He suffered a black eye and a split cheek.

"She's lucky I won't sue her," were the first words from his mouth when Julia rushed to the room to defuse the situation. She had to give Mama Rose a sedative to calm her so she could put her to bed.

"It's her sickness, Nolan. She had a memory lapse and forgot who you are. She never would have attacked you otherwise." She begged his reflection in their bathroom mirror for understanding as she stood behind him while he tended to his cuts and bruises.

His cold stare met hers in the mirror. Chills ran down her arms. He vibrated with anger, but he held himself in check.

"She needs to go into a home, Jules."

"This *is* her home."

"She's only going to get worse."

Julia's shoulders dropped. Of course she knew that. She just couldn't accept Mama Rose's mental deterioration had reached this point. She was going to lose the first and only person who genuinely loved her.

Nolan turned around, and her gaze dropped to the welts on his chest and collarbone. They were red and inflamed. She gingerly touched the marred skin. His muscles rippled under her fingers, the only sign that he was in pain. She whipped back her hand.

"I'm so sorry."

"So am I."

"It won't happen again."

"It will happen again."

She looked past him at the wall reflected in the mirror. She couldn't meet his eyes even though she knew he spoke the truth. It had happened before. Mama Rose had been violent with her on a few occasions, pulling Julia's hair or shoving her for no reason. As the disease progressed, it would happen again, and more frequently.

"You're right. I know that. It's just . . . I feel like I'm abandoning her. That I'm giving up on caring for her when she spent her life caring for me."

"You aren't doing us any favors keeping her here, your grandmother included."

Julia's mouth opened only to clamp shut. She didn't have anything to say to that.

At her silence, Nolan continued, "It's her or me, Jules. One of us needs to move out."

Her eyes snapped up to meet his. Pain and resolve hardened his expression. She expected the pain, but the resolve? Fear skittered across her nape.

"What do you mean, exactly?"

"I mean, if you don't move her into assisted living, I'm moving out. I can't live like this."

A match lit inside her. The nerve of him to make her choose. "Well, excuse me for wanting to take care of her."

"Without any regard for yourself? Do you plan to quit your job and stay with her all day?"

"No."

"Then hire a nurse. Or find her a place where you'll both be happy and comfortable."

They stared at each other. Julia crossed her arms and glanced away. She couldn't make herself agree.

Nolan exhaled with frustration and left the bathroom.

"Where are you going?" She followed him into their room, the room she'd grown up in. He dragged his suitcase from under the bed and stalked to the closet. "What are you doing?"

"Since you can't make the decision, I'm making it for you." He pulled a clean shirt over his head and grabbed an armful of clothes.

"You're leaving me?"

He didn't look at her. He kept packing, going from the closet to the bed and back.

Her heart raced. "Nolan, no. Let's talk about this."

"We have. I've tried." He finally looked at her, and she shamefully couldn't meet his eyes. He'd brought Mama Rose's condition up on plenty of occasions. But she'd rejected, deflected, and ignored his pleas because she was in denial. Her mother had left her. Her grandmother was going to leave her too. She had no idea who her father was other than a blank line on her birth certificate. She had thought she'd have Nolan, but—

"Look, honey," she pleaded. "I know it's been tough—"

"It's been painful, Jules. And I'm not just talking about her hitting me." He gestured at his torn cheek, and she cringed. "You've given up so much for her, I have to wonder at what cost."

"She gave up years for me. She raised me because my mother dumped me on her." And now it was Julia's turn to take care of her.

His eyes softened. "I know that. But you dropped out of college for her, and you've cut back on your hours. You don't keep in touch with any friends from school. And lately"—he straightened from the suitcase and took a breath—"lately I've felt that I'm next. That you're going to give me up."

"I'd never do that. I love you."

"That's why this hurts so much." He zipped the case and dropped the wheels on the floor, popped the handle.

The match inside her flared with her rage. "Oh, so you're going to leave me before I leave you?"

"It doesn't have to be this way."

"So, what, if I tell you I'm moving her, you'll stay? You won't break up with me?"

"I never said we were breaking up."

She tightly folded her arms. "It sure feels that way."

He moved to embrace her. "Jules—"

She lifted a hand. She didn't want to hear his excuses or feel his goodbye.

"She could live another fifteen to twenty years," he said.

"The doctors said eight to ten." That was four years ago. Julia was determined to spend as much quality time with Mama Rose as she could. One day, her grandmother would forget who she was, and she feared that day would come soon.

"They don't know that for sure. It could be longer. Is this how you want to spend your life? Spending every minute watching over her? At some point, you'll have no choice but to watch over her twenty-four seven. How are you going to support yourself?"

Her hand sliced through the air between them. That was the wrong thing to say to her, and he knew it. After everything Mama Rose had sacrificed for her, she'd give up her life for her grandmother if it meant Mama Rose could die peacefully in her home.

He swallowed audibly. "This isn't how I imagined us. You deserve more. *I* deserve more."

She flinched, his words echoing her mother's when she'd left Julia with Mama Rose.

She stepped aside for him to pass. "Goodbye, Nolan."

His face fell. He held her gaze until she looked away, hurt, and unnerved. He'd forced her hand, and she made her decision. She didn't choose him.

"Julia." He spoke her name with resignation.

Then he was gone.

The next morning, she came downstairs to find Mama Rose seated at the table, her hands folded around a steaming cup of tea. She was lucid but had no memory of the previous night when Julia asked her about it. She then told Mama Rose that Nolan had moved out. After six years together, they'd broken up.

Mama Rose didn't ask, but Julia suspected she knew it was because of her. Ever so quietly, she told Julia that it was time for her to move out too. And Mama Rose knew exactly the facility she wanted Julia to place her in.

The whir of the laptop's fan brings Julia back to her room. She stares at her mother's name in the search bar. An option, Lenore told her, encouraging her to reach out. Lea is Ruby Rose's daughter, and in a perfect world, Lea would step up to her responsibilities and take on some of Julia's burden.

But Lea abandoned Julia and Mama Rose. And Julia doesn't want to invite that kind of heartache into her life again.

She'll have to find another option if she's to keep her promise to Mama Rose.

CHAPTER 21

MAGNOLIA BLU

August 17, 1972

It's been a month since my last entry. Liza has been keeping me busy. I've finished designing and overseeing the build-out of a secluded garden nook Liza can escape to for outdoor naps and reading. She's been occupied with her charities and hosting backyard parties. I don't know what she'd do without Adam and Sally. They make things happen in her absence.

When she's home, she spends a lot of time with them, Adam especially. He's been joining us for breakfast more frequently, and he and Liza often share dinner in the kitchen in Matty's absence. I suspect Liza's lonely for his company because Matty is working endless hours on his current film project. When he's not on set, his team sends him from one social engagement to another. But his face often greets me in the grocery store checkout line. He's on almost every magazine cover. And it's his face I see when my eyes close at night.

I'd been so preoccupied with my latest fantasy—living together in the garden studio, but the studio is on the beach, and it belongs to us—that he startled me this afternoon. I was cutting back the vine overtaking the shed and didn't expect anyone to be outside. Adam had told me Matty was sleeping and that Liza would be out all day. But I heard someone swearing. Then I heard whispers and what sounded like someone sneaking down the gravel path. Superfans have tried to break into the yard before to get a peek at Matty. There have also been a series of robberies in the neighborhood.

Thinking a thief had found a way onto the property, I put down the clippers, grabbed the shovel, and tiptoed toward the garden nook. I could hear the intruder pace. He grumbled incomprehensibly, and after several deep breaths, I worked up the nerve to confront him. I leaped from behind the tree and swung the shovel. The Holloways would not be robbed on my watch.

Matty shouted and I shrieked. The booklet in his hand flew in a wild arc. He leaned back in the nick of time, narrowly avoiding the shovel head.

"What the fuck?" he bellowed.

I dropped the shovel and profusely apologized for my stupidity. I told him that I'd thought he was a thief and that I should have looked to see who it was before I had attacked.

"You thought somebody was robbing us in broad fucking daylight?"

"It could happen. And Adam said you were sleeping."

"I should fire you. You could have cracked my cheekbone." He nailed me with a look he never would have shown me in my daydreams, and I was mortified. I felt silly for having the fantasies, and I felt horrible I'd almost seriously injured him. I didn't know how to make it up to him, so I kept apologizing like a moron. I deserved to be fired and turned to go pack my things.

"Don't go. Liza will be more upset with me than she already is if she comes home and finds you gone."

"Wouldn't she be upset if she found you injured by me?"

He picked up his booklet and flipped through to the page he'd been on. "I doubt it."

His gaze flew to mine before lowering again, his expression guarded. He didn't seem standoffish. More like he was ashamed he'd admitted to me Liza's lack of concern for him.

I hesitated leaving for that very reason. Somebody should be concerned about him. I also didn't want to leave him.

Curious, I asked him what he was reading. It looked like a manuscript. He told me it was the screenplay to the movie he's filming, the sequel to last summer's blockbuster *Season of the Gods*. I was intrigued, and I said that I'd have to go see the first one so that I could watch this one.

"You're kidding?" He laughed. "The only person on the planet who hasn't seen the movie and she lives in my backyard." He laughed again, his face softening.

I pushed my hands into my pockets. "Is that a problem?"

"That you haven't seen my movie or that you live in my backyard?" He angled his head to the side. "I'd say both."

"I offered to leave."

"Don't." He grinned. "I think you're growing on me."

That made me smile. I felt warm inside like I had the first time we'd met.

I nodded at the screenplay. "You seem frustrated. Is it not good?"

"The screenplay's great. Better than the first movie. But I can't seem to please the director on this one scene." He shoveled his hair back, his voice taking on a worried note. "No matter how I play it, he doesn't like it. He wants more emotion one take, less on the next. I can never get it right. We're filming tonight and I'm already wound up." He shook his arms, trying to loosen up.

He was under pressure, and I knew exactly how to help him relax so he could focus.

I grabbed two pillows from the nook's couch and dropped them on the flagstone. I sat cross legged and gestured for him to do the same. He balked at first, but when I explained that I wanted to show him how to meditate and how it could relax him, he sank onto the pillow with a dramatic sigh that made me smile.

We faced each other, our knees touching, my heart racing at the contact, and I tapped into my inner balance before I lost myself. Matty has a strong presence. He draws people's eyes when he enters a room. I've seen it happen at Liza's parties. And even with just the two of us, even though we were outside, I was very much aware of him. Almost too aware. He smelled of ocean and pine from his cologne and salt from a nervous sweat. And his eyes. I hadn't realized how intense the color hazel could be, or how ruggedly handsome his mouth was this close up. No wonder women swooned for him. No wonder I fell for him within moments of meeting him despite his abrasiveness, which I know is just a front to keep people away. They'll take anything they can get from him—a strand of hair, a wink, a smile, a grope—if he lets them. He has to protect the side of himself that isn't in the public eye.

I cleared my throat and told him to close his eyes.

"Why?"

"So you can focus on your breathing. Trust me, this will help you." I smiled again when I realized I was making him uncomfortable. Was it possible he was just as affected by my presence?

His eyes held on to mine for a beat before closing. I followed suit and instructed him to breathe in for four counts, then out for four counts. We did it together twice more when I felt him looking at me again. I opened my eyes.

"What?"

"You're beautiful. I hadn't . . ." He shook his head. "Never mind. Ignore me."

My internal temperature went from warm to infernal. Every nerve in my body woke up and was firing, angling toward him. Could he tell I've been fantasizing about him? I took a steady breath. "Close your eyes," I whispered. He did, and so did I. He synced his breathing to my count, and then I stopped counting and we just breathed. It was the most intimate thing I've ever experienced, hearing his breaths, feeling the heat of his body where his knees pressed into mine, his scent filling my lungs. My skin tightened with desire.

"Are Liza and Adam close?" he asked.

My eyes snapped open. "Excuse me?" Matty was watching me.

"I don't know." He shrugged. "I get the feeling there's something going on with them."

"They spend a lot of time talking. They're friends, but I don't think it's anything more than that." I'd seen them enjoy meals together, but nothing beyond that.

Matty's gaze dropped to my mouth, and my heart rate picked up. I unconsciously scraped my teeth over my bottom lip, and his eyes flared. Then he seemed to remember himself and where he was. We both did. He grabbed the discarded booklet, and I popped to my feet, reminding myself this was Liza's husband.

"I should let you get back to work."

"Agreed."

I picked up the shovel and started to walk away. A cold shower sounded like a good idea.

"Magnolia?"

I turned around. "Yes?"

"This helped, the meditating." He pointed at the pillows. "Thank you."

I smiled, pleased. "You're welcome."

Sunday

CHAPTER 22

MATT

Matt opens his eyes, the top lids unsticking from the bottoms like packing tape peeling off cardboard. He frowns at the drawn curtains. They're too bright for 4:00 a.m.

He grabs his phone off the nightstand and swears at the time. It's past noon. What happened to his alarm? Convinced he must have turned it off rather than tapping the snooze, he checks the app only to see he set the alarm for 4:00 *p.m.*

He also sees Dave texted twice and called once. Lenore and Julia both called a few hours ago.

"Goddammit." At some point last night, he silenced his phone.

He throws off the sheet and scrambles around the room, repacking his duffel. The place is a mess, littered with chip bags and empty beer cans. He finds the bottle of Jack, a decent portion drained.

"Fucking hell." No wonder he feels like an elephant stomped him to death.

He pops an edible and calls Dave on his way to the bathroom.

"I've been trying to reach you," he answers. "Where are you?"

"Some motel." He takes a piss and brushes his teeth.

"How's Grams?"

"Haven't seen her. I'm not there yet." He talks with his mouth full of foaming paste.

"It's noon. They aren't open to visitors?"

He spits and rinses his mouth. "No, I'm not in California."

"Where the fuck are you?"

"No idea." He packs his toiletries and explains to Dave what happened, everything from the canceled flight to his decision to drive thinking he'd save time, and meeting Magnolia.

"You picked up a hitchhiker?" Dave shouts into the phone.

"Spare me the lecture. And she wasn't hitchhiking." But Magnolia was an excuse to put off Elizabeth.

"Still . . . Are you all right? Is something going on with you? Talk to me."

"I'm fine," he says, fully aware his actions yesterday tell a different story.

He leaves the bathroom and adds the toiletries bag to his duffel, then zips that bag.

"You're not. It sounds to me like you're having some sort of crisis."

"I'm fine, honest." He'll push through the mental muck as he always does.

"Where are you? I'll fly in."

"Are you saying I can't handle my shit?" He comes off defensive, but he's not angry at Dave. He's pissed off with himself for screwing up his alarm.

He stalks the room, making sure he's got everything. He surveys the empty food containers he doesn't remember picking up. He sniffs at the half-eaten burger and cold fries. When did he go on a food run? He swears he didn't leave the room.

"I'm not saying that. But you've got me worried."

"Ford's photos will get done. I'll work on them some before I leave and send you what I've got." Without downtime on the plane, he didn't make any progress yesterday. "You'll have the rest by Tuesday morning."

That'll give him a day to make changes if Dave doesn't agree with the selection.

"I'm talking about you, asshole. The photos can wait."

Matt yanks open the curtain. Daylight blasts into the room. He squints against the glare and the punch the light sends to his head. He jerks the curtain closed.

"I'll be fine. Honest."

"So I don't need to remind you about Le Mans?"

"No, you don't."

"Good. I'll check in with you later. You better be in California by then."

He will.

Dave hangs up, and Matt glares at the room. What a disaster. Even the bed looks like he was fighting something in his sleep. He dreamed about his mom and one of the last conversations they had. They'd been sitting side by side on the seawall and sharing the blanket he brought to keep her warm. She spent so many hours on that wall after his dad died, gazing out to sea.

"Your dad's out there," she told him. "He's living on a small island now."

Matt wanted to believe that was true. "Where?"

"There." She pointed to the horizon. "You can't see it from here. It's just a speck, smaller than the stars."

Matt glanced up at the sheet of glitter above them. "How do you know he's there?"

She smiled at him, brushed back the hair that had blown in his face. "I just do."

He was confused. She knew his dad had died. Why did she say he was alive?

"There are coconuts and shrimp there," she explained. "More than you can eat in a lifetime. He's waiting for us."

The paradise she described sounded fantastical. Miraculous. But Matt knew his dad's island was nothing more than a story to help his mom cope.

His mom, though . . .

He thinks she started to believe her own tales. He shakes the images from his head, doing his best to put them behind him.

———

It's after 1:30 p.m. when Matt fires off the first batch of edited photos to Dave, bites off half an edible for his headache, and checks out of the motel. He settles in his car and is about to leave when something in the passenger footwell catches his eye.

He grabs the leather fringed satchel and swears. Magnolia's purse. How'd he miss this?

He searches the bag for a wallet or something with her phone number so he can call her, but he finds only a lighter, rolling paper, and weed.

Air fills his cheeks. He blows it out. Yesterday's high with her was phenomenal. That was some good shit. And she left it behind. He should keep it.

No, he shouldn't.

He can't keep it.

The stash belongs to her, and he doesn't need the temptation.

He also doesn't have time to return her bag.

But where did she sleep last night? Did her parents show? Could she still be waiting outside, or did she find a way in?

The not knowing will bug him all the way to California unless he does something about it.

With a frustrated groan, he leaves the parking lot, turning in the opposite direction of the freeway and toward Magnolia. He tells himself he's doing this for his peace of mind, that he's not intentionally procrastinating. He needs to know Magnolia is all right. He'll return her bag, and then he'll go.

The drive to her parents' house is quicker than he remembers from last night. She isn't out front, so he knocks on their door. He knocks again and again, and he rings the doorbell twice when nobody answers.

She could be in the backyard.

Quick strides take him to the side gate, which is locked. He hollers for her over the fence, growing more concerned when she doesn't answer.

Where did she go, and what the heck is this fascination with her? Why does he care?

And why does he need to see her again?

She intrigued him.

She aroused him.

She's unlike anyone he's met before.

He backs up a step and assesses the fence. He could leap over it in a snap.

Then he notices the security camera overhead and dismisses that idea.

Staring at the lens, he holds up her bag. If she's watching this live and is here, she'll come out. He returns to the porch to meet her and notices the next-door neighbor washing his car, watching him suspiciously.

"Hey," Matt calls out to him and walks over. "Have you seen Magnolia?"

"Who?" The neighbor tosses a soapy sponge into the bucket and meets Matt at the property line on the other side of a low hedge.

"Magnolia Blu . . . umm, Ruby Rose Hope. Her parents live here. I dropped her off yesterday. She left this bag in my car."

"I don't know of a Ruby Hope. The Sheppards live there."

"Not the Hopes?" Matt looks over his shoulder at the house.

The neighbor shakes his head. "Don't know anyone by that name. The Sheppards have lived there for well over fifteen years."

"Huh." Matt clasps his nape and turns back to the house. Did Magnolia lie to him? Why would she tell him this was her parents' house if it wasn't? Is it possible she was worried enough about seeing her parents again and feared their rejection? Is that why she had him drop her off several houses down or even several blocks over from their real house?

That can't be it. It doesn't add up. She asked him to come to the door with him. She'd been genuinely worried.

Maybe her legal name isn't Hope either. Maybe it's Sheppard.

Or maybe, she's in some sort of trouble.

He turns back to the neighbor. "Did you see a woman with long dirty-blonde hair here yesterday? She was wearing jeans and sandals and had a couple pieces of luggage with her?"

"Haven't seen anyone around here matching that description. Sorry. Wish I could be of more help."

Maybe he could be.

"One sec." Matt lifts a finger and returns to his car. He doesn't stop to think about this need of his to find Magnolia when he should be in California with his grandmother by now. He retrieves a business card and gives it to the neighbor. "She goes by Magnolia Blu, but her legal name, I believe, is Ruby Rose Hope. If she shows, would you tell her I'm looking for her and want to give this back?" He shows the man her bag. "That's my cell number on the card."

"Sure thing, Matt Gatlin." He slaps the card on his palm before tucking it into a pocket.

Matt glances at the date on his phone. Two full days until the end of the month and Elizabeth is on the street. He can spare one more day, can't he?

"If you see her, tell her I'll be in town until the morning." He'll leave at first light.

"Will do." The neighbor retrieves the sponge and squeezes out the excess water.

Matt nods distractedly, watching the neighbor wash his car a moment before turning to his own. He then notices the house Magnolia said was Benjie's. There's a FOR SALE sign on the lawn.

"Huh." Was it there yesterday?

On the off chance the neighbor Magnolia spoke with yesterday saw where she went, he jogs over and rings the doorbell. When no one answers, he peeks through the door's side window. He can see through the living room and into the dining room. The house is empty. Where'd the furniture go? Where's the man who answered the door?

Scratching his head, Matt returns to his car, wondering what's going on. Something about this neighborhood doesn't sit right with him. Did he imagine what happened yesterday?

Impossible.

But still . . .

He drives back to the motel. She'll come looking for him. She'll show him that she's all right. Then he'll know she's real.

CHAPTER 23

———

JULIA

Julia greedily took the Sunday shift at the spa when Hollis, one of the two deep-tissue massage therapists, called in sick. She texted Matt that she'd have to miss their meeting for coffee but knew he'd understand. It's well after 7:00 p.m. when she arrives at Rosemont to visit Mama Rose. After a full day where she worked straight through lunch to bill for extra time, her feet hurt and thumbs tingle. Exhausted, she tries to rub life back into her hands and wrists.

She wonders when Matt got in and is surprised that she hasn't heard from him yet. He didn't text or call back. With back-to-back appointments, she hasn't had time to research Lenore's list, and she worries Matt will be disappointed since she offered to. That could be why she hasn't heard from him. He's been busy touring facilities and researching options for Liza, exactly what she should have done today for Mama Rose.

Julia scans the parking lot for a New Mexico license plate. Guiltily, she stalked him online last night, tumbling down the internet rabbit hole for over an hour after their call. Aside from a brief bio and a few headshots, most of what she found about him had to do with photography and cars. She's never been interested in aerodynamic designs and Formula 1 racing, but after a deep dive into his portfolio, she's curious how he captured such magnificent shots at those unique angles. Now, in addition to her initial worry for him—because she's convinced that he did make it to Rosemont today as he'd promised—she's also curious about him.

Because let's face it. Matt's a great-looking guy. He isn't smiling in his headshot, but his wavy hair and shadowed jaw lend a dash of mystery to him. The intelligence in his eyes drew her in. There's a gentleness about him despite the rough edges. The photo doesn't appear staged. He doesn't look like he's posing. His expression is too pensive, as if his mind were far from where he was. She wondered what he was thinking about right then.

Julia pops a mint and brushes her hair. She gathers the diary and bag of assorted foil-wrapped chocolate squares she picked up at the store on the way over. They're Mama Rose's favorite, and she hopes they'll soften the blow when she tells her grandmother that she has to look for a new home for her. Of course, Julia has to work up the nerve to admit she can't honor the one promise Mama Rose swore her to. With her luck, that promise will be the one thing her grandmother does remember.

Julia enters the facility. The day shift staff have gone home, and Steve is behind the reception desk. She waves.

"Evening, Julia." Steve's greeting is chipper. "It's game night. Trevor wheeled your grandmother to the common room thirty minutes ago."

"Thanks." Julia heads in that direction, eager to see if Matt's there with Liza so she can apologize for not following through on the research she promised to pass along.

The room is lively and bright. Poker tables have been set up along the far wall. Dealers shuffle cards, and players count chips, heckling each other. A movie plays on the flatscreen on the opposite wall, a classic in faded color Julia recognizes but can't recall the title of. She spots Mama Rose in her wheelchair, her back to the room as she looks out at the garden. Liza, of all people, sits beside her. And they appear to be actively engaged in conversation. That's new.

Did Mama Rose finally recognize Liza? What could they be talking about?

Disregarding Lenore's warning to avoid Liza, Julia cautiously approaches. She doesn't see any sign of Matt, who could help her around Liza. He might have already left for the day. But she wants to listen in on their conversation.

Mama Rose is smiling as Liza chats, a good sign. Julia prays her grandmother is lucid enough to discuss the diary. Liza catches Julia's glance, and her face slackens. She whispers to Mama Rose before leaning back in her chair with what Julia can only interpret as a superior smile.

Mama Rose twists around and looks up at Julia with a gasp.

"I didn't mean to interrupt. Keep talking." Julia starts to back away so they can continue their conversation. She'll hover nearby where she can eavesdrop.

"What are you doing here?" Mama Rose grips the wheelchair arms as if she's about to launch from the chair.

Julia glances between the two women, wondering what Liza said to her. "I came to see you. How was your day?"

Mama Rose's withered hands jerk at the wheels. She grunts, trying to push herself forward while nervously glancing from Julia to Liza and back. "Unlock them," Mama Rose complains of the brakes when the chair doesn't budge.

"Ruby," Liza says.

Julia crouches beside Mama Rose since all the chairs are taken. "I brought your favorite chocolates." She shows her grandmother the foil bag. "Do you want one? Liza?" She tilts the bag toward Matt's grandmother.

"Not from you." Mama Rose spits on the floor, and Julia rocks back on her heels.

"Mama!"

"Never from you." She backhands the bag out of Julia's hand. Chocolates scatter across the floor.

"Mama Rose." Julia's hand smarts where her grandmother hit her. Ever watching out for others and never herself, Julia retrieves the pieces around Mama Rose's chair before someone trips on them, putting her head within her grandmother's reach.

Mama Rose grabs a fistful of Julia's hair and yanks. Julia shrieks at the sharp, unexpected pain. Mama Rose bellows, "You undeserving, spoiled brat." Then she screams, pulling again at Julia's hair.

The entire room goes quiet for one heartbeat, and then all hell breaks loose.

Chips tumble and cards fly across tables as residents rush over to see what's happening. Chairs scrape across the floor in people's haste to get closer.

"You can't have her, Lea! You no-good piece of trash. She's mine. Mine!" With Julia's hair fisted in her hand, Mama Rose yanks Julia's head side to side. Julia stumbles left to right on her knees, holding on to her hair so it isn't torn from her scalp. Her eyes burn from the pain. She tries to loosen her grandmother's grip, but Mama Rose is strong, fueled by a rage Julia has witnessed only twice before: when she attacked Nolan with her cane and the day Lea abandoned Julia.

Julia fears Mama Rose is reliving that day.

"It's me, Mama. It's Julia." She manages to get to her feet.

Rosemont staff rush toward them. Liza rises from her chair, backing out of the way.

Trevor and two other caretakers surround Mama Rose. They try coaxing her down, holding her arms, but she won't release her grip on Julia's hair.

"Julia is mine," Mama Rose shrieks. "You can't have her back. You'll never get her back."

"What is she going off about?" Alice, the night-shift nurse, asks.

"She thinks I'm my mother," Julia explains over Mama Rose's screeching.

"I've never seen her like this. Get the benz," Trevor orders Alice. "I'll try to get her back to her room."

The common room is in chaos. Residents who can walk on their own hurry away. Those needing assistance cry out for it. The curious crowd them.

"Back off, everyone. Return to your games," Trevor orders.

"Calm down, Rose," Liza yells, and Julia wants to yell at her. What did she say to Mama Rose right before Mama Rose noticed Julia?

Mama Rose screams nonsense. She struggles against Trevor as he keeps her firmly planted in the chair. Julia squeezes her grandmother's wrist, and Mama Rose finally lets go. Julia stumbles back with a cry. Trevor hugs Mama Rose from behind, restraining her in the wheelchair. He talks in her ear, but whatever he's saying isn't registering. Then—

Rap, rap, rap.

"Mags."

Liza bangs her cane on the floor again.

"Calm down this instant, Magnolia."

Mama Rose stills at Liza's command just as Alice returns. The nurse injects Mama Rose with the sedative, and they all watch her body go lax.

Julia hates they had to sedate her. But she's never been this out of control since the walking cane incident with Nolan. For the first time in her life, Julia was afraid of her.

And to think Julia had argued against moving her to assisted living after she'd attacked Nolan. Imagine if Mama Rose were still living at home like Julia had wanted. They both could have been seriously injured.

She watches the staff tend to her grandmother and the other residents. They take such good care of them. These caretakers truly love them. Where will Julia find this level of care at a price she can afford? Nowhere, she's afraid.

Trevor puts a hand on her shoulder. "Are you all right, Julia?"

Her scalp burns and her heart aches. But she nods. "I will be."

"Go home and get some rest. She'll be better tomorrow." Trevor wheels her sleeping grandmother from the room.

Pressure builds in Julia's chest as she watches them go. They turn the corner into the hallway and she loosens her pent-up breath. Trevor will write up a report, and Lenore will assess if Mama Rose poses a risk to other residents or herself. Rosemont could terminate her contract for behavioral problems. Even if Julia does find an additional income source, she may be forced to relocate Mama Rose anyway.

Julia picks up the remaining chocolates and notices Liza watching her. "What did you say to her? Did you tell her I was Lea?" Surely Liza couldn't be that cruel. Granted, Julia upset her yesterday, but to take advantage of Mama Rose's condition?

Liza is a tall woman. She looks down her nose at Julia. "Not that I owe you an explanation, but I said, 'Your granddaughter is here.'"

Julia gets up off the floor. "She's never attacked me like that."

"She's getting worse. She must have misheard me. I didn't expect—" Liza stalls. A shadow darkens her face.

"Didn't expect what?"

Liza shakes her head. "Adam was wrong. My time here has been pointless." Sadness tints her sea-green eyes a shade darker before she blinks and they clear. She walks away with the support of her cane. *Step, step, clack. Step, step, clack.*

Liza's remark settles like the fertilizer Mama Rose sprinkled over freshly planted seeds, and a new thought sprouts. "Did Adam convince you to move to Rosemont? Isn't he your POA? Wasn't he also your butler?"

Liza stops. She angles her head toward Julia. "He was more than my butler."

From the sound of it, he was also more than Liza's power of attorney. That six-worded statement was loaded.

But Adam's gone missing. He's been unreachable for a month. Which reminds Julia . . .

"Was Matt here?"

An arched brow meets Julia's question. "My grandson?"

"He said he'd be here today. We were supposed to meet for coffee. I was hoping to see him."

Liza harrumphs. "Honey, don't get your hopes up that he'll show. I sure haven't."

"Why not?"

"That boy will never come through for the likes of me."

CHAPTER 24

MATT

Matt checked back into the motel after leaving Magnolia's house, but he didn't go to his room. He went across the street to the bar to watch the ball game and wait for Magnolia's call. He orders a beer and another and keeps peering at his phone, face up on the bar top.

Several hours and the same number of drinks later, Matt still hasn't heard from her, and he questions why he's stalling. Why is he unwilling to give up on a woman he hardly knows when he should be well on his way to California, if not already there?

He drops an edible on his tongue, the answer as clear as the glass he just emptied.

Returning to his grandmother is revisiting why he was sent to live with her in the first place. It's acknowledging that he never mourned his dad. It's remembering what happened to his mom. It's admitting he wasn't enough for her to stay. It's remembering it all. He could have saved his mom; he could have *at least* tried. But he didn't. And the memory of his inaction is an oil spill gliding across the surface of his mind. Slick and toxic.

Which is why he chooses not to remember, and why he's choosing to wait here until he stops remembering. Hence, Magnolia. He needs a distraction.

The game finishes shortly before eight, and Matt closes out his tab. He returns to his room and eats half a gummy to take off the edge, sinking further into himself. And when that doesn't settle his mind, he rolls a joint from Magnolia's stash, turns off the lights, and settles back on the couch to stare at the gray ceiling. The curtains are drawn, the room cast in shadows, and Matt closes his eyes.

"Thank you very much, Mags," he whispers to the room, taking a hit, and he sinks into oblivion. Spicy smoke wraps delicate, smooth arms around his mind, and she is there, in the room with him. He feels her over him, on him, dulling his headache and muting his buzz. She unravels the tightness binding his lungs, and he can breathe again. Like fog retreating to the coast, his restlessness eases.

He goes willingly and hungrily with her. Tumbling, falling, drowning until he feels nothing. No ache or throbbing pain. No knife cleaving his skull. No tortured memories from the past. Just her.

He definitely feels her.

Fingers trace his jaw, his neck. His hand follows hers down his torso and under the band of his jeans. He cups himself and groans. His body melts into the cushions.

Music plays in the distance, warm, brassy notes. Melodic voices grow louder. He knows that sound. He needs to answer that sound . . .

Matt jerks up on the couch. His gaze flies to the phone he left on the table among discarded food cartons and beer cans.

He scrambles off the couch and answers. "Matt Gatlin."

"Thank God. I've been trying to reach you for hours," Julia says.

Matt glances at the screen. It's almost midnight. Christ, he must have passed out.

"H-Hey." His voice cracks as much from his shock over her concern for him as from exhaustion.

"Are you okay? Where are you? Liza said you never showed up today."

"I'm—" He rakes back his hair and sinks into the couch. "I fell asleep."

Pause. "Are you still at the same motel?"

Shame floods him, and he hesitates before answering. "Yeah."

"Are you still drinking?"

And smoking. But that was earlier.

"Right now, no." He rubs his eyes, past caring that he's procrastinating getting to Elizabeth. His gaze narrows on what's left of the joint he must have snuffed out hours ago. He reaches for a tin and chews an edible. "What of it?"

"I don't know," she says. "I'm trying to picture this good-looking, award-winning professional photographer I read up on that everybody sings praises about as this slacker getting drunk by himself in a motel room when he should be in California helping his grandmother, and I'm sorry. The pieces don't fit."

If he wasn't awake before, he is now. He should be offended, but he can't help the goofy smile. She googled him. "You think I'm good looking?"

"That's what you got out of everything I said? Are you listening to me? Liza needs you, and instead you're wherever you are having some sort of breakdown. That or you just don't care."

"I care," he fudges because the truth means admitting he's having a breakdown and needs help, which he doesn't. He just needs to get himself under control.

"About her. You don't care about her. You sure aren't acting like it. Your grandmother said you'd flake. I didn't want to believe it."

Not surprising. Elizabeth never thought highly of him. But despite that, he senses something out of orbit in Julia's world. She launched into him like a cat with claws drawn. "Everything all right with you?"

"No." Julia sighs. "It wasn't a good day. My grandmother . . ." Her voice catches.

"It's okay. You can talk to me," he offers, eager to redirect the conversation's focus on her.

"I told myself I wasn't going to cry over this," she says as she does cry. "Oh, gosh. This is embarrassing. I'm going to hang up now."

"No, don't."

"Let me spare us both and get off the phone. I'm usually not like this."

"Like what?"

"Emotional and melodramatic."

"You're not."

"I'm normally a very private person. I don't dump my problems on people I hardly know."

"You aren't. I'm not taking them on. I'm just listening. That's all." Matt waits for her to collect herself. "You still there?"

"I'm here. Okay, yes, I need to talk this through. She had an episode. She thought I was my mother, and she . . . she hurt me." Julia then tells him what happened, and he wishes he knew how to comfort someone over the phone. But for a guy who's spent his entire adult life avoiding emotion, let alone meaningful relationships, he lacks the experience to connect. So he does what he told her he would and simply listens. "It was Liza who finally got her to calm down," Julia explains. "I don't know if it was her tone or that she called her Mags, but Mama Rose stopped screaming. Now I'm afraid if I can manage to meet the fee hike, Rosemont will cancel her contract anyway for behavioral issues."

"They won't," Matt says. "From what you've told me, it sounds like they love your grandmother too much."

"That's the other thing. I don't know where else I'll find a place with a staff as wonderful as Rosemont's. But you should have seen her, Matt. It was terrible. I was afraid of her, and I've never been afraid of her before. I hate feeling like this about her."

"I'm sorry that happened to you."

She's quiet for a few beats. "After Trevor, her caretaker, wheeled her away, that's when Liza said that about you. She said, and I quote, 'That boy will never come through for the likes of me.' I wanted to tell her she's wrong. Please tell me she's wrong."

Matt pinches his nose bridge. At least Elizabeth's expectations of him haven't changed. He doesn't have to live up to the impossible on top of everything else. "She isn't wrong, Julia," he says quietly.

"Why, Matt? Help me understand. She selected you as her secondary power of attorney. You. There has to be a reason."

"That's the thing, Julia. There isn't a reason, none that I've come up with." Other than Elizabeth wanting to torment him.

"You're the only person who can help her."

"I can't be." People swarmed her at her garden parties. She was always entertaining guests, buzzing off to some meeting. Anybody is a better option than him. This is his punishment for her daughter's death.

"Whether or not you believe it shouldn't matter. You mean something to her because she picked you. Yet you're there, wherever you are, choosing not to be here, and I have to wonder—" She pauses. "Do you need help? I can call someone. I can . . . I can come get you."

"No, you have too much to worry about. I'm fine." But a sliver of something bright, something that has been dormant for a long time, flickers to life. He'd call it hope. He wants to grab it and hold on to it, store it in a safe place. But any hope that he could be enough for someone abandoned him years ago.

"You sure?"

"Yes, I'm sure."

She's quiet again before she asks in a hesitant voice, "How did she hurt you?"

It takes a second to make sense of what she's asking. "What's your fascination with my grandmother? What is she to you?"

"I'm not sure. I mean, I don't like anyone to feel lonely or unloved. But there's something about Liza. Now that I know she and my grandmother were once friends, I feel sort of an affinity with her. Mama Rose had many friends, but most are old like her and in homes or have passed on. There isn't anyone left who visits her. Nobody I can talk to about her."

"You can talk to me."

"Thank you for that."

They're quiet for a few moments, neither volunteering to get off the line. Matt guesses she's as lonely as him. "Do you have your grandmother's diary on you?" he asks to keep her on the line.

"I do."

"Will you read it to me? That is, if you're planning to read more of it."

"Okay. Yeah, that's a good idea. It'll get my mind off today." He hears rustling on her end and pages flipping. "August nineteenth, nineteen seventy-two. Matty was in between projects . . . ," she starts, picking up where, presumably, she left off yesterday.

Matt cracks open a beer, drains half, and lights another joint, opening the door for fresh air as he listens to her read about their grandparents. He takes the joint and phone out on the balcony and deeply inhales the night's air.

Below him, someone splashes in the pool, a woman swimming alone. Lithe limbs leisurely cut through the water. Long hair fans across the surface behind her. She reaches the far end and pushes off the wall, flipping onto her back. His breath catches. She's nude.

The woman opens her eyes and looks straight up at him. She smiles and everything inside him tightens. Blood rushes to his center as he stares down at her, not quite believing his eyes. But his reaction doesn't lie.

It's her. Magnolia Blu.

Yeah. Change of plans. He's not going to California.

CHAPTER 25

MAGNOLIA BLU

September 23, 1972

A month has passed since the day I meditated with Matty, and up until this week I rarely saw him at home. I should say he wasn't home more than usual, or from what I've seen of him throughout summer. But it's hard not to believe that he's avoiding me after what happened between us in the secluded garden nook. I could also be overthinking what I felt with him—I would pay anything to know if he felt it too, that hum resonating between us—because I haven't been able to stop thinking about him. Our encounter only made my fantasies more vibrant.

It's wrong of me to have these feelings for him. He shouldn't be on my mind every waking moment. Liza's my employer. More importantly, she's my friend. My only one in California. She trusts me. And while Sam and I had shared partners, while I'd been able to love without restraint for five years, and while Liza confessed that sharing her husband with the world was part of her marriage, I know she would not be open to me loving Matty.

So I've been keeping extra busy, which hasn't been too challenging. There's plenty of work to do around the property, and Liza's rarely home. The arts council gala is next month at the Beverly Hills Hotel, and planning is in full swing. She invited me up for breakfast on the patio the other morning. She seemed tired and unusually quiet. Basically, she wasn't her chipper self, and I remarked upon it. She insisted that she was fine and expected the gala to go off without a hitch. I asked her how she and Matty were doing. If I'm being honest, I was more curious about him, hungry for any morsel she'd direct my way.

Her lips pursed. She pushed her eggs around her plate and set down her fork.

"I have to go." She scooted her chair back and stood. "I won't be home tonight. We're working late at the hotel and celebrating afterward. It'll be easier to stay there than drive home."

"All right," I said, taking her avoidance as a cue to not ask again about her and Matty, and I tried not to feel disappointed that both would be away.

"Sally will be home if you need anything." She retreated to the house. Just inside the door, Adam caught her elbow. I'd never seen him touch her so boldly. He whispered in her ear, she nodded, and then she left. Adam turned his attention to me, his expression troubled. I got the feeling he wanted to help Liza but either she wasn't letting him or he didn't know how. There was a trace of yearning that lingered just long enough for me to notice, something I probably shouldn't have seen. I felt like an interloper. I dipped my head and shoveled a spoonful of scrambled eggs into my mouth.

True to her word, Liza was gone all day and night. That evening after I showered and dressed for bed, I took my flute to the porch. But the loud music coming from the house made it difficult for me to play. All the windows were open, every room lit up. I watched Matty aimlessly move from one room to the next, and I longed to go to him, help ease his restlessness. Even from a distance, I could tell that he was drinking. And it didn't take long for him to appear on the patio. He brought a glass to his mouth, and he looked up at the sky. For a while, he stared into the dark openness. Then his gaze swept over the yard, searching, and landed on me. Our eyes locked and my breath came faster. He stepped in my direction, and my legs unfolded underneath me and I stood. I hurried into the studio and closed the door behind me before I made a move I'd regret. He'd told me the day we met to stay away from the house while he was home. Nothing good could come of me going to him.

I wanted him to come to me. I desired him so.

"Stop it, Mags," I ordered my reflection in the bathroom mirror. "He isn't yours. You can't have him."

But I wanted him.

He knocked on my door.

I should have told him to go away. It was late and I needed to sleep.

I still opened the door.

He casually leaned against a porch pillar, lazily knocking a half-empty tumbler of scotch against his thigh. "Saw you watching me."

"I wasn't watching you," I denied in a desperate attempt to prove I wasn't interested. I wouldn't make Liza's marriage more complicated than it already was. "I was already looking up at the house when you came outside."

"Why didn't you come up?"

I didn't answer, and I didn't remind him he'd asked me to stay away either.

His eyes held mine for a beat, and he glanced away with a quick smile. "Probably wouldn't have been a good idea."

"Probably not. Liza still out?"

"Yep."

"Adam?"

He scowled. "I fired him."

That took me aback. "You did? When? Why?"

"He was fucking my wife."

Shock rippled through me. "He told you that?"

He shook his head. "Not so much in words."

"Liza say something?"

He nodded.

I opened my mouth to tell him how sorry I was. That confession from her had to hurt. But I stopped short of saying anything. This could be good. Hadn't she told me she suspected Matty slept around? Or was I just assuming that for my own benefit? Was I looking for justification to be with Matty?

"I didn't know. She didn't say anything to me. She . . . She isn't at the hotel tonight for the gala planning, is she? She left you."

"Why do you think I'm drinking?" He lifted his glass in a mock toast, then fell silent. I watched him trace a finger around the lip, wondering what must be going through his mind, when he announced, "I should be in bed. We're filming at the crack of dawn, but I can't sleep."

I wondered where Liza had gone. Was she expecting him to go after her, prove his love like she'd once told me? I didn't ask him. Instead, I heard myself whisper an offer. "Do you want to stay? We can talk."

"I'd like that." He dropped into one of the chairs on the porch. "Got anything to drink? I'm on empty." He set the tumbler on the table.

"Yes. What would you like?"

"Water?"

I smiled. "Coming right up."

We talked on the porch for over two hours about everything and nothing. He wanted to know about life in the commune and was especially curious about why I'd left home and Benjie and Sam. He wanted to know if I'm happy here. I told him that I'm happier than I've ever been because I'm doing this—living here, working in the dirt—for me. California was where I wanted to be when I first ran away.

He told me what his life had been like growing up. He was a nobody with a deadbeat dad and an alcoholic mom. He'd never had acting lessons but auditioned for a small part on a whim. He didn't believe he was talented. He thought he was getting by on his charm and good looks. He'd milk those as long as he could. But despite all the glitz and glam of the life he led, he missed people being real. He missed being real himself. He peered at me, his beautiful hazel eyes holding mine, and told me that I was real. That was why he liked being around me. Why he hasn't stopped thinking of me since that day we meditated in the garden. His words wove a spell. He was opening himself up to me, telling me things I'm assuming he'd only shared with Liza. He was making it too easy for me not to just fall for the movie star or my dear friend's husband, but for the man himself. For Matty.

I felt hot, flushed, and shot to my feet. "I need something stronger than water."

"Was it something I said?"

"No, it's me." I touched his shoulder, moving around him into the studio, and he snagged my fingers. A jolt shot along my arm. My gaze lifted from our hands to his face. His eyes dilated with desire. Then he suddenly let go.

I poured vodka over ice and reached for a second glass. "Do you want one, or am I drinking alone?" I called out to him.

"I'll share yours," he said from right behind me.

My breath caught in my throat as his arms slipped around my waist and drew me back against his chest. I could feel the heat of him through my thin nightgown. He kissed my shoulder, a soft, lingering kiss, and reached for my glass on the counter. He took a deep drink and gave me the glass, turning me to face him as I took a sip. Eyes fixed on mine, he took the glass from my hand and set it on the counter.

I then forgot all about that glass.

I forgot about Liza too.

And Sam, and Benjie, and my parents.

I only thought of me with Matty.

I lifted my nightgown over my head, and his gaze followed the satin as it pooled at our feet. His eyes hungrily swept up my body, landing on my mouth. I'd never felt so desired.

"Mags." His voice was strained, grainy. He grasped my face with both hands and brought his mouth down on mine. The kiss was fire. My hands were on him, stripping off his shirt and unbuckling his jeans. We didn't stop kissing or touching as he walked me backward toward the bed. We fell naked onto the mattress, and I drew my legs up by his hips. I cupped his jaw and he broke the kiss, lifted his head. I saw his hesitation, his questions.

"I want this," I whispered the reassurance.

"I want this too, but I also want you."

My soul soared, and he took my body in ways that seemed only right with him. He made me feel things I never could have with Sam, as if he were trying to make me forget him. I wanted us to forget Liza. And for a stretch of time—an hour, maybe two—I think we did.

CHAPTER 26

MATT

Matt jogs down the steps to the pool, convinced his eyes are tricking him. Magnolia Blu can't be here. He'd only left his number with the neighbor, and she never called him. How could she have known where he is?

No matter. She's here now. That's definitely her in the pool.

The chain-link fence creaks when he opens the gate to the pool deck. She swims to the side to meet him. He kneels at the edge, and she grins at him from under damp lashes.

"Hello, Matt."

"How'd you find me?"

"You're really not coming to California?"

He shakes his head with a short laugh and tips back his beer. "Nope."

"Then get in." Magnolia pushes away from the ledge with a flirty smile.

"I don't have a suit."

"Do you see me wearing one?"

"You're trouble." He shakes a finger at her. He glances back at the motel. A few room windows are lit, but most are dark. Could they get away with skinny-dipping?

She treads in the water. "Everyone's asleep. No one will know."

He levels her a look. He'll know.

Magnolia does a slow backward somersault. The peaks of her breasts break the water, and the rest of her follows, leaving nothing to his imagination.

"Fuck me." Any objections he had about jumping in the pool leave the building.

Matt finishes off the beer and drags his shirt over his head. He drops his jeans and turns toward the pool. Magnolia shakes her head and points at his boxer briefs. He's either all in or chickenshit.

He shoves down his briefs and dives in. The water is shockingly cold, exactly the temperature he needs. Numbness will set in in no time. He breaks the surface with a whoop.

She presses a finger to her lips, reminding him to be quiet, and swims to the deep end. Matt follows. They grasp the ledge, facing each other. Their bodies backlit by the pool light, their legs swirl in the water.

"I drove back and looked for you today. Where'd you go?" he asks.

She shrugs. "Around."

"Did your parents show up?"

She sinks underwater and surfaces behind him. Her nipples graze his back, her legs brush his. Heat rushes to his center. He turns around with a groan. "What are you doing?"

"Have you ever been in love?" Her words douse his arousal.

"What kind of question is that?"

"An easy one. Yes or no?"

"No."

"Why not?"

"None of your business." He closed himself off to love a long time ago.

"Interesting." Magnolia traces a finger across his collarbone. His skin pebbles.

"How so?"

"It implies you've made a conscious choice not to fall in love."

He clears water from his ear. Her observation hits too close to home.

She tiptoes her fingers over his chest, and he flattens her hand. "Stop that."

"How'd you lose your mom?"

He shakes his head and looks away.

"It helps to talk about it."

"I don't talk about her," he says, feeling like a song on repeat.

She tilts her head like an inquisitive bird. "It couldn't have been all bad."

"It wasn't." Until the end, it was idyllic. He couldn't have asked for a better set of parents.

"Then tell me something good."

Words escape his mouth like birds released from a cage. "She was radiant." The sun in his universe. And the memories of her are suddenly there, vivid and dynamic. Him waking up to her singing "Good morning" as she opened the blinds in his room. Him running home after school to the scent of oranges on her fingers from the snack she'd made for him. The notes she'd leave him in his lunch bag, positive affirmations that disappeared with her. The kisses she'd bless him with every evening before bed. Her checking in on him at night before he drifted to sleep. Moments he's forgotten in his struggle not to remember that last day with her. They knock the wind from him.

"I wish I'd had the chance to meet her," Magnolia whispers.

So does Matt.

He shoves off the wall and crosses the pool with an aggressive stroke. On the opposite side, he stands in the shallow end and wipes the chlorine from his eyes. Water falls in rivulets off his shoulders. Magnolia doesn't give him a chance to get sucked into his dark thoughts. As if she knows she's the distraction he needs, she swims to the shallow end and, like a nymph, rises from the water with her head tipped back. Her hair falls in a glistening sheet behind her shoulders, her breasts polished and gleaming in the single lamp lighting the pool deck, thoroughly distracting him.

Everything inside Matt tightens. It hurts to breathe.

"You're fucking hot." The words slip from him.

Magnolia's hands rise to cup his face, and eyes locked onto her mouth, Matt feels himself leaning over. She kisses him, and he jolts, her touch an unexpected shock. Then he's melting into her arms as his wrap around her, lifting her as he straightens. Her legs cradle his hips, and he groans into her mouth. She kisses him and kisses him, her fingers tangling in his hair.

Matt has never felt anything like this. He's never felt so lost and found—*understood*—at once. His head is spinning. He feels himself falling and falling.

They crash into the water. He comes up gulping air, disoriented.

Magnolia comes up sputtering. "You!" she shrieks, laughing.

Matt holds up his hands. "My bad." He lost his head with her and eyeballs the empty beer on the side of the pool. He tries to calculate how much he's had tonight, what he's taken, when a shout comes from outside the fence.

"Quiet down in there," a man wearing nothing but a rumpled cotton shirt and loose boxers hollers.

Magnolia yelps and sinks to her shoulders.

"Pool is closed," he complains.

"We were just leaving," Matt says.

The man glowers, then returns to his room.

Magnolia stares at Matt with swollen lips and huge eyes. Water sparkles like black diamonds on the tips of her lashes. "We should go," he whispers.

"What about California? Your grandmother—"

"I can't—" He stops before he says more. The very idea of confronting Elizabeth is triggering. Someone else will come through on her behalf. Best to return home tomorrow and coordinate her relocation from there. As for tonight . . .

Their eyes meet.

"Stay with me."

"I have nowhere to spend the night," she says at the same time.

They share a smile.

She kisses him lightly on the mouth and wades to the steps, climbs out. Matt follows. They gather their clothes, and he grabs her hand. Naked and giggling, they stealthily jog up the stairs. She walks backward into the room when he lets her in, dropping her clothes by the door, and crooks her finger, backing up toward the bed.

Matt likes what she's thinking. He kicks the door shut behind him.

CHAPTER 27

JULIA

Julia presses her phone to her chest and shuts her eyes, mortified. She asked Matt, a man she hardly knows, if he's ever been in love. And that's not the worst of it. She wouldn't shut up about his mom. She kept pushing him on what he's doing about his grandmother.

Meddlesome, that's what Mama Rose would call her. It's what got Matt's attention when she had Liza's personal belongings shipped to him. She hasn't stopped butting into their business since. But she couldn't help herself. After he remarked yesterday that his parents are deceased, she hazarded a guess that Matt's reluctance to assist Liza stems from more than whatever's going on between them. That the death of his mom, Liza's daughter, could be one of the reasons for the estrangement. Julia knows a thing or two about grief and keeping people at a safe distance to minimize the risk of getting hurt again. Goodness, she's doing it with her own mother.

She glances at the clock and cringes at the time. She and Matt spent over two hours on the phone. Most of their conversation was her reading Mama Rose's diary to him, but they did chat about themselves some. Matt has issues with his mom, and he's tight-lipped about them, which only makes her more curious about who she is and what happened to her. Aubrey's her name, if Julia recalls correctly from Liza's brief mention of her daughter while Julia boxed her things.

Admittedly, it was bold of her to pry into Matt's history. But she can't help who she is. She does feel an affinity toward both Matt and his grandmother. She and Matt lost their mothers, and Liza faces what Julia fears for herself: dying alone.

Has Matt really changed his mind about coming here, or was that just the alcohol talking?

Worried she's partly to blame by interfering in his personal life, she sets her alarm to call him first thing in the morning. She's starting to care for this man who's becoming less of a stranger and more of a confidant with every phone call. Hopefully she can catch him before he leaves for home and convince him otherwise.

She leans over to set her phone on the bedside table, and the diary slides onto the floor. It lands open on an entry dated eight years ago, exactly a month after Mama Rose was diagnosed.

"That can't be right." The journal entries only go until midyear 1973. How did she miss this one?

Julia picks up the book and skims the passage. "What?" she murmurs and reads it again more slowly. Then again, and again.

The last entry in the Magnolia Blu diary isn't an entry at all but a letter to Liza. It explains why Mama Rose insisted Julia promise not to move her away from Rosemont. Mama Rose was waiting for Liza to find her there. She hoped this journal would find its way into Liza's hands.

But that discovery isn't nearly as alarming as what else the letter reveals to Julia.

Monday

CHAPTER 28

—

MATT

Matt lies naked on his side. Sunlight bounces off the faceted crystal he studies. He doesn't recall Magnolia wearing the necklace last night, but she had it on this morning.

The piece is unique. Bound by gold wire to the chain, it rests between her breasts. "Where'd you get this? It looks custom made."

"It is." She exhales the spicy-scented smoke from the joint they're sharing and tucks her chin to look at the charm. "My friend June made it. She said it's a time-link crystal."

"A what?"

With the joint pinched between her pointer and middle fingers, she lifts the crystal to the light and studies it. "She said it's supposed to help me get in touch with earlier parts of my life so I can rebalance them or something like that."

"A type of healing crystal?" He's heard of those before.

"I guess." She shrugs. "It's also supposed to help me access my future. Sounds far out, doesn't it?" she says with a laugh when he makes a face.

"Not sure I believe that."

"Doesn't make it untrue. You'd like June. She's radical." The crystal drops against her chest, and she gives him the joint, rolls onto her side. Hair flows over her breast. He tucks the wayward tresses behind her shoulder and glides a knuckle across her nipple, watching the bud tighten.

They've been awake several hours, staring at the ceiling as they pass her weed back and forth while discussing the most random facts. Until a few minutes ago, he didn't know peaches were in the rose family or that a sunflower isn't just one flower, but a thousand individual flowers. She hasn't nudged him about his mom or grandmother since they left the pool, but he hasn't stopped thinking of either despite his efforts to get his mind off them. He and Magnolia collapsed, exhausted, at four thirty this morning, only for him to wake at eight eager to bury himself in her again. She's been willing and giving, and he can't get enough of her. But it's more than a physical relief he craves with her.

Warm fingers gently touch his rough jaw. "Where'd you go?" Magnolia brings his mind back to the room. An old Bogart movie is muted on the TV. Morning light spills across the bed, highlighting the fine hairs on her arms. They glisten like dew. Thoughts tumble over each other in his head to land solidly on his mouth.

"I was thinking about why I'm here, and . . ." He pauses, swallows. "Why I can't seem to leave," he says with a tight chest, and he's back there again, treading beneath the surface of his memory: the pitch-black sky and inky, cold water. The tang of rotten fish and cool metal of the boat. The infinite stretch of silence behind the steady lap of water. The outline of his mom's body sinking into the abyss.

"When I was sent to live with my grandmother after my mom died," he hears himself explaining, "she asked me what happened. Elizabeth knew the basics, that she'd drowned and I had been in the skiff with her. My neighbor must have told her, or the coast guard, I can't remember. But she wanted details. Things like the last thing my mom said, why we were in the boat in the first place, how we managed to get so far from shore, where were the oars, how did she fall overboard, did I jump in and try to save her. On and on and on. I was already reeling from my dad's death. He was lost at sea during a storm. They never found him."

"Matt," he hears Magnolia whisper. He feels the warm press of her hand over his, and it breaks the levee.

"I was in shock," he continues, unable to stop the words from flooding his mouth. "I couldn't tell her. I didn't *want* to tell her. Talking about it made it more real. It meant my mom was really gone. Elizabeth tried a few times to get me to talk, but I was stubborn. I really hated being there with her, and she wasn't too thrilled having me, especially since I was tight-lipped about what happened. So she decided that since I wouldn't talk to her about my mom, I wasn't to talk to her at all. Unless spoken to, of course. Oh, and that it was my fault my mom died."

"She didn't."

"She did."

"And then she neglected you."

"Pretty much." He takes a long drag on the joint. "Her form of punishment, I guess. Kind of messed me up." Though he was already well on his way after losing his parents within a month of each other.

"You've never talked to anyone about this, have you?" He shakes his head.

"Why me?"

"Because I don't think you're real." He gently pokes her sternum to punctuate each word. Nobody cares how he feels. She can't be real.

He wants her to be real.

Her delicate laugh sounds like a wind chime. "I'm real. You're talking to me, aren't you? And stop changing the subject. You always do that."

"Right." He clears his throat and flips his hand. "Ask away. What's your question?"

"Not a question. Just an observation."

"What's that?"

"You haven't grieved, not really. No wonder this trip is hard."

"What's the point of grieving if I can't stop once I start?" He gives Magnolia a hit, takes one for himself. A tin of edibles sits open between them. An almost-empty half liter of Jack leans against her hip. He takes a swig of courage. "That saying about time healing all wounds is bullshit." He rolls to his back and stares at the ceiling.

"Okay, let's say I agree with that, and I think I do." She leans forward to peer down at him. "Grief is for life, but it's a process. Time won't make it go away, but conversation could soften the edges."

"What are you saying?" He turns his head to look at her, meeting her blue-gray eyes.

"Talk about it with your grandmother. Tell her what happened. What she did to you was wrong. I mean, you were what—ten? Talking might make interacting with her more bearable."

A short laugh escapes him. "Yeah, right." Elizabeth might have something she wants to share with him about his mom. It's what finally motivated him to agree to help her move. But an iron vise tightens around his chest at the very thought of going into specifics with her about his mom's death. To relive that night in real time? No thank you.

Magnolia rolls to her back and joins him in staring at the ceiling, which kind of gives off the same effect as if they're talking on the phone. He can feel her, but he can't see her, making his next admission come easier.

"You were right last night. I have made a conscious effort not to fall in love. I tend to push people away."

"You aren't pushing me away."

No, he isn't, not anymore, and he frowns at that.

"Are you afraid?"

"Of falling in love?" He shakes his head. There's a flutter of nerves inside his chest at the thought of revealing something he's hardly admitted to himself, but he's on a roll and plows over the cliff. "I'm afraid of what happens after. What if I'm not enough for someone to stay?"

He hears a small catch of breath beside him and chances a look at Magnolia. She turns to look at him. Her gaze darts between his eyes, realization bright in hers. "You believe your mom left you because she didn't love you?"

"Couldn't love me enough to stay," he clarifies, his eyes closing as the weed and alcohol suffocate his inhibitions, take control of his brain. "I am unworthy of love."

A warm hand fits to his cheek again. "Matt."

His eyes snap open, and confusion clouds his mind. He could have sworn it was Julia's voice he heard.

Magnolia gently presses a thumb to his lips. "My mom didn't love me enough to stay with me either. But it doesn't mean I'm not lovable. Mama Rose showed me that. She loved me as much as any mother could. I'm sorry Liza couldn't do that for you."

Again, it's Julia's voice coming from Magnolia. He stares at the joint and, as if separated from his body, watches himself stub it out. His pulse pounds in his ear. His breathing shortens. What the fuck is wrong with him?

He takes another swig of Jack.

Fingers gently probe his jaw. He turns back to Magnolia. Her smile grounds him. He comes back into his body.

"Life isn't worth living if we don't allow ourselves to love."

He knows that, because in some ways, he stopped living the day his mom died. He also knows he's starting to trip, which means he's done talking.

He leans into her, kissing her, and Magnolia rolls to her back, pulling him over her. Her legs brace his hips, and he sinks into her while somewhere in the room his phone rings and rings and rings.

CHAPTER 29

MAGNOLIA BLU

November 11, 1972

You can't help but love Matty.

Liza's words couldn't have been truer. I wish I'd known they also served as a warning. I'm in love with Matty. Even though Liza left to live with a family friend in San Diego and I haven't heard from her for almost two months, I still feel like I'm betraying her by loving her soon-to-be ex-husband. Matty didn't go after her when she left. He didn't profess his undying love. He asked for a divorce.

Matty stays with me every night in the studio. I don't want him to stop coming to me, and I selfishly haven't asked him not to. Instead, I take my guilt out on the yard, aggressively yanking weeds and digging up plants I've become bored with. Liza hasn't been here to guide me with her vision. But I haven't been fired, and Sally keeps bringing me cash, so I kept working, prepping the yard for winter.

I was in such a state today—sweaty, dirty, and exhausted—that I didn't hear the sliding glass door open and her approach.

"Aren't you a sight for sore eyes."

My hand spade clattered onto the patio. Liza stood above me with the sun to her back. She wore a wide-collared flared dress that reached just above her knees. Her hair was combed off her face and fell in loose platinum waves down her back. Her face had filled out some, but she looked tan, fit, with a glowing smile behind sunglasses so large they covered half her face.

Happiness over seeing her after all these weeks warred with my guilt over what I've been doing in her absence. I bounced to my feet and lifted my chin for her air kisses after I told her I was too filthy for a hug, and that's when I saw him. Hands on narrow hips, Matty glared at his wife's back. I didn't know where to look, so I stared at Liza's neck, unable to meet her eyes.

"Why so peculiar?" she asked me.

"I'm not. I mean, I don't mean to be," I babbled, rattled. "I'm just surprised to see you." Matty had given me the impression she'd never be back. *She left me,* he told me. But I should have known. This house had once belonged to her father. Of course she wouldn't leave for good. If either of them moved out, it would be Matty.

"That makes two of us," Matty said, terse.

Liza flicked her hand. "I know, I should have called first."

So he hadn't been expecting her. He was just as surprised by her arrival as I was.

"You should have signed the divorce papers I sent."

Liza pouted. "I brought them with me. I'll sign them if that's what you want," she said, sounding heartbroken. I could tell it wasn't what she wanted. "Can we talk first, please? Inside?"

Matty gave her a curt nod and tilted his head toward the house.

Liza squeezed my arm. "Don't go anywhere. I'll be out in a bit. I'll catch you up on everything. Come along, Matty."

He scowled at her retreat, then turned to me. "I'm sorry," he mouthed.

"It's okay," I said, knowing full well it wasn't. Liza was going to fight him on the divorce. She could be persuasive, and I worried Matty's love for me wasn't strong enough. She'd sway him to stay with her. He'd give in to her demands.

I was dying inside. It felt like the beginning of the end of something that barely had time to stretch its wings.

"Mags," he pleaded, fearing what I'd do, where I'd go.

I told him that I'd be okay. I was going to wash up and go to the nursery in the afternoon, and we could talk later.

"Don't. Not yet. I'll come see you when I'm done. She won't stay long."

But I knew Liza. She hadn't signed the papers yet for a reason.

Numb, I stumbled to the studio, neglecting to clean the mess I'd left on the patio. I shouldn't have stuck around these past months. I should have left the moment I'd heard Liza had left. Yes, I would have lost my job, my home, and our friendship. But now, I feared I'd lose the man I loved too.

I knew I couldn't stay and watch them work it out, not when Matty was never mine in the first place. I dragged my suitcases from under the bed and got as far as unzipping them before I burst into sobs. Where could I go? Not home. I couldn't go back without something to show for what I've accomplished, something to convince my parents I'm destined to be more than a housewife and to please, please love and accept me for me. And I certainly won't return to the commune. That life isn't for me. I don't know how long I was crying when a knock came on the door.

"Magnolia, are you in there?"

My gaze whipped wildly around the room. I couldn't let Liza see me in that state. She'd want to know why, and I feared I couldn't hide my love for her husband from her.

"Magnolia, it's me. Open up." She banged on the door.

I desperately dried my face, choking on a loud sob, and the door flew open. Liza rushed to my side. "Darling, goodness, are you all right? What's wrong? Are you hurt?"

I shook my head, sobbed harder.

"Come here. Sit down." Liza tugged me to a chair and nudged my shoulders until I sat. I heard running water, and a glass appeared before me. "Drink this."

I sipped the water and tried to get myself under control. "I'm sorry. I'm sorry," I babbled.

"Whatever for?" She kneeled before me and rested her hands on my knees.

I shook my head, squeezing my eyes shut. I couldn't tell her. I couldn't bear for her to hate me like my parents do, not when she's been so generous to me.

"Well, whatever it is, I'm sure it'll work itself out." She patted my knee. "If anyone should be sorry, it's me. I left you so suddenly and never called you. You must have been worried about me. But fear not, I'm good. I'm more than good. Yes, I was shocked Matty found out about Adam and confronted me. Yes, it was wrong of me. But it's not like he's been a saint either."

I stared at the water glass in my lap.

"You remember that day we met, how upset I was? I'd just learned Matty had slept with his costar. Again, mind you."

The water I'd drunk wanted to come back up.

"Listen to me going off. I'm so happy to see you. You're still here. I thought for sure you would have left. I've missed you terribly. And wow, Magnolia. You are a wonder." She walked to the window. "What magic did you work over my garden? It's November and it's still beautiful. It's in better shape than my marriage." She laughed, and a flush of shame crawled up my neck.

"So, you're staying married? Matty's forgiven you?"

"I wouldn't go that far, but yes, we're still married. For now."

"I'm happy for you." I felt sick inside.

"I was hoping you would be because I have the best news." She rushed back to my side and pulled me up from the chair. "Well, *we* have the best news, Matty and me."

Dread sloshed with the water in my stomach. I was too afraid to ask.

"I'm pregnant!" She squealed, a very un-Liza-like noise, and hugged me. "Can you believe it? You can hardly tell, but I'm already five months along." She grabbed my hands and stepped back so we could both look at her belly's slight protrusion.

No, I couldn't stay. I had to leave.

"What is it?" Liza squeezed my fingers. "Aren't you happy for us?"

I told her I was happy as my eyes fell to the opened suitcases on my bed. Liza followed my gaze. She looked back at me with shock. "Are you leaving?"

"I . . ."

"You can't! I need you now more than ever, don't you see? Winter will be slow. You won't have to garden every day. You can help with the nursery. And when this little girl comes"—she patted her stomach—"I want your help with the baby, especially with Matty's career taking off. He's only getting busier. Please say you'll stay."

Just tell her.

But if I told her, it would ruin any chance of them having a happy little family. It wasn't just about Matty, and Liza, and me anymore. The one time I wanted to be selfish and I couldn't. I had to think about what was best for their little girl.

"All right. I'll stay," I agreed to appease her. I didn't want to further upset her in her delicate condition. But I know I'll have to leave eventually—if not tonight, soon. I have no other choice.

"I'm so pleased." She hugged me. "These next few months are going to be wonderful." She fanned her face. "Look at me, I'm positively glowing."

I was shrinking inside.

She then told me that Matty needed her back up at the house but that she'd be by again later to fetch me for dinner. I had to join them to celebrate, she insisted.

I dreaded seeing them together, but I heard myself agreeing. And the moment she left, I hurriedly packed. What Liza didn't know wouldn't hurt her. I'd leave quietly and quickly through the side gate. Without Adam around, and with Matty and Liza busy with each other, nobody would know I was gone until it was too late. I'd be far away by then.

I was just about to leave when there was another knock. I quickly shoved the packed suitcases under the bed and opened the door. Matty stood there looking broken. He told me that dinner had been called off. Liza's pregnancy was high risk and she'd been experiencing some cramping after today's excitement. She was resting in bed.

He then cupped my face and lifted my chin. My breath hitched with emotion, and his eyes watered. "I'm so sorry. I didn't know she was coming back. I didn't know—"

"I don't blame you."

"But you're leaving." He could read it on my face. That, or Liza told him I was planning to until I let her think she'd convinced me otherwise.

"I can't stay."

"Why not?"

"I can't watch you love her when I'm in love with you."

"Then I'm going with you."

"You can't. You're having a baby. Your little girl will need her daddy."

"But I don't love Liza. It's you, Mags. I love you. I want *you*. And we don't even know if she'll carry to term. Luck hasn't been on our side, and that's the truth of it." His face twisted.

I stepped out of his embrace and shook my head. "You need to go. You leave Liza and you'll break her heart. You can't risk the baby."

"What about your heart? What about mine?" He tried to touch me and I turned away.

"Go, please."

He was quiet for a long time before he said, "We'll talk tomorrow. Please tell me you'll still be here."

I honestly couldn't tell him. At my silence, Matty came around in front of me. He pressed a kiss to my forehead, whispered against my lips that he loved me, and left.

The door clicked shut, and a sob ripped from my throat. I cupped a hand over my mouth and rested the other over my stomach, the news I'd planned to share with him tonight in shambles.

I raced to the bathroom and threw up.

CHAPTER 30

JULIA

It's late afternoon by the time Julia arrives at Rosemont. She spoke with Matt early in the morning but didn't get the chance to ask if he meant what he'd said last night about not coming for Liza before he hung up on her. She'd listened to him ramble about flowers and crystals, and she admittedly got sucked into talking about love. Her heart broke when he told her about his mom. Their circumstances are different, but if anyone understands the agony of being left behind, it's her.

She hurries toward the administrative offices. Lenore's door is open, and she's seated at her desk. Julia called earlier and gave her a heads-up about Matt, that she suspected Matt was high when they spoke and had started drinking before their call. He probably won't remember that she called him. Lenore didn't know where he's been staying when Julia asked her. If she had his address, Julia would have sent an officer to do a wellness check. She's worried about him. But, as Lenore reminded her, what Matt does and where he's gone is not their responsibility. Though he could use a friend or confidant.

She pokes her head into Lenore's office. "Any word from Matt?"

Lenore looks up from her monitor. "I was just going to call you with the same question. No, I haven't heard from him."

"Me neither. It looks like he's not coming." She chews her bottom lip with worry.

"That's disappointing. Well, no matter. I wasn't betting on Matt making it here in time anyway. I received word a few hours ago that Liza's officially a ward of the state. Her guardian is moving her tomorrow. If by some miracle you speak with Matt, tell him to call me. Say it's urgent."

Julia thinks of Liza. The elderly woman is lying in the bed she's made, but Julia feels for her all the same. "I'll let him know."

"What about you?" Lenore asks before Julia can escape. "Have you found a new place for Ruby?"

"Not yet," she hedges. Magnolia Blu's diary and Matt have kept her occupied.

"Julia," Lenore implores and pushes up from the desk. "As the director here, I'm pleased you want her to stay with us, and to say I'm impressed you'll do what it takes to keep her here is an understatement. But as your friend, I'm going to remind you again Ruby isn't the only person you should be considering, especially after what happened yesterday."

Julia sags against the doorjamb. She wondered when Lenore would bring this up.

"Are you okay? Trevor thinks she might have hurt you."

Her scalp was tender this morning, but that isn't what worries her. "Are you canceling Mama Rose's contract because of this?"

"Right now, no. But if she becomes a danger to the staff, they could put in a request to have her moved." Julia's mouth draws down, and Lenore's expression softens. "I'm forewarning you so you aren't caught off guard."

"I know. It's just . . ." She shakes her head. Lately, it's been one thing after another with her grandmother. But Lenore is right. Julia can't put off her search any longer. She at least knows now why Mama Rose wanted the diary. She'll share the last passage in the diary with Liza as she suspects her grandmother would have wanted her to, which is most likely the reason she asked for the diary. Mama Rose's most recent entry makes it clear she terribly regrets how Liza learned about her relationship with Matty. Unbeknownst to Julia, Mama Rose had attempted for some time before her Alzheimer's diagnosis to reconcile with Liza. Hopefully, Liza will forgive her and Julia can relocate her grandmother with the knowledge she's fulfilled Mama Rose's last request where Liza is concerned.

"I'm here if you want to talk."

"Thank you."

"Hope your grandmother is doing all right today," Lenore says, returning to her desk.

Julia doesn't mention she isn't here to see Mama Rose. "Me too."

She locates Liza in the dining room. She's seated alone at a table near the back with a half-eaten bowl of yellow custard, a deck of cards, and a forgotten mug of coffee. Creamer powder floats in patches on the coffee's surface.

Julia stands across the table. "Hello, Liza."

Liza briefly meets her eyes as she shuffles the cards.

"I'm sorry about yesterday. I didn't mean to interrupt your conversation with my grandmother."

"That doesn't seem to have stopped you from bothering me today." Liza splits the deck.

"No, I . . . uh, thank you."

"Whatever for?" She lays out the cards for a game of solitaire.

"For helping Mama Rose. You calmed her last night when you called her Magnolia. I think she knew who you were." Julia had never seen anything like it. It lasted a split second, and she would have easily missed it if she'd been looking the other way. But her grandmother went absolutely still at the name. She stared up at Liza in shock before the nurse stabbed her arm with a sedative and she passed out.

Liza scoops up the cards with an irritated swipe and reshuffles the deck.

"I've been reading the diary. I believe I know why Mama Rose asked me to find it. There's an entry from eight years ago. It's a letter to you."

The only sign Liza gives that she heard is a slight bobble of the deck. A card slides across the table. Julia sends it back.

Liza tucks the card into the deck. "Do you know how to play gin rummy?"

"What? Yes."

"Then sit."

Julia hooks her bag onto the chairback and takes a seat. Liza deals ten cards each and positions the partial deck between them, flipping the top card to the side, face up. Julia sorts her cards into sets and potential runs. "I heard you're leaving us tomorrow."

"Mm-hmm." Liza moves her cards around. "You have first move."

Julia selects a card from the deck, the ten of hearts, and adds it to her set of tens. She discards a five. "I'm sorry Matt isn't going to make it. I tried to convince him, but he seems set on not coming."

Liza selects a card from the stack and discards another. "I see he's been talking to *you*."

"Yes, we've had several calls. But, Liza, he's your grandson. He should be here. The state shouldn't have had to intercede."

"But you did."

She deflates, thinking of the boxes. "I did. I'll arrange for the boxes to be forwarded to your new address."

"Don't bother. The next time you speak with Matt, you can tell him it wasn't my idea to appoint him as my secondary. I'm sure he's wondering about that."

"Then why did you? Why get him involved at all?"

"Adam suggested him. And—"

"You want to reconcile?" Julia interrupts, hopeful. Maybe apologize for neglecting him? He was only a child.

Liza's mouth pinches. She looks at the cards on the table. "There was no one else but Matt."

"Surely that's not true. You had plenty of friends. Your garden parties—"

She dismisses Julia's remarks with a curt wave. "Superficial, all of them. People didn't come to my parties to be with me. They came because of what I could do for them. Hollywood is greedy. It was no different then than it is now."

"Not everyone must have thought that."

"I wouldn't know. I didn't—" Her eyes glass over before she blinks and shakes her head. "Never mind. It isn't important."

Julia is of the mind to disagree. Liza's relationships might have ended because they were superficial, but from what she read in Mama Rose's diary, she finds it difficult to believe they started that way. If Liza was anything like the woman she is today, she likely kept herself apart from others, erecting an unconscious barrier between them and herself. Losing a husband, a daughter, friends like Mama Rose, not to mention the multiple miscarriages Julia read about, all had to have taken their toll. Loss of that magnitude changes the very core of a person. This revelation gives Julia new insight into Liza and Matt's estrangement, although she can't be sure it's accurate. Liza's disregard for Matt's emotional state when he came to live with her might have had less to do with her indifference toward him and more to do with her incapability to open herself up to love after losing so many. Much in the way Matt explained himself to Julia.

Liza selects a card and re-sorts her hand. "Why do you care what happens to me, Julia? Do you enjoy tormenting me by dredging up the past with your curiosity?"

"I—No, I don't mean to. But if I may bother you with one more thing, I'll get out of your hair." Julia folds her cards and rests her hand face down. She retrieves the Magnolia Blu diary from her bag and puts the book on the table, her palm on the cover. Her heart races in her throat, recalling what she read last night. "Have you known all this time who I am?"

Liza's hands tremble. She sets down her cards and coolly glances away. "Magnolia isn't the only one who lied."

"What do you mean?"

Liza turns back to her. The facade that always holds her face rigidly in place has fallen away, revealing a fragility hidden underneath. "Matty still wanted to divorce me despite the baby. I threatened to use my connections so that he'd never get another movie deal. I threatened to ruin him. He was unfazed. He was still going to leave me. Unbeknownst to me, he'd planned to leave Hollywood before he met Magnolia. *Season of the Gods II* would have been his last movie. Nothing I said or did could convince him otherwise."

"I'm sorry for everything," Julia says. "I know my grandmother regrets the role she played."

"That's because of me. I let her believe she was responsible for everything that had gone wrong in my marriage. Don't get me wrong, she did play a part in its demise. But I was as much at fault." Liza gathers up the cards, finished with the game and, apparently, their conversation. Cool eyes drop to the diary under Julia's hand. "I'll read Ruby's letter, but I make no promises it'll change how I feel about her."

Julia pushes the book to Liza's side with an air of accomplishment and relief. She's fulfilled what she believes is one part of Mama Rose's request, that Liza read the final entry, the letter Mama Rose wrote to her. "That's all I ask. Thank you." She rises to leave. It's late, and Liza has yet to answer Julia's question about whether she knew who Julia is—it would explain why Liza barely tolerated her company—but she doesn't want to deter Liza from reading the diary by asking her again and pushing for an answer. She'll try tomorrow when she returns for the diary.

Liza snatches her wrist, stopping her. "There's more."

Julia's fingers flex in Liza's grasp. "More?"

"It's about Aubrey, Matt's mother. There are things Matt must know about her and his family, and I don't know if he'll give me the chance to tell him."

CHAPTER 31

—

MATT

Matt sits up in bed. His gaze coasts around the motel room. Faint light frames the curtains, hinting that the afternoon has eased into twilight. The sheets are bunched at the bottom of the bed, and the stiff comforter is piled on the floor. Empty bottles and food cartons clutter the table. The TV plays, the sound still muted. A talking head points at a weather map. Nothing but sunshine across the Southwest. Whenever he gets motivated, the drive home will be easy. The downpour they had at the airport when he first set off won't be an issue.

A muffled ring comes from somewhere under the bed linens. He digs for it, finds his phone. He thinks he answers but feels a hand glide up his spine. He feels her behind him as if she's a sun with its own center of gravity, luring him back to her. He looks over his shoulder at Magnolia. "I thought you were asleep."

She stretches, catlike, with a deep arch in her back, and yawns. He looks at the clock on the bedside table. It's after eight in the evening. His stomach growls, reminding him they missed dinner.

"Shouldn't you go see your grandmother?" She trails a fingernail over his hip.

Doesn't she remember? He already mentioned he's going home once he's motivated to check out.

He turns the conversation back on her. "Shouldn't you call *your* mom?"

Her face sours. She scoots up the bed, pulling the sheet along with. "I don't want to talk about her."

"I thought you missed her."

"I never told you that."

The first conversation they had when he met her turns over in his mind. "Aren't you trying to reconcile?"

"I don't know what you're talking about. I haven't seen her for years. She left me."

He frowns. She isn't making sense. "What about Benjie?"

"My grandfather? He died before I was born."

Matt stares at her, confused. He didn't hear her right. She doesn't sound anything like herself.

The bed shifts as Magnolia presses her front to his back. She rests her chin on his shoulder. Her breath tickles his earlobe. "What's wrong?"

"For a moment there—" He tugs at his ear with a dry laugh. "Never mind." She'll think he's lost his mind. He's starting to believe he has. Magnolia doesn't just sound like Julia—she's talking as if she is Julia. Julia's mom left her. Benjie was Julia's grandfather.

His stomach growls again.

He feels Magnolia smile against his skin. "Hungry?"

"Starving."

"I'm craving pizza."

"Perfect. I'll order in." He kisses her pert mouth and smacks her rear, rolling out of bed. Somewhere around here is a flyer for the local pizza parlor. He finds it with a stack of take-out menus in a drawer and calls in an order for a meat lover's pizza. He adds on a six-pack of pale ales. After popping an edible and downing the rest of the Jack, he slides back into bed. The alcohol weaves through his system, relaxing fatigued muscles, and the gummy does more than calm his mind. Magnolia is back by his side. Her arms close around him, and he burrows his head in the curve of her shoulder. He isn't ready to let her go. He isn't ready to face the real world. So he decides he won't.

CHAPTER 32

MAGNOLIA BLU

June 7, 1973

I left California almost six months ago, only to return when my parents refused to see me, and I haven't written anything in almost a year because I didn't know how. I've been renting a room in a house with three other unmarried mothers, struggling with everything I've lost. I still don't know how to express how I'm feeling other than putting this pen to this paper and getting it out. I have to get it out.

Matty had returned later the same night that Liza told him she was pregnant, afraid that I would leave before he could express what he'd wanted to say to me. As stunned and excited as he was about being a father, he said he could not and would not remain married to Liza. No, he hadn't been faithful to her, but he'd never loved the other women he'd been with, not as he loved me. He'd come to realize those women had been escapes, that he desperately wanted out of his marriage. He didn't love Liza. Sure, she was gorgeous, and for a while their marriage had had a good run. But her love came with conditions, and too many miscarriages had broken the two of them.

Matty proposed a plan. Liza was under the care of an excellent physician. From his viewpoint, him staying or leaving wouldn't affect the pregnancy. The state of their marriage wouldn't prevent him from being a good father. As much as he didn't want to be married to Liza, he wanted to be involved in their daughter's life. But it wasn't fair of him to stick around if he didn't love her. So he would move out, and he wanted me to go with him.

I wasn't entirely sure about the idea. I had a job. We both had reputations Liza could ruin if she found out about us. But I couldn't deny my love for Matty. It pained me to see him so torn. He had a colleague who had an empty apartment he was willing to rent to Matty until he found a place to buy. I'd go live with him there. In fact, we agreed the sooner we moved out, the better. He had a full schedule at the studio the following day, but he'd pick me up in the evening and off we'd go.

After Matty left, I spent the evening packing, but I didn't have the heart to visit Liza when she called me up to the house the next morning. So I wrote her a goodbye letter, begging her forgiveness for abandoning her before the baby came. I stopped short of apologizing about Matty. She'd find out about us sooner or later, and I knew that her forgiveness would be nothing short of a miracle. I also believed I didn't deserve it. Then I passed the time cleaning the studio, scrubbing it from top to bottom.

The hours crawled slowly, and when the time came and went for Matty to come get me, I worried that he'd changed his mind. I kept looking up at the big house, expecting to see both him and Liza in the windows. But I saw no sign of either of them. Just as I was about to fix myself tea to relax my nerves, there was an urgent knock on the door.

"Ms. Blu, it's Sally. Are you in there? Ms. Blu, open the door!"

I rushed to answer, my immediate thoughts going to Liza and the baby. "Is Liza all right?" I asked when I swung open the door. "The baby?"

"It's Mr. Holloway. Quickly, you must come."

A thousand questions tumbled through my mind as I raced up to the house with Sally. Did he need help with Liza? Was he intoxicated and Sally needed my help to get him under control? I followed her through the back door, where Liza's anguished wail slammed into me. All thoughts of Matty burst apart like balls on a billiard table.

"The baby!" Sally yelled, startled.

I looked wildly around. "Where is she?"

"Upstairs."

I chased after Sally to the second floor and down the hallway to the room Liza and Matty shared. Liza was bent over an armchair. Heaving sobs tore from her diaphragm. Her face contorted in pain.

"Mrs. Holloway! What are you doing out of bed?" Sally hurried to Liza and beckoned me over.

Liza collapsed against me. "Oh, Mags," she cried.

"What's wrong? What can I do?" I met Sally's panic-stricken face. She shook her head.

"Please, Mrs. Holloway," Sally begged. "Come back to bed."

"No," Liza cried. "Not this bed."

"Think of the baby," I said, trying to coax her to lie down, but she resisted.

"I can't sleep here. Not without him."

I looked at Sally again for some sort of explanation.

"It's Mr. Holloway. The police were just here."

Unease sliced through me. "Was he hurt on set?"

Sally did that pitiful shake of her head again, and this time fear punctured my chest. "What happened to Matty?" I asked her and looked to Liza. "What happened to him?"

"He's gone," Liza wailed.

"What do you mean, 'gone'?"

"He's dead, Ms. Blu. Car accident. He was speeding home and ran into a tree about a mile from here."

Sally could have pushed me down the stairs and it would have hurt less than her words. I felt my knees buckle under Liza's weight.

Sally watched me closely, Liza clinging to us both, and I swallowed, and then I swallowed again. Sally knew about us, I realized, me and Matty, and she wasn't saying a word. I wanted to scream. I wanted to shatter every glass perfume bottle and vase in the room. Matty was gone. Dead. I would never feel his arms around me again. I'd never feel his lips on mine again. But I had no right to mourn, not at that moment. I wasn't his wife, and Liza needed me.

I inhaled an unsteady breath.

"Will you be all right, Ms. Blu?" Sally asked tepidly, missing nothing.

I nodded tightly.

"Good. We need to get Liza to lie down before she loses the baby."

I could barely register where I was, and for a split second, I couldn't focus on anything. I forced my head to clear. "Is there another room she can sleep in?"

"Across the hall."

Sally and I half carried, half guided a devastated Liza into an immaculately decorated guest room. Sally whipped back the covers, and I gently guided Liza under them.

"He's gone, Magnolia. My darling husband is gone." Liza cried into the pillow.

"I'm so sorry," I whispered, unable to look at her, fearing she'd see my own misery.

I pulled up the covers and Liza grasped my hand. "Don't leave me. I don't want to be alone."

"I'm not going anywhere." As soon as I spoke the words, I knew it as truth. I would stay until my condition kept me from staying. Matty had been rushing home for me. His daughter would never meet him because of me. I owed that baby and Liza whatever time I could give them.

I crawled underneath the covers and spooned her back as Sally bustled about the room, drawing the curtains and dimming the lights.

"He was so excited to be a father," Liza whispered.

Her words cut like a knife. "I know."

"Aubrey."

"Who?"

"Aubrey. That's the name he wanted for a girl. What do you think of it?"

"Of the name?"

"I didn't like it and I told him so. Now, though . . ."

I choked on the sob swelling in my throat. "I think it's a beautiful name."

"I think so too. I can tell her, when she's old enough and understands, that her father named her. That he loved her very much."

I was going to die from the strain of holding on to my tears. "She'll treasure that knowledge."

Liza murmured her agreement and soon fell asleep.

Behind her, my face crumpled, and I silently grieved for Matty. For the life we wouldn't have together.

For the next month, we lived harmoniously. I gardened a few days a week. On the other days, I helped Liza prepare for Aubrey's arrival. I'd moved into the big house, but I never had the chance to meet her. Five weeks after Matty's death, I found Liza in the guest room I'd been using. She was sitting in the armchair by the window that overlooked the circular driveway reading this journal. The goodbye letter I'd written her when I planned to leave with Matty was open on her lap.

I stopped in the doorway, and my heart landed in my stomach. Liza picked up the letter when she felt my presence. "Ironic that you apologized for everything but the one thing you did that would have gutted me. Matty was going to leave me? With *you*?" She spoke with disdain, referencing what I'd written about us in my journal.

"Liza," I implored, stalling. Really? What argument did I have? None.

She dropped the letter, and to my mortification, she read from the journal, "'He sucked my breast into his mouth, and his tongue swirled my nipple. His teeth nipped at the raised bud, and my hips rose to meet his. He pushed into me repeatedly, and I was lost. I clung to him as he whispered in my ear, "It's you. Only you," and I fell deeper in love with him.' Oh, please. This reads worse than the smut they print in *Cosmopolitan*." She slammed the journal closed. "Do you know how many women he said those exact words to? You're looking at one of them. I'd bet there are dozens more."

"Please don't."

She rolled her eyes. "Don't what? Don't speak the truth? Don't read it? Then you shouldn't have written it."

I only meant for her to stop tormenting herself. I didn't want her to put too much strain on the baby. Matty hadn't loved Liza, not like she thought he had. But Liza was right. I sounded utterly selfish.

"I was looking for a matchbook," she said quietly.

That explained how she'd found the diary. I'd left it in the night-stand, never thinking anyone would come into my place. Fool that I was. It wasn't my house. I didn't own the nightstand. There wasn't an inch of space inside the room that was off-limits to the homeowner.

"Were you ever going to tell me?" she asked.

"How are you so calm?"

"Oh, I'm not calm. The only reason I'm not trying to kill you is that I don't want to lose my baby. I've already lost Matty. Lying, cheating bastard that he was, I still love him. Can you believe that? I'm a fool."

"I'll leave."

"Yes, I think that's best." Liza held out my journal, waiting for me to take it. I crossed the room and grabbed it, but she didn't let go. Our eyes locked. "I trusted you."

"I know."

Liza let go. She stood, pausing with a grimace, and out of habit, I reached to assist her.

"Don't you touch me," she hissed, and I lurched back, apologizing as she walked to the door. "I want you out of this house and off my property within the hour."

I looked at the blue shag carpeting. "Yes, ma'am."

"And Magnolia? I'll die before I ever forgive you. You didn't only ruin my marriage; you killed my husband. Matty died because you were selfish. I never want to see you again."

So I left California for home, only to have my parents turn me away at the door. Not only did I run away on my wedding day, but I'd also returned home penniless and pregnant. I'm nothing but an embarrassment to them.

Tuesday

CHAPTER 33

JULIA

It's barely 8:00 a.m. when Julia arrives at Rosemont to retrieve the diary—and, hopefully, the answer to her question—from Liza. Her entire life she's believed Benjamin Stromski was her grandfather. Why Mama Rose would mislead her, she may never learn, but if what she wrote is true, Matthew Holloway is her biological grandfather. Which explains the animosity between Mama Rose and Liza, and why Mama Rose sought her forgiveness.

Julia is headed down the hallway toward Liza's room when Lenore intercepts her. She's breathless and less put together than her usual self. Her silk blouse is untucked and sleeves pushed up. Flyaway hairs have escaped her topknot.

"Have you spoken with Matt Gatlin?"

"Not since last night." She'd asked about his plans for Liza, but either he hung up on her again or his phone died. She didn't know which, and he hadn't answered when she called back. She looks over Lenore. "What time did you get in this morning?" She's usually not on-site until 8:30 a.m.

"I've been up since three. Just got back from the hospital."

Alarm spears Julia. Instinct tells her the news isn't good. "Liza?"

Lenore grasps her hand. "She had a stroke late last night."

Julia doesn't allow herself to consider that the diary could have been the trigger. She refuses to let her thoughts go there. "Ookay. How . . . How is she?"

"Critical. Tell Matt she's at Huntington if you can get through to him. He isn't returning our calls. Her doctor isn't confident she'll last the day."

"I'll—I'll call him right away." No telling if he'll answer, but it's worth the shot. Why didn't she ask which motel he's at? If she knew where he was, she'd call the front desk and insist someone knock on his door.

"Thank you." Lenore squeezes Julia's hand before rushing off.

"Lenore," Julia calls after her. "Liza has something that belongs to my grandmother—a book. It's important."

"Her room is open if you want to have a look."

Julia's hands shake as she rummages in her bag for her phone. She calls Matt on her way to Liza's room and is immediately dropped into voicemail, where she's notified his box is full. She dictates a text. "Lenore has been trying to reach you. It's Liza. There's been an emergency. Call me."

Unless Matt had a change of heart and drove to California last night or can get on a plane within the next hour, it will take nothing short of a miracle for him to get here. He's at least an eight-hour drive away, and there's much Liza shared with her last night about his mom that she regrets not telling him when he was younger and it mattered. It still matters. Matt needs to sit with her before he loses her.

Liza's door is open, and the lights have been left on. Aside from the floral bed covering, the room lacks any personal touches since Julia boxed and shipped most of Liza's possessions to Matt. But there's a lamp, a pair of reading glasses, and a cup of water on the nightstand. Along with a particular light-blue book.

Julia swipes it up, and a slip of stationery flutters to the floor. She flips it over to find a note.

Dear Matt,

I'm not surprised you didn't come for me. I wouldn't have either, not after the way I treated you. But there is something about your mother, and indirectly about yourself, you should know.

Julia tucks the note back into the diary before she's tempted to finish. It isn't hers to read, and if this secret is different from what Liza confessed last night, it certainly isn't for Julia's eyes.

Intent on going straight to the hospital, she calls the spa to cancel her clients for the day. She doesn't know if Liza is conscious, but she can't let her spend her last hours alone. Someone needs to be at her side.

Again, she tries to reach Matt. He doesn't answer.

On her way toward the exit, she passes the dining room and spots her grandmother at breakfast with two other residents. Julia jogs over to say a quick hello.

"Morning, Mama Rose." She touches her grandmother's shoulder. "How's breakfast?"

Mama Rose blinks at the scrambled eggs and toast on her plate. "It's delicious." She squints at the diary Julia holds and waves a fork at it. "That thing again. I told her I don't want it back. Tell her to keep it. It's hers."

"This? Who did you say that to? Liza?"

"Of course. Who else would it be? She came to my room last night and tried to pawn it off on me. She wanted to apologize for some silliness, but I didn't believe anything she said about me and wouldn't hear any more of it. I told her she was wasting her breath. Did she talk you into giving it to me? She never could take no for an answer."

"You—you spoke with Liza?" Julia sputters with disbelief.

"Ruby, who's your friend?" the woman with tight salt-and-pepper curls seated across from Mama Rose asks.

"It's me, Mrs. Zimmerman, Julia. Your massage therapist?" she adds to jostle the woman's memory when she keeps shaking her head. Her phone vibrates, and she glances at the screen, hoping it's Matt. A message displays from the spa that her appointments have been rescheduled.

She needs to get to the hospital.

"I'll come back later," she tells Mama Rose. She isn't confident her grandmother will remember this conversation and they can pick up where they left off, but it's worth a try.

CHAPTER 34

MATT

Matt opens his eyes, feeling a moment of panic when he doesn't recognize where he is. The gold-speckled popcorn ceiling comes into focus, and he remembers he's been staying at a motel. His mouth is drier than Death Valley, and his body feels like a massive paperweight pressing into the mattress. He drags his hands down his face and startles at the short beard. How long has it been since he shaved?

A sharp pain slashes across his skull, and he groans into his cupped palms. What time did they fall asleep last night? Or was it this morning when they finally crashed?

He reaches for Magnolia and finds cool sheets and an empty side of the bed.

He lifts his head. "Mags?"

She doesn't answer.

He swings his legs off the bed and hobbles to the bathroom, nudges the door open. She isn't there either, and from the looks of the bathroom, it hasn't been used recently. Her hairbrush is no longer on the sink counter. He looks back in the room. Her clothes are missing and her purse is gone.

Did she leave him? No—he shakes his head in denial—she wouldn't have left without saying goodbye.

Thinking she might be down at the pool, he peeks out the window at the overcast sky. He can't tell if it's morning or afternoon, but the pool deck is deserted.

She'll be back.

The curtains fall into place, and he returns to the bathroom to take a leak, watching himself in the mirror. He looks like death warmed over, his beard that of a broke musician with bloodshot eyes and dark circles the size of tea bags. And he stinks. He sniffs his armpit, his nose crinkling. When did he last shower?

He splashes water on his face and debates returning to bed to wait for Magnolia when the time on the digital clock jumps out at him. It's ten past noon. Who the hell knows what day it is.

He pulls on jeans and a wrinkled navy shirt, swishes with mouthwash, and leaves the room to look for her. On the way downstairs, he runs into another guest. The man looks familiar, and Matt snaps his fingers when it clicks. He's the guy from the pool the other night.

Matt stops him. "Have you by chance seen the woman I was with? Long brassy hair?"

"You're the jerk-off who woke me and half the hotel."

"Ah . . . okay." Matt didn't realize they'd been that loud. "Have you seen her?"

"Don't know what you're talking about. Nobody was in that pool but you."

A nervous laugh escapes Matt. "Seriously, have you seen her?"

"Imagine yourself a fake girlfriend all you want, bro. But it was just your naked ass in the water." The man stomps up the staircase, laughter trailing him.

"Asshole." Matt jogs down the steps and past a housekeeping cart as he heads for the front office on the off chance Magnolia is there. When he recognizes the maid cleaning a room, he pokes his head in.

"Hey, hi," he says when the maid startles at the sight of him. "I'm the guy in room 208. Have you seen the woman who's been staying with me?"

"Room 208? No." She shakes her head. "No woman with you. Just you."

Matt scoffs. There aren't many rooms in this motel and Magnolia is memorable. "She answered the door when you came by. You spoke with her."

"I remember. You answered the door. You told me to shove off." With that, she shuts the door in his face.

Addled, Matt backs up and, hands on hips, looks vacantly around. That's not how he remembers what happened. "What's wrong with these people?"

They're screwing with him.

He enters the front office and questions the clerk. The young woman behind the plexiglass insists the only person in Matt's room has been Matt. He hasn't had any visitors other than a pizza delivery. She saw the guy dropping off food yesterday.

"Huh." Matt rubs nervously at his neck and returns to his room. He opens the door and is assailed with an odor that sends him reeling back. Soiled food and stale beer. There's also an undercurrent of vomit. "What the fuck day is it?"

"Tuesday," answers a guest walking past Matt's room.

"The hell?" Matt frowns after him and swings his gaze back into the room.

For the first time in what he figures has been three days since he checked in, Matt sees the mess in the room for what it really is: eau de three-day binge. A careless, irresponsible waste of time.

"No. Nonononono." He claps his face. He should have been to California and back by now. He's supposed to be home prepping for the Le Mans race with Dave. He did not just spend—*fuck*—seventy-two hours holed up in a motel bingeing on booze.

A small crinkled paper bag on the table catches his attention as if waving a neon-orange flag. It's the bag Dave gave him. He upends it. Two tins are full, but one is about empty, the very one Dave warned him about because of the potency. The edibles Dave cautioned are homemade. Matt must have mistaken them for his headache gummies because they're the same shape and color.

"Are you kidding me?"

Matt crumples the bag and chucks it across the room. Empty beer bottles are everywhere. There are also two empty whiskey bottles. The marijuana he smoked is gone. That, or it never existed. Same with the purse Magnolia left in his car. Gone, gone, gone.

He cups a hand over his mouth and turns a circle.

He did not just wake from a three-day bender. The last seventy-two hours were not a lucid dream. Mags was here. She is real. She has to be. He spoke with her. He touched her. He can still taste her. There's no way he imagined her. He picked her up on the roadside. He drove her to her parents'. He swam with her.

He thinks of the guy he ran into on the stairs and his deprecating laugh. The maid and her wary once-over when she recognized him. And Julia. He remembers Julia, and slowly, his mental fog parting like a curtain, he recalls the hours upon hours they spent on the phone. Her reading Magnolia Blu's diary to him, sharing stories about his grandmother he hadn't wanted to hear but had listened to because he loved Julia's voice. He was craving her company. He was craving *her*. Their long calls about everything and anything. Intimate, revealing confessions he's never wanted to share with anyone. Somehow his mind twisted it all into some sick fantasy. His stoned-out brain.

How pathetic is he?

Julia had begged, pleaded, and demanded that he pull himself together and get to California. Yeah, his relationship with Elizabeth sucked. Yes, she'd been exceptionally harsh with a kid suffering from PTSD. But did she deserve to be abandoned during her sunset years? Julia hadn't thought so. She even offered to help Matt. Had gone so far as to offer to come pick him up herself.

But he was too damaged. How could he help anyone, especially Liza, when he never sought help for himself? He's an expert at quashing grief and trauma, burying both with drugs, liquor, and avoidance.

And that's not the half of it. He not only failed his grandmother and Julia. He failed his best friend and business partner. He promised to have the Ford photos to him by today and he's not even half-done curating the thousands of photos he took.

He owes his buddy a call and an apology.

Matt locates his phone between the couch cushions. The device is dead. He plugs in the charger and takes a quick shower. When he's done, the phone has enough juice to power on. It steadily chimes with text and missed-call notifications, dozens from Dave, Lenore, and Julia. Dread is a heavy stone in his stomach.

On instinct, he calls the most recent number on his phone. Julia's. She answers after the first ring. "Matt? Thank God. We've been trying to reach you all morning."

Her tone sets off alarms. He suddenly feels excessively anxious, like he's late for a flight and stuck in traffic.

His tone is cautious. "What's wrong?"

"It's Liza. She's in the hospital. How soon can you get here? She doesn't have much time."

CHAPTER 35

MATT

Matt stares at the slight form in the hospital bed. Elizabeth is a fraction of the size of the intimidating woman he remembers. A monitor tracks her vitals. A ventilator keeps her alive. She hasn't woken since her stroke, and her nurse told him that she'll go quickly when she's taken off the machine, as her advance health care directive dictates. He's been left alone so he can say goodbye.

How does he say goodbye to the person who loathed him?

After his call with Julia, he ignored everything else—voicemails, texts, the state of the motel room and his mind—and drove to the nearest airport. Shock propelled him onto the first flight to Burbank, but once he was settled on the plane, he argued with himself about why he needed to go. There wasn't anything he could do for her. He doubted she would have wanted him there.

Standing over her, he remembers how cold she was toward him when he couldn't talk about his mom, and in a snap, he's that orphaned boy again who only wanted to be told everything would be all right. Who only wanted to feel safe and loved. Instead, Elizabeth not only left him to contend with the trauma of losing his mother on his own but also reinforced his belief that he was to blame.

Intense feelings of regret and failure that he didn't do more leave him shaken. He holds up his hand and watches it tremble. He knew being in his grandmother's presence would trigger his PTSD.

He forces out a long stream of air and makes a fist. The tremors stop. He retreats one step, then another, intent on leaving. Why did he come? What's he supposed to do? What can he say? Does it even matter? She's in a coma. She can't hear him. She doesn't know he's here. And nothing he says will change the past or what he believes of himself.

"It'll matter to you," comes a gentle voice behind him.

He turns to find a woman who just reaches his shoulders looking up at him with a mix of curiosity and concern. Her brown hair is a knotted mass atop her head. Freckles sprinkle her nose like a dusting of cinnamon. And her eyes—they're a startling shade of green bordering on blue that study him with a degree of familiarity. She's wearing a navy-blue smock of sorts with white pants and Crocs, and if he hadn't recognized her voice, he would have mistaken her for one of Elizabeth's nurses.

"It's you."

"Hello, Matt." Julia's smile is kind, and all at once, he's relieved, embarrassed, and furious. Relieved she's here. Embarrassed by what he revealed of himself to her over the past few days. Furious because he let Elizabeth get under his skin and didn't arrive in time for her to share with him what she had to say about his mom. Now he'll never know, and he'll spend the rest of his life convinced it was something important.

He clears his throat behind a sweating palm. "I, uh . . . I didn't realize I said that out loud." The part about not knowing what to say and whether it mattered. He glances between her and his grandmother.

"I'll give you some privacy." Julia turns toward the hallway, and his reflex is to follow her out. He feels useless. There isn't anything he can do.

Julia stops in the doorway, her expression warm and open with understanding. "It's okay to just sit with her if you don't know what to say. But if there's anything you've wanted to get off your chest"—she tilts her head toward Elizabeth—"now's the time."

He blinks at the empty doorway, Julia's advice winding through him until it settles with meaning. He doesn't need to stay for his grandmother. He needs to stay for himself.

He mechanically turns back to Elizabeth and moves to her side. His gaze slides from her matted hair down her arm and back to the mask cupping her mouth and nose. Her eyes are unmoving under the tissue-thin eyelids.

Magnolia's advice—or maybe it was Julia's—comes back to him. *Time doesn't heal relationships, but conversation does.*

Even if it's one sided?

He dares to touch the back of her flaccid hand and wonders if she ever felt anything for him. Thinking back on those first weeks that he lived with her, it occurs to him that she must have. That she, like him, perhaps felt too much in the aftermath of his mom's death. And that also like him, she didn't know how to process the loss. She'd already tragically lost so much, and his very presence was a reminder that she'd never see her daughter again. She'd never have the chance to resolve whatever it was that had his mom fleeing California with his dad. So she pushed him away, thereby neglecting him.

He vividly recalls entering her library to retrieve a book only for her to rise from the chair where she'd been reading and leave the room without acknowledging him. Numerous times she had Adam remove him from the patio before she went for a swim. It happened time and again with almost every room in the house until Matt looked for reasons not to go home after school. He remembers the despair and guilt he felt on a daily basis. No wonder he left on his eighteenth birthday and never looked back.

She shouldn't have ignored his suffering. Though she probably couldn't see his through her own. It still doesn't excuse how she treated him or make him inclined to forgive her.

Rage simmers, and contempt pushes the words from his mouth. "I was just a kid," he begins. She doesn't react, and he doesn't know if his words will register. But he pulls up a chair and tells her what he saw and felt—still feels—about his dad, his mom, and her. He shares his fears and shame and regrets. He gets everything off his chest short of forgiving her. He's not ready to. He doesn't know if he ever will be.

When he finishes, he touches his grandmother's hand one last time. Then he leaves the room.

———

Several hours later, Matt heads toward the floor's sitting area, where he knows Julia has been waiting. He returned to Elizabeth after he spoke with the nurse and remained at his grandmother's side until she took her last breath. He didn't leave the room until her body was removed and the bed stripped of its linens. He feels like an empty shell.

Julia notices him immediately and gets up to meet him. "How are you feeling?" Her eyes search his face, and he takes an internal reading. Only then does he become aware that he's been clenching his teeth.

"Okay." He rubs the ache where his jaw hinges. "Thanks for what you said back there."

She smiles a little. "I'm glad you stayed."

"Me too." His eyes roam over Julia, clocking her wrinkled attire, the floppy bun of hair, and the dark shadows under her eyes. "How long have you been here?"

"Since one this afternoon. I came right after we got off the phone."

She's been worried about Elizabeth since before they first spoke on Friday. She's a better person than he is.

He glances around, past the windows behind him, and realizes how late it is. He inhales deeply, taking in the subtle odor of bleach and antiseptic. "Mind if we get out of here?" There isn't anything else for him here, and he needs fresh air. He figures he'll check into a motel for the night and leave first thing in the morning.

"Uh, sure." She blinks, turning toward the elevators and back to him as if trying to figure where they should go. "We can get coffee."

"Okay, but not that coffee." He points at the cup with the hospital logo in her hand, and she blinks at him, looks at the cup, then grins.

"It's pretty watered down."

Matt drags in a sharp breath. Her smile is stunning. It's also Magnolia's smile, and a shudder moves through him. How could there be a resemblance between them when he's never seen Julia before today and he thinks—*believes?*—he imagined Magnolia.

Exhausted from abusing his body over the weekend, spent after venting to Elizabeth and then watching her die, he's one beat away from cracking.

"Actually," he says, changing his mind, "can we get dinner? I haven't eaten all day." For once, he's man enough to admit he shouldn't be alone right now. Not after the mental trip he went on this weekend.

She glances at her watch. "It's late. I'm not sure anything is open, but we can try. Where are you parked?"

"I don't have a car. I took an Uber from the airport."

"We can use mine." They walk to the elevators, and she pushes a button. She then snaps her fingers and looks up at him. "I know it's late, but do you mind if we swing by Rosemont? Lenore said she'd be working late. She needs to talk with you and wanted me to ask if you could manage a visit tonight."

His hands begin to shake. He shoves them into his front pockets.

"Are you up for it? I don't think it'll take long."

Lenore probably just wants to settle what Elizabeth owed Rosemont. Best to get it over with tonight so he can get back to Dave and their project at first light. "Sure, fine." Still, he breaks out into a sweat.

CHAPTER 36

JULIA

Julia had just returned from stepping out for a cup of vending machine coffee when Matt arrived. She recognized him from his photos, but more so, he felt familiar. Startling, given they'd never met in person. She had to restrain herself from hugging him like a friend she hadn't seen in ages.

Matt now fills the space beside her as she drives them to Rosemont. He rubs his hands over his thighs and stares out the front window with a glazed expression. Sweat sheens his forehead. She can feel his agitation as her own. There's an underlying turbulence about him. He's likely feeling the effects of a hangover and withdrawal as well. She considers taking him straight to a hotel. What is Lenore thinking? His grandmother just died.

"How far is the drive?" Matt asks when they stop at a light. He clasps his knees, then drags his hands up his thighs. Clasps his knees again.

"Not far. A few miles. Are you okay?"

"Not sure."

Maybe she should overrule Lenore. Matt's on edge. His thoughts must be chaotic. On top of that, he's famished. "Let's get dinner instead. Lenore can wait until morning."

"No, let's get it over with. I'm fine, honest," he adds when Julia hesitates after the light changes.

"All right." She drives through the intersection rather than turning right toward an all-night diner she knows of. They reach Rosemont, and she parks near the entrance. She doesn't spot Lenore's car. "I'm not sure she's here."

"We can look. Since we're here, can you show me where Liza lived?"

His interest surprises her. "Sure." She points down the hallway opposite Lenore's office when they're inside. "Her room was down there."

He looks at her with lifted brows. "Come with me?"

"Of course." Julia tells him the room number, and he stops in the doorway to take in the barren room.

"This is it?"

"She had a few items left. I can ask where they are."

Matt moves into the room and stops at the window. He peers into the darkness. "How's the view?"

"The grounds are beautiful. This room overlooks the back garden."

"Elizabeth had a rose garden. It was a sight to see. But you already know that."

Their eyes meet, and an invisible tether pulls her across the room. Surreal to think her grandmother once oversaw that same garden. Even more bizarre to be standing here with Matt as if their families have come full circle. As if she's known him her entire life. As if they were meant to have met all along.

She pulls her gaze from him, embarrassed by her ridiculous thoughts. Just because they've had several long, intimate conversations doesn't mean they'll ever speak again once he leaves for home now that Liza has passed.

She hopes their calls continue.

"Everything all right?" Matt asks.

"Mm-hmm." Mouth pressed into a thin line, she nods.

He peers at her with a slight tilt of his head, opens his mouth only to close it and shake his head. She wants to ask what he was going to say, if he, too, is feeling whatever this is between them. But he looks around the room and asks, "Was she happy here?"

"I wouldn't call Liza happy. But I don't think she was unhappy here if that helps."

Matt nods and doesn't say anything further.

"Let's go find Lenore," she suggests, guessing he must feel strange in Liza's room given they hadn't been on good terms. "Steve's at the front desk. We can ask him about Liza's things."

"I don't want anything of hers. I already have to figure out what to do with the stuff you sent me."

Julia winces. Her bad. "If it's too much for you, I can help. Ship the boxes to me and I'll sort through them. I can put aside anything that seems important for you when you're ready and donate the rest." It's the least she could do for the inconvenience.

"Thanks, but they're already with me. I'll get around to them eventually."

They return to the lobby and approach the front desk. "Do you know what they did with Liza Holloway's personal effects?" Julia asks Steve.

"Got her things right here." Steve retrieves a box from under the desk. "It's addressed to Matthew Gatlin to be shipped tomorrow."

"That's me. I'll take it." Matt picks up the box. "Is there someplace I can go through this?"

"You don't want to wait until you get to your hotel?" She'd be an emotional wreck going through Mama Rose's things and would want privacy.

"Here's fine. I'm sure someone could use whatever's inside. It's probably just clothes."

"That's kind of you. The dining room should be empty at this hour."

They walk past the common area on their way to the dining hall. It's movie night, and Julia automatically searches for Mama Rose among the small gathering in front of the TV.

Matt stops to stare into the room. "Is your grandmother here?"

"Yes, she's sitting over there." She points at the wheelchair in the far corner.

"I want to meet her."

She's surprised he wants to, but pleased nonetheless. "All right, but fair warning. She won't know who I am."

Matt's mouth turns down. Just a glance from him and he makes her feel like she isn't alone in this. She leads him into the room and around the residents parked in front of the screen. Just as they reach Mama Rose, Matt stops abruptly. She glances back to see what grabbed his attention. He gapes at Mama Rose. Disbelief pulls at his face while Mama Rose gazes up at him with the smile she reserves only for those she knows. It's the smile she used to give to Julia.

"Magnolia?" Matt's voice croaks. The box drops with a thud.

"Matty." Mama Rose grasps his hand. "You came back for me."

CHAPTER 37

MATT

Matt gapes at the woman who's pressing his hand to her cheek like a long-lost lover. Her skin is cool and speckled with age spots. Her eyes, though—faded, the milky whites veined with the decades separating their ages—are Magnolia's blue gray. They sparkle with mischievous joy, as they did at the motel, her smile shimmering all the same.

Impossible. Age aside, he couldn't have pictured Magnolia Blu this accurately based solely on the diary entries Julia read to him.

"What's going on?" Julia's gaze pings between him and her grandmother, reminding him that he's in a room surrounded by strangers. This isn't the place for a psychotic breakdown.

"I don't know." When he woke this morning and found Magnolia gone, he couldn't believe she'd left him. When he searched the motel for her and three people denied they'd seen her with him when he swore they had, he figured between the alcohol, the edibles, and the stress of having to see Elizabeth again, he'd been hallucinating. That he'd experienced a drug-induced, alcohol-soaked psychotic trip fueled by stories of Magnolia through conversations with Julia.

Because *that* was logical while *this* is not: Magnolia Blu recognizing him.

"Who do you think he is, Mama Rose?"

Magnolia, or rather Ruby Rose Hope—Julia's *grandmother*—smiles up at Matt. "He's my Matty."

"She has dementia," Julia tells him. "She confuses me with my mom on occasion, but mostly she thinks I'm one of the caretakers on staff. I'm guessing she's thinking you're Matthew Holloway."

"I—I'm not so sure," Matt says more to himself, peering at the pendant she wears. It's an exact replica of the one Magnolia was wearing yesterday morning.

His skin prickles as time warps, confusing reality with his fever dream.

He drops to his knees.

"What are you doing?" Julia whispers roughly.

"It's you, isn't it?" Matt startles at the question coming from his mouth. He sounds crazy to himself. Too late. It's done, and his apparent psychosis is visible to all. He didn't even have to sell tickets. *This is a free show, folks.*

Ruby Rose Hope cups her hands over his and shocks him further. "Have you allowed yourself to love yet?"

"What?" His voice croaks. If he was hallucinating this weekend, Julia's grandmother wouldn't have been privy to their conversation.

Unless she was there.

"I don't understand," he whispers.

"I'm not understanding either," Julia says above him.

Ruby Rose's eyes fill with love. "So much grief. So much anger. You have to go back, Matty."

"Back where? The motel?"

"Back to where it all began." The creases around her eyes soften. "You have to let it go." She rests her palm over his heart, and he jolts at the contact. He'd felt something similar when she touched his hand the day they met on the roadside.

"Sorry I'm late, Ruby." A tall, beefy man in matching teal pants and shirt with glaringly white sneakers grasps Ruby Rose's wheelchair handles. He unlocks the wheels, and the chair jerks back. Matt's hands slip from hers. He notices the movie has ended and the lights have been turned on.

He jumps to his feet. "Where are you taking her?" They aren't done talking. He needs to know where he's supposed to go back to and why. What does he have to let go?

"Ruby needs her medication and sleep."

"Who are you?"

The man's brows rise at Matt's aggressive tone. Julia touches his arm, startling him. He whirls on her.

"This is Trevor, Mama Rose's caretaker."

Matt pulls himself back and mumbles an apology. He's losing his head.

"Excuse us." Trevor swings the wheelchair around. "Good night, Julia."

"Good night, Trevor. I'll see you tomorrow."

Matt watches Trevor take Magnolia away. His heart clangs in his ears. They need to finish their conversation.

He starts to follow them.

Julia grabs his arm. "Matt."

"What?" he snaps at her and goes to shake off her hand when he notices how pale she is. "I don't know what I was thinking. I didn't mean to freak you out." He's freaking out.

"Why are you acting like you know her?" Her tone is wary accusation.

He glances in the direction Trevor took Ruby Rose, but they're gone. He turns back to Julia. "I don't know. I don't understand it myself. Over the weekend, I thought I was . . ." Tripping? Maybe he still is. The drugs could still be in his system and his brain is short-circuiting.

Julia stares hard at him. She isn't going to drop this.

He scrubs his jaw, frustrated. "Before tonight, I've never met your grandmother, at least not the way she is now. I spent the weekend with a woman. Sometimes she had your voice, sometimes not. But she looked like a younger version of your grandmother. Her name was Magnolia Blu."

Julia gives him side-eye and warily moves a step away from him.

"I was a mess this weekend," he rushes to explain before she calls a doctor to have him committed. "I was drinking, there were drugs. We had those conversations and you told me those stories. I must have projected her. For a while there, I thought she really was there with me."

"Were you hallucinating?"

"I must have been because it's impossible your grandmother was really there with me when she was here, right?"

"Right."

"She felt so real, though," he says, impassioned, unable to hold himself together. He can still smell the chlorine in her hair and taste the weed on her tongue. "I swear I wasn't alone this weekend."

"You and I spent a lot of time on the phone."

"But she was in the room with me."

"Then who were you with?"

He opens his mouth to say "no one," but the words lodge in his throat.

"Just say it, Matt."

"It was her, Magnolia. She had the same necklace as your grandmother. I don't know." He tosses up his hands. "Maybe Ruby mistook me for my grandfather, Matty. We probably look alike." While it doesn't explain how Julia's grandmother brought up parts of their conversation from the motel, it's the only explanation he can make any sense of.

Julia cuts a hand between them. "Not possible."

"How so?"

"First of all, I'm the one who asked you about opening yourself up to love."

"Did you tell her that?"

"No."

"Then how could she have asked me about that?"

"I don't know." Julia looks as freaked out as he's feeling. "But there's something else you need to know."

"What's that?" he asks, desperate to make sense of this weekend.

"It's impossible you look like Matthew Holloway. He wasn't your grandfather. Adam is."

CHAPTER 38

MATT

Julia is speaking nonsense. In fact, this entire trip hasn't vibed with him. He fell asleep Friday night and woke up in an alternate universe. He almost laughs at her. This is a poor time to joke.

"We both know Adam's not my grandfather." He's been told since he was a kid it's Matthew Holloway. Elizabeth had been pregnant with Matt's mom in the last entry Julia read to him. His grandmother had just announced the news to Magnolia. Isn't that proof?

Julia remains straight faced and silent. She isn't joking.

"Adam?"

He thinks of the man who picked him up at the Burbank airport when he flew to California upon his parents' deaths. Adam was the only person who went out of his way to purchase Matt clothes when he outgrew them. Adam signed him up for baseball. He went to some of Matt's games. He would have told Matt if he was his grandfather. Adam knew how lonely he'd been those first months when Elizabeth couldn't bear the sight of him.

"Liza told me last night," Julia says.

An angry laugh bursts from his throat. "Of course she did. Don't you see? She would have been evicted today had I not shown up. She thought I'd bailed on her."

"You did bail on her. Would you have come if she didn't have a stroke?"

He waves a dismissive hand. "Point is, she was trying to hurt me."

"I don't think so. She didn't believe she'd get the chance to tell you herself. She made it very clear to me nobody knew your mom was Adam's daughter. She asked me to tell you."

Matt scoffs. He doesn't want to believe Julia. But she has nothing to gain by lying. Was this the elusive news Elizabeth had to tell him about his mom? Why not tell him when he was a kid and thought she was his only family?

He thinks of all the time he spent with Adam, and acid churns his stomach. Had Adam known? Did he intentionally keep their relationship secret? To what end? To further torment him?

"What took you so long to tell me? I got to the hospital hours ago."

"Liza was dying. I didn't want to lay that on you too. I didn't mean to tell you just now either."

"When, then?"

She throws out her arms. "I don't know. Later sometime?"

"Pardon to interrupt."

"What?" they both snap at the woman he didn't see approach. Startled brown eyes widen behind thick-framed glasses.

"Whoa." The woman lurches back with palms facing out.

Julia winces. "Lenore, hi. We were coming to look for you."

"Steve told me you were on-site. You must be Matt Gatlin. Lenore Pullen."

"Hey. Matt." He briefly clasps the hand she offers.

"I'm sorry about your grandmother," she says.

"Yeah, well, it is what it is." His hand shakes when he swipes his fingers through his hair. Only Elizabeth could hurt him postmortem.

"Matt." Julia's tone tells him he couldn't have meant what he said.

Lenore's gaze pans between them. "Either way, I'm sorry. We enjoyed having her with us."

"Not from what I've heard."

Julia frowns at him, and he hates that he's acting like a dick again around her, but he isn't himself. His headache is back.

"Yes, well. When you're ready, we have the remainder of her things. Clothes and a few books. Some framed photos. You're welcome to take them."

"Already got them." He looks around his feet, spotting the box he doesn't remember putting down. He picks it up.

Lenore glances at Julia before saying to him, "May we speak privately?"

"I'll go." Julia points toward the door.

"Don't," he orders, and exhales heavily. "I didn't mean it to sound like that. Do you mind waiting for me? Please?" he adds when she hesitates. "I won't be long. This won't take long, will it?" he asks Lenore.

She shakes her head.

"I'll be in the lobby." Julia smiles uneasily at them both and offers, "Want me to hold on to that?"

Will he ever get over how nice she is to him? Though *nice* doesn't come near to what she's done for him. She's kind, compassionate, and beautiful, inside and out. Matt hasn't met anyone like her. She makes him rethink how selfish he is with his time, how closed-minded he's been. He gives her Elizabeth's box with an awkward "Thanks."

"Let's go to my office," Lenore suggests, and he follows her down a hallway to a door marked FACILITY DIRECTOR. She gestures at a vinyl armchair as she rounds the desk to her own chair. "Have a seat."

"I'll stand." He's too restless to sit. He crosses the office to a glass door he figures leads to a patio. He can't see anything other than his gloomy reflection at this hour.

"I sense you're upset, Mr. Gatlin."

"Matt, and I'm fine." He isn't going to try to explain the trip he's been on since Friday. But he does turn to her, wondering if she knows about Adam too. Is what Julia told him true?

"All right." Lenore dips her chin but doesn't press him. "Like I said, I'm sorry about Elizabeth. Her death was sudden. I also regret how we've handled things on our end. We shouldn't have shipped her personal property to you without consulting you first. The board of directors was on me about keeping our rooms occupied with paying residents only, and I was desperate. I let one of my staff—" She clears her throat behind a fist. "Excuse me. One of my volunteers talk me into the idea."

Stacks of boxes are the least of his worries. He presses a finger to the middle of his forehead to relieve the ache. "It's fine," he says tightly. "I don't blame Julia." In reality, she's helped him on numerous levels.

He puts a pin in that thought to mull over later.

"Good, because I take full responsibility. Understand I'm not a callous person. If it were up to me, I would have found a way to keep Liza here rent-free. But it's not up to me, not anymore. My board—"

Matt cuts a hand between them. "Doesn't matter. It's in the past now."

Lenore's shoulders rise on an intake of breath. "Yes, but there's more regarding your grandmother's situation. I know you and Julia have spoken, but she doesn't know the full story, not where Liza's concerned."

He spent his weekend procrastinating with an imaginary woman, only to arrive hours before Liza's passing. He then discovers the woman he spent the weekend with might not have been a figment of his drugged imagination because she's here, just older. And she knows what they spoke about in the motel.

Then he's told Adam is his grandfather, not Matthew Holloway, whom he's believed was his grandfather for as long as he can remember.

Wham, bam, more surprises for you, man.

He stares at Lenore wondering, *What now?*

Sensing a need to sit down, he takes the chair Lenore offered.

She settles in her seat. Vinyl creaks under her weight. "Liza moved to Rosemont just for the year. She paid her fees up front." Almost reflectively, she adds, "In a strange sort of coincidence, today marks a year to the exact date she moved in."

A chill ripples across Matt's shoulders. "Are you saying she planned to die today?"

"No, she had a stroke. I just find it—" She stalls.

"Odd?" Matt supplies. Liza wasn't just out of money. She was short of time too.

"I guess." Lenore shrugs.

"So why move here for just a year? She had a house in Beverly Hills. She had money."

"From what her power of attorney told me, she sold her house last year and donated her estate across several charities and philanthropies, including the Hollywood Arts Council, Hollywood Chamber of Commerce, and the SAG-AFTRA Foundation, if I remember correctly."

He leans forward. "Did she come here because of Julia's grandmother?" Julia had wondered if there was a connection.

"I don't have an answer to that. I do know she and Ruby Rose had history and that Liza was frustrated Ruby couldn't remember her. On multiple occasions I had the impression Liza had something important to tell Ruby."

"Do you know what about?" It couldn't have been what Julia told him about Adam. He doesn't see how that information would be relevant to Julia's grandmother.

"I don't, but you can ask Adam."

His ears tighten at the name, which has new meaning to him. "You found him?"

"His daughter reached me a little over an hour ago."

"His daughter?" If Adam is his grandfather, that would make her his aunt. He sinks back into the chair.

"Adam suffered a fall. He's recovering from a broken femur and a concussion. He only remembered his duty to Liza this evening and asked his daughter to call me. Siobhan said her dad was acting strangely, mumbling something about Liza dying and that her spirit had visited him. He's sorry he wasn't there when she passed."

"I was with her. He might find some comfort in that."

"I'll be sure to let him know," Lenore says.

"Where is he now? I'd like to pay him a visit." Matt wants to ask him if it's true. Is he Matt's grandfather?

"You can call Siobhan." Lenore writes the phone number on a sticky note. "She'll let you know if he's up for visitors. I imagine there are a few more things to be settled with Liza's estate now that she's passed."

"Thank you."

Matt and Lenore both stand.

"I'm sorry things didn't turn out differently, but I'm glad you finally came. Liza would have been pleased to know you were at her side."

A note of disagreement rumbles in his throat.

They shake hands, and Matt leaves to meet Julia in the lobby. She jumps out of her chair when she sees him and rushes over. "I'm so sorry about earlier. I feel horrible springing that on you about Adam."

"It's all right. I shouldn't have snapped at you. It's been one thing after another today." He looks down at the paper with Siobhan's phone number and can barely read the numbers because his hand is shaking so much.

Julia rests a hand on his, steadying the tremors. "Come home with me. I'll cook dinner. We can talk."

Emotion presses behind his eyes. He nods tightly, way past the ability to make any more decisions today. He picks up Liza's box from the floor near where Julia sat, and together, they walk to her car.

CHAPTER 39

JULIA

Julia waited longer than she should have, risking injury to Mama Rose and herself, before moving her grandmother into assisted living, and now she's dragging her feet to move her to a more affordable place.

She excels at procrastinating, but she isn't known for her patience.

She told herself she'd wait until Matt ate before she plied him with questions. Commendably, she made it through a quick shopping trip to pick up food for dinner—an unseasoned pork loin, fresh broccoli, and fingerling potatoes. And she's contained herself as they work in tandem in her kitchen, prepping the food as if this were something they did together every day.

Strange how they fell into sync, salting the pork and drizzling olive oil over the vegetables. She attributes their easy banter while doing so to their extended phone conversations. It feels like they've known each other for years rather than days. They're also dodging the heavier topics, like what happened back at Rosemont between Matt and Mama Rose or what Lenore had to speak to Matt about that was so important. When he came out of the meeting with her, he looked like the husk of the man Julia had seen at the hospital, and even then, he had appeared pretty beaten up. She knows she's partly to blame for his shell shock, blurting the news about Adam the way she had.

She still needs to tell him the rest of what Liza shared with her. But when they slide the food in the oven to roast and she offers him a glass of wine, her patience gives over to concern. Matt's complexion hasn't improved since they left Rosemont, and she noticed his hands shook as he washed the potatoes. He drags a chair from under the kitchen table and collapses in the seat as if his legs give out.

"Are you okay?" She's immediately at his side.

Elbow on the table, he drops his head in his palm. "Headache."

She doubts he's eaten today. His blood sugar is most likely low. He also spent the weekend drinking and smoking weed. Who knows what else he took. She wouldn't be surprised if he's still hungover.

She puts down the wine and glasses and sets a tumbler of orange juice in front of him. "Drink this."

He lifts his head and chugs half. "Thanks." He wipes his mouth and rubs his temples.

"Do you want something for the headache?"

He shakes his head.

"Do you get them a lot?"

He nods. "Edibles help. But after this weekend, I think I should stay away from them." He looks up at her, amused.

"So there was more than alcohol and weed involved."

"My friend Dave gave me something that had a bit more kick than what I'm used to."

"Ah. That explains the hallucinations you mentioned."

He looks uncomfortable she brought it up.

She rubs her hands to warm her palms, then holds them by his head. "May I?"

Matt's gaze lifts from her hands to study her face, and his close vicinity boosts her heart rate. "I might be able to help. With the headache," she adds when he continues to just look at her.

He slowly nods and leans back in the chair.

Julia rotates her hands to loosen her wrists and moves to stand behind him. She combs his hair off his forehead, and with her fingertips, she applies gentle pressure to his temples, moving her fingers in a circular motion.

His head falls back, and he groans. "Fuck me."

She smiles briefly, loving that first touch when she can feel her client's tension melt away. But Matt isn't a client. He's just a man whose family's history is intertwined with hers, one with a throaty voice that sparks a heated awareness inside her even when they're arguing. And he's even more appealing in person, something she didn't anticipate.

It's been a long time since she's felt anything for anyone, and she's definitely attracted to him on multiple levels. Though she'd argue *attraction* doesn't come close to describing what she feels for him. Whatever this is, it feels deeper, more meaningful. She has to continuously remind herself they met over the phone just days ago and she shouldn't be overly friendly with him.

She massages his scalp along the hairline, applying firmer pressure. He groans again, making the discomfort in her overworked wrists worth it.

"Feel good?"

"So good. It's been so long . . ." He groans as she moves her fingers in circular patterns over his scalp, and he trails off before finishing his thoughts. She digs her teeth into her bottom lip so she won't ask him what he meant. So long since he had a massage or since a woman touched him? She wants to believe it's the latter, but he mentioned spending the weekend with a woman. Who happened to be a younger version of her grandmother with Julia's voice. She can't decide if she should be jealous, flattered, or repulsed.

She has a lingering sense of all three feelings when Matt's shoulders rise with a sharp breath as if he's about to speak.

"What?" she asks when he doesn't say anything. She deepens the pressure behind his ears.

"Elizabeth." He stops and so does she, her fingers stilling. "What else did she say about Adam?"

Julia was wondering when he'd bring up his grandfather. She resumes her ministrations. "Not much other than he's your grandfather and that she'd only recently told him too."

Matt's back goes rigid. "So he didn't know."

"Apparently not." Julia imagines things would have turned out differently for Matt had Adam known about their relationship. To think his daughter Aubrey grew up right under his nose and neither of them knew. "Liza told Adam last month. She believes that's why he disappeared. He left her quite upset and broke off contact."

"He fell and hit his head. Broke his leg too," Matt says. "Lenore told me. His daughter called this evening to say he had amnesia and forgot about Liza."

"You have an aunt." He could have uncles and cousins too. A whole family of relatives. Jealousy slithers underneath her skin. "Are you going to call him?" she asks of Adam.

He's quiet for a breath. "I want to."

The combined longing and hesitation in his tone is unmistakable. She knows from Mama Rose's diary that Adam was married and had his own kids while working for Liza. She imagines Adam's family, especially his wife if she's still alive, might not take kindly to the news that Adam had a child with his employer, or that he has a grandson through her too.

The probability of them rejecting him is high and might not be something he wants to explore given what he went through with Liza. She hasn't reached out to her mom for that very reason. Lea rejecting her once was too much. But to go through that twice? Julia won't risk her scarred heart.

Matt has gone quiet, presumably lost in thought like her. His head falls forward as she moves down his neck to relieve the tension in his shoulders. "This is . . . awesome. Thank you."

"My pleasure." She squeezes his shoulders, her thumbs pressing into the muscles between the blades, and a sharp pain shoots up her forearms. She makes a noise in the back of her throat.

"You okay?" Matt twists to look up at her.

"Yeah, fine." She shakes out her wrists, and his gaze drops to see her rubbing the base of her palms.

"You're not fine." He grasps her hand and tugs her into the chair beside him.

"What are you doing?" she asks. But once she's seated, the tension she's been holding on to all day pours out. She falls back against the chair, and his smile is slight, understanding.

"Who massages the massage therapist?" He smirks and they fall into a companionable silence. He's massaging her hands, and she wants to melt into a puddle at his feet. Their eyes make contact, and something indiscernible passes between them. An understanding of sorts, a common goal—she doesn't know. But whatever it is, it's steadily growing, and she's sorely tempted to explore it.

Matt studies her hands as he draws his knuckles along her forearm. She stares at his fair scalp where his hair parts. Questions she's been dying to ask bubble to the roof of her mouth.

"So, you weren't with a woman this weekend. You were hallucinating?"

He pauses midstroke and then starts up again, applying firmer pressure. "I honestly don't know what happened this weekend. I've been trying not to think about it."

"You don't sound delusional, if that's what you're worried about." She was raised by a woman who regularly smoked pot and hosted 420 parties well into the early 2000s. Mama Rose had an eclectic group of friends who frequently saw illusions, as they'd describe them, when they were high. Their visions sparked lively conversations that often led to deep introspection about what they meant.

"Do you think it was those gummies your friend gave you?" she asks.

"Must have been."

Julia chews on that a moment. "So, you were drugged and stoned—"

"And drunk," he adds with a self-deprecating smirk.

"—imagining yourself with Mama Rose."

He clears his throat. "Magnolia Blu. That's who she told me she was."

"Right. And all this was happening while you were talking with me, while I was telling you about Magnolia Blu and reading from her diary, and during all that other stuff we talked about?" Like falling in love and whether life is worth living if you don't allow yourself to love.

He nods. "Strange, I know."

Julia nibbles her lip. "What were you imagining yourself doing with her while you were talking with me?"

With fascination, she watches a flush move up his neck to his cheeks.

"Matt?"

"Nothing much."

She takes a steadying breath. "Do you remember our conversations?"

He freezes for a second before starting up again, moving to her other hand. "Pretty much."

"So what were you hallucinating about while we were talking?"

His flush deepens.

"Were you fantasizing about having sex with—"

"Stop."

"Jesus." She looks away, face heated.

His touch softens on her arm. When she looks back at him, his expression is contemplative. "It was really for you. Those feelings I was having while I was . . . they were for you. I—Never mind." He stares at his fingers pressing into her forearm. "I'm not expecting anything from you if that's what you're worried about. Frankly, I'm wiped and just want to find a hotel and crash."

Her arm is warm where he's touching her. She wasn't expecting anything from him either. But she is grateful he's being open about his feelings despite not having a phone to hide behind. She wants to delve deeper into what he said, but he's out of his seat and crossing the kitchen to where she dropped her bag on the floor. Peeking out the top is the Magnolia Blu journal she collected from Liza's room earlier in the day, and the object of Matt's interest.

"Is this the diary?" He picks up the book.

"You're welcome to read the rest if you want." She didn't get the chance to read him Mama Rose's last entry, or her more recent note to Liza, which he might find of interest.

"No, I think I'm good. No offense, but I've had about all the earth-shattering news I can handle today. Not sure I can take any more."

"You pretty much know everything." Other than that Matthew Holloway is her grandfather.

Best she hold on to that nugget since he's already overwhelmed.

He fans through the pages, and a piece of paper drops to the ground.

"Except that." Julia jumps from her chair to grab it. "It's for you. Liza left it in the diary."

He exchanges the diary for the letter, his complexion further waning. He really should eat soon. She glances at the timer and notices dinner is just about ready.

"She had the diary last night. I asked her to read the most recent passage." Julia returns the diary to her bag and retrieves the hot mitts. Matt folds the letter and tucks it into the front pocket of his jeans. "You aren't going to read it?" She'd be tearing through the letter if it were her.

He shakes his head. "Later. Not tonight. Do you, ah . . . Do you have a photo of your grandmother from when she was younger? When she used to go by Magnolia Blu?"

"Yeah, one sec." She turns off the timer and takes out the meat and veggies. Leaving the pork to rest, she leads him into the front room and grabs a framed photo off the bookshelf of her grandmother, arm in arm with a tall blonde woman. "Mama Rose has had this forever. She once told me the woman with her was an old friend she's no longer in touch with. She looks like Liza, and now that I know the story, I believe it's her. The color is faded, but look at the roses behind them. That must be her garden at her house."

Matt makes a gruff sound and snags the frame from her. He stares at the photo and weaves on his feet.

"Oh." Julia grabs his elbow the same instant he throws out a foot for balance.

"Did you show me this photo before?" he asks. Julia shakes her head. "Texted it to me? Emailed me?"

"No."

"You swear?"

"I've never shown you that photo."

He stares hard at the image.

"What is it?"

"It's her."

"Who?"

"Magnolia Blu. The woman I picked up this weekend. This is her."

A chill runs down her neck, tightening her skin. She looks warily between him and the picture. "Are you sure?"

"That's exactly how I saw her."

"But that's my grandmother. That picture was taken over fifty years ago."

"I know. How is that possible?"

Julia is speechless. She looks from Matt to the photo.

He throws up his hands. "That explains it. I'm losing my head." He shoves the photo back at her and paces the room, dragging his fingers through his hair.

"You're not." Julia returns the photo. "I'm sure there's another explanation."

"One aside from me having a psychotic break?" Matt turns to her, his eyes bright with the need for answers. "What about your grandmother? She recognized me. Those things she said . . . It felt like she was talking to me."

"All of which has an easy explanation," Julia reassures. "You must have seen a photo like this at some point and your subconscious tapped into it."

"Maybe." He sounds doubtful.

She tries another angle. "You lived with Liza for what, eight years? You probably saw a picture there. As for my grandmother, she wasn't seeing you, Matt. She saw Matty. And what she said about you coming back, it makes perfect sense. The night Matty died, he was supposed to come back for my grandmother. They were going to run away together."

Matt frowns. "I don't remember that part. Was it in the diary?"

"It was. I didn't get the chance to read it to you. I think you hung up on me or your phone died." Julia returns the photo to the shelf.

"What happened to Mag—your grandmother after Elizabeth told her she was pregnant with my mom? Did she stay with her?"

"For a short time, until Liza found the diary and read it."

"She read about Magnolia's affair with Matty. Liza made her leave."

"Yes, though I think Mama Rose would have left anyway. She was pregnant."

Matt follows her to the couch, sitting beside her. "Sam's kid?"

Julia shakes her head and sees the instant it registers with Matt. His eyes flare. "Matty Holloway is *your* grandfather?"

"I think so. Mama Rose said as much in her last entry."

"So, what happened?"

"As you can imagine, that was the end of their friendship. Mama Rose returned home and tried reconciling with her parents, but they refused. She eventually ended up back in California, married Benjie, and started her business. This was their house."

"And they lived happily ever after."

"For a while."

Matt fixes his attention on his hands clasped between his knees, his expression pensive. "She seemed so real to me. I could smell her. I was touching her."

"Maybe—" Julia stalls.

Matt looks at her. "What?"

She shakes her head, feeling embarrassed. "You'll think it's foolish."

A sharp laugh bursts from Matt. "After what I experienced this weekend, not a chance."

"All right." Julia rubs her palms over her thighs and thinks of Mama Rose's life, everything she's enjoyed, everyone she's loved. All the things she's forgotten. Melancholy is a heavy blanket that bows her back. "Alzheimer's is horrible. It steals your life while you're still living."

"I'm sorry." Matt tucks a curl that escaped her messy bun behind her ear. Her skin warms at the contact. Her heart flutters at the kindness and concern she feels behind the gesture.

"When she started forgetting things, I'd picture those fragments or bits of memories as books disappearing off a library shelf. Or these shelves here in this room." She waves a hand at the bookcases buttressing the fireplace. "The shelves are slowly emptying, but the books aren't necessarily gone."

"You want to believe her memories have been checked out, like library books?"

Julia's eyes widen. She clasps both his hands. "Exactly. I've read up on the disease, about how the brain cells die off, severing neurons so memories can't be retrieved, and then enough cells die that the memories themselves disappear. But I wonder if they're truly gone.

"Let me explain," she says at his bewildered expression. She scoots closer to him, her hands gesturing as she talks. "Our brains run on energy. Memories are nothing but electrical impulses. Energy can't be created or destroyed. But it can transform. This will sound far-fetched, but honestly, it's helped me cope with what's going on with Mama Rose. It's too difficult for me to watch her lose a life's worth of memories. To think that they're gone forever. But what if when we die, our memories don't die with us—they're just released into the universe, where they manifest in some other form? Then there are people like Mama Rose with Alzheimer's. What if her memories aren't disappearing? What if they're being released to the universe *before* she dies?"

"And manifesting elsewhere?"

"Like the motel you were staying at."

"Wouldn't that be something?" Matt knocks his knee against hers and gives her a warm smile.

Julia shrugs. "It's just fanciful thinking."

"I like your fanciful thinking."

Matt's eyes meet hers right before they drop to her mouth, and Julia feels the heat of his gaze to the center of her body. She has the urge to kiss him. He must feel the same because she swears the inches between them are decreasing. How easy it would be to close the distance. Her hand starts to move to his chest.

Matt's phone rings, jarring them out of the spell they've fallen under. He glances down at his thigh, where the phone is tucked inside a pocket. He digs it out and looks at the screen. "It's Dave. I have to take this."

"Of course." She blinks, leaning back. "I'll just . . ." She stands and gestures toward the kitchen. "I'll heat up our food."

He gives her a brief nod and heads for the front door. "Dave, hey," he answers. The door quietly shuts behind him.

CHAPTER 40

MATT

"I've been trying to get a hold of you for hours." Dave isn't happy.

"I'm sorry. No excuse. I—things have been weird." Matt steps off the porch. Long, purposeful strides take him to the sidewalk.

"I knew this shit with your grandmother would get to you. Are you okay?"

"I'm fine." For the moment. No telling how he'll feel after he reads Elizabeth's letter. He walks to the street corner and turns around, retracks his steps. "I made it to Pasadena. She had a stroke and passed a few hours ago."

"Matt. I'm sorry." He pauses. "How are you holding up?"

"Okay," he manages without elaborating. He should feel sad, but he doesn't. He doesn't miss her either. If he feels anything, it's frustration and anger. He expected to feel better after sitting with his grandmother and getting his thoughts off his chest, but that was before Julia told him about Adam.

"How's everything on your end? Did you get the photos off to Ford?" Matt had powered through a batch on the plane and uploaded them with a note for Dave to finish the rest.

"That's why I've been calling. They loved them. They went with one you edited and two I did."

Pride floods Matt. "Told you that you had it in you."

"Yeah, I'm pretty pumped about it. So, what's your plan? Are you flying to the race from there? We're supposed to leave tomorrow."

The instant Dave asks, Matt knows he's not going.

"I'm not shooting the race."

"Excuse me?"

Matt stops in front of Julia's house and claps a hand on a tree trunk. He bumps his shoe against an exposed root. "I have some things I need to take care of."

"But you worked so hard for this. *We* worked hard to get this assignment. You're giving that up?"

His inner photographer shouts for him to rally and get on a plane. But he thinks of Adam. His *grandfather*. The only man who showed him any kindness after his parents' deaths.

"No, I'm not giving it up for us. You're going on our behalf, and you're going to kill it and get us invited back next year."

Dave hesitates. "I—I don't know."

"I can't get back yet. There's someone here I need to see. You got this, just like you did with my photos from the shoot. I have total confidence in you."

"All right. I'll do it. But only because I don't want to lose Ford as a client. Don't blame me if I screw it up."

"You won't."

"Ugh, whatever. Promise you'll deal with what's going on with you. I'm worried about you."

"Promise." Matt thinks of Elizabeth's letter in his pocket. He might as well read it before he goes to bed tonight.

"You need anything, I'm here for you. Say the word, and I'll ditch the race and fly home."

"Will do." Matt hasn't had a family for decades, but he won the lottery when it came to best friends. "Thanks, Dave."

Matt returns to the house as Julia comes out of the kitchen carrying two plates. She sets them across from each other at a small dining table with two place settings. "Dinner's ready."

He doesn't have much of an appetite anymore but takes a seat.

"Everything okay with your friend?" Julia asks as they dig into their meals.

"He's going to cover for me at Le Mans."

Julia's fork pauses midway to her mouth. "You aren't going? I thought working that race was your dream."

"It was. It is," he corrects. His mouth quirks. "Next year."

"What's keeping you from going?"

Family. You.

Those are his immediate thoughts. Then: *I don't want to be alone.* He thinks of his house in New Mexico. He always considered his domain the perfect bachelor pad. Now when he thinks of home, he feels empty and lonely.

He'll never open himself to love. He's too damaged for that. But he's been alone for longer than he cares to admit. He's been without a family. Solitude has served him well over the years, but now the thought of going home to an empty house makes him miserable.

"Since Elizabeth had no one else, I should see about finalizing her affairs before I go. I'm also going to visit Adam. Try to, anyway."

"Really?" Her eyebrows rise in surprise. "Aren't you nervous?"

"Very." But not necessarily about Adam. It's his family he's worried about. Will his daughter let Matt see him?

"You're lucky you still have family."

"Well, they aren't family yet. I don't know how they'll feel about me, knowing who I am."

"Either way, I'm happy for you." Julia fidgets with her fork, looking down at her plate.

Matt frowns. She doesn't seem happy for him. "Did I say something wrong?"

Her head snaps up. "No, not at all."

He isn't buying it. But before he can comment on it, she scoots her chair back and picks up her plate. "I was thinking while you were on the phone that you probably don't have a hotel room."

"I haven't had the chance to book one yet," he confirms.

"I have an extra room. You can sleep there if you want to."

He does want to. "Thank you."

She smiles tightly before heading to the kitchen, and he can't help thinking she seemed upset.

———

Julia shows Matt the room upstairs. She brings him fresh sheets and towels, and when he declines her offer to help make the bed, she says good night.

Matt showers and changes, but he doesn't try to sleep. He's restless, like he guzzled a pot of coffee, and he still needs to read Elizabeth's letter.

That's going to require a drink first.

He slides the letter into his pajama pocket and heads downstairs. But at the last second, he veers away from the kitchen and sinks onto the couch. Alcohol is the last thing he needs.

With shaky hands, he turns on the table lamp and unfolds the letter.

> *Dear Matt,*
> *I'm not surprised you didn't come for me. I wouldn't have either, not after the way I treated you. But there is something about your mother, and indirectly about yourself, you must know.*
> *Do you remember my butler, Adam Nulty? He was in my employ for almost four decades. You were with me for eight of those years, so, clearly, you must recall him. Your mother knew him, but she didn't*

know the truth about him, not in relation to her, and neither did you. Adam is—well, there's no easy way to put it but straight. He's your grandfather. Then again, if you're reading this letter, you might already know this. Julia Hope may have told you.

Your mother grew up believing my late husband, Matthew Holloway, was her father. She didn't know otherwise. Now, you're surely wondering why I lied to her, and in turn, to you and everyone else. I could sugarcoat this and tell you I didn't know who her father was, or that I wasn't thinking clearly, or wasn't ready to deal with it. I could say that I didn't want to be judged for having an affair with the butler. If Hollywood loves anything, it's a good story. But I've never been one for sweets. Give me a strong martini over a strawberry cheesecake any day.

Quite simply, Matt, I wanted Aubrey to be his, Matthew Holloway's. Hate me all you want. I'm not writing to ask for your forgiveness. I'm also not going to get into a long-winded explanation about the difficulties of losing my mother at a young age when you know that trauma firsthand yourself. But Matthew was my last connection to Hollywood and, in essence, to my parents. What I do know is that Matthew and Aubrey are gone, and there's no reason for me to be keeping secrets. A shame it's taken me decades to admit this. To be a fly on the wall and hear what you have to say about me when you visit Adam! I've always loved stirring up drama.

As of tonight, Julia knows. (Oh, the irony! She has the look of him, you know.) You've been talking with her, and I asked that she pass this letter along. I wasn't sure you'd ever give me the chance to explain.

But for once I came to my senses and figured you at least deserved to learn directly from me if for nothing other than confirmation. Adam also knows about you. The old sod left in quite a huff after I told him last month. I don't blame him for disappearing on me. It was rather poor of me to keep this from him for so long. Not one of my better decisions. Perhaps I loved him too much after all. Knowing the truth early on would have put him in a precarious position, and I'd already done enough damage to my own family. But if he asks, tell him I'm not angry he abandoned me. I deserve every speck of his condemnation.

Lastly, and certainly not least, I am sorry, Matt. You deserved better from me.

Well, there you have it, the truth. What you do with it, that's up to you.

Sincerely yours,
Grandmother Elizabeth Holloway

Wednesday

CHAPTER 41

JULIA

Matt is asleep on the couch with Liza's letter crumpled in his hand when Julia comes down in the morning. She doesn't have the heart to wake him and ask about it, and she's already running late for work. She leaves a note telling him to help himself to the eggs in the refrigerator. By the time she arrives at the country club, he's texted once, thanking her for the eggs and for the talk. When she reaches her locker, he texts again about his neck. It's cramped. He didn't mean to fall asleep on the couch, and she smiles at that, wondering if he'll let her massage his neck later.

But she doesn't see his third text mentioning he's going to call Adam's daughter, his aunt, until she's walking into Rosemont to visit Mama Rose during her lunch break. She should be using this time to interview and tour other facilities. She should also take a moment and text Matt back. What if he wants to talk with her first before he calls Adam's daughter, walk through what he's going to say? But during an aromatherapeutic session with a young woman recovering from a sprained ankle, Mama Rose flashed to mind and Julia felt compelled to see her as soon as possible. She doesn't like the sense of dread she's been feeling all morning or the shortness of breath that's come along with it.

"How is she today?" Julia asks when she runs into Trevor in the hallway.

"She was feeling ill this morning, but she's resting now." Trevor sorts a stack of clipboards. "All's good, Julia."

"Thank you." She's relieved to hear that. She goes straight to Mama Rose's room, needing to see for herself. She quietly enters to find her grandmother asleep, her face turned toward the window framing the garden that had sold her on Rosemont. The newly planted shrubs are thriving under the noon sun.

Julia's racing heart eases for the first time in what seems like hours. She pulls a chair to the bed and sits down. She rests her cheek on the quilt by Mama Rose's hand and carefully, so as not to wake her, slides her hand under her grandmother's. She weaves their fingers together and closes her eyes.

It's been months since she held her hand. She can't remember the last time they hugged without Mama Rose being offended Julia had touched her, believing her a stranger. Both of them were affectionate people. Up until recently they touched all the time. A hand squeeze of reassurance here. A kiss hello there. They hugged to greet the morning and end the day. They danced arm in arm through the house whenever Julia or Mama Rose put on a record.

She used to believe she'd have all the time in the world with her grandmother. Back when she was a child, this age and this day seemed forever away. Mama Rose would talk to her of angels and fairies and where people went when they died. Once, they'd been sitting knee to knee digging in the dirt in the backyard, planting bulbs that would bloom into daffodils the following spring. A bee had found its way into Julia's shirt. She could feel its wings beat against her stomach and chest. It buzzed angrily, looking for a way out. Julia was petrified. She'd never been stung by a bee before and she panicked, swatting at her shirt and screaming.

Mama Rose lifted Julia's shirt and scooped up the bee, which immediately buzzed off to a nearby rose, flapping its wings when it landed on a petal as if it were just as flustered.

Teary eyed, Julia flopped onto the grass and cried, "I never want to garden again."

"Because of one little bee?" Her grandmother tsked.

Julia nodded, wiping her eyes and getting dirt on her face in the process.

"Bees are our friends. Without them there'd be no flowers."

"But they're so mean."

"Yes, they can be when they're angry . . . or frightened."

She sniffled. "Bees get scared too?"

"Of course they do. That little bee helps in our garden, so we have to help him. We don't beat him, or smash him, or give up on him. We love and nurture that little bee, just like Mama Roses love and nurture their little Julias." Mama Rose squeezed Julia to her bosom and rained kisses on her hair, making her giggle.

Julia remembers wishing at the time that Mama Rose would live forever. She thought that as long as she was living, Julia would never feel unloved, unsafe, or afraid. Mama Rose filled the void her mother had left.

Mama Rose's hand twitches under Julia's cheek. Julia lifts her head with a soft gasp. Mama Rose stares at her with clear eyes.

"Mama?" Julia whispers.

"I'm sorry." Her grandmother's voice creaks like a door on rusted hinges.

"For what?"

"I was wrong to make you stay away."

"I'm right here, Mama."

"I shouldn't have kept Julia from you."

Julia's heart sinks. Mama Rose thinks she's Lea again. "It's okay," Julia says, crestfallen.

"It's not okay. Julia needed her mother, and I kept you two apart. You lost so much time with her, time I'll never be able to make up for. I should have given you another chance when you came back for her."

Julia's lip quivers as her grandmother's confession sinks in. "My mom came back for me?"

Mama Rose pats Julia's hand. "Not much time."

"No, no, we have time." Julia tightly clasps Mama Rose's hand. "You have plenty of time."

"Julia is going to need you, and she doesn't know where you are. It's my fault. You were struggling, and I did nothing to help you. What sort of mother am I? I failed you."

Julia shakes her head, fighting to maintain her composure. "You didn't fail me. You were a wonderful mother," she says, despite knowing it's not her Mama Rose is talking about.

But Mama Rose doesn't hear her. She's fallen back to sleep.

CHAPTER 42

MATT

That afternoon, Matt rings the doorbell of the remodeled ranch home in West Hollywood. Inside, a dog yips with excitement. Nails scratch at the side window, and a wet nose presses to the glass. The dog sees him and wiggles with glee.

Matt wipes his palms on the back of his jeans, not the least surprised to find them damp. He rubs them together and presses a hand to his abdomen below his rib cage to calm his nerves. He follows ringing the doorbell with a knock.

"Vinnie, hush," a woman's voice orders before a face appears in the glass to see who's at the door. Matt gives her a little wave and the woman smiles. The dog continues to bark until the squirming ball of fur squeaks when the woman abruptly picks him up and tucks him under her arm like a football.

A bolt flips, the knob turns, and the door opens. The woman is tall, almost eye level with him. Her dark hair is streaked with gray, and thick black-framed glasses sit low on her nose. The flared loose pants and white tunic she wears make him think of an artist, or a writer. Then she smiles. It knocks the wind from him. It's his mother's smile.

"You must be Matt."

"Yes," he croaks, shifting his weight before schooling his expression into neutrality. "Yes, I am. Siobhan?" He called just an hour ago, and she didn't hesitate to invite him over when he introduced himself by name, mentioned he was in town, and asked to visit Adam. She said without hesitation, "Can you come by this afternoon?"

The dog kicks its stubby legs to get to Matt. The woman's laugh is flustered as she scolds the dog. "Vin. Quiet. Sorry about that. Siobhan. We spoke over the phone. Pleasure to meet you." She takes Matt's proffered hand.

"Likewise."

"Please, come in." Siobhan opens the door wider, inviting him into the open-concept home. "We're glad you called. We didn't know if you would."

This shocks him. He's an outlier in their family, his mother the product of a broken vow. But Matt still worked up the nerve to call. The worst Adam's family could do was refuse to acknowledge they're related. But he wants to hear the truth from Adam directly. Was Aubrey his daughter? He half expects Adam to deny it. It's still possible Elizabeth lied. What was it she wrote? *I've always loved stirring up drama.*

Matt moves into the foyer and has to force himself not to stare at his mom's half sister. Their coloring isn't the least similar, but their smiles, and the little quirk of Siobhan's hand when she sets the dog down and orders him to his bed, makes his heart palpitate. He feels like he's watching the ghost of what his mom could have been had she had the chance to age. Vinnie trots through the living room and hops onto a leather couch covered in beach towels.

"That's his couch," Siobhan explains, closing the door behind them.

"I can see that."

"How long are you in town for?"

"Not sure. I promise not to keep Adam long."

"He'll probably nod off while talking with you, but don't let that keep you from coming back as often as you want. You're family." Matt is taken aback. Siobhan makes a face. "Was that too forward? I don't mean to come on too strong, but we're a close family, my sister and brothers and I."

Matt slides his hands into his pockets. "How many do you have?"

"There are four of us. Five, I guess. I have two brothers and a sister, now a half sister. Or we did. I'm sorry about your mom."

"It was a long time ago. I didn't find out about Adam until yesterday. I don't think my mom knew she had half siblings."

"I mean no offense, but that was probably for the best. Dad had been married to our mom for almost forty years before she died. He worked for Liza Holloway our entire lives, but he never told Mom about his affair with her. And Liza never told him about Aubrey. We were all in the dark. He hasn't mentioned it, but I have to believe he suspected something. How could he not? He practically raised her alongside her nanny."

Matt's shoulders lift to his ears. "I wouldn't know. I lived there for eight years and he didn't say anything to me about it."

"I remember when you were there. We didn't meet, but Dad mentioned you once in a while when I saw him. I know he liked you, but he also felt for you. Said you were a good kid who got a sour deal. You know how Liza can be."

Matt's mouth flattens. "She wasn't a fan of me."

"I loved her flair and the way she spoke. Very old Hollywood. Glamorous and rich. It was kind of cool when I was a kid. But she was a cold woman. Dad said she wasn't always like that. She lost herself when she lost her husband, and even more so after Aubrey died. Once you left, she became a bit of a recluse. She stopped hosting guests. She stepped back from her charities, donating money rather than her time. She only put you down as her secondary because my dad practically browbeat her into agreeing."

"Why me, though? We hadn't been in touch."

"You were her only living relative, and my dad is a happy-ever-after sort of guy. Family is important to him. Liza had lost touch with everyone but him before she moved to Rosemont. I think he sort of hoped she'd come around and reach out to you."

Siobhan's voice takes on a benign note and she leans toward him as she says, "She only told Dad the truth about Aubrey last month. He just remembered it yesterday. There were a lot of phone calls going back and forth among us well into the night. We didn't get much sleep with all the talk about you and your mom, and what we should do."

"I'm surprised you're okay that I'm here."

"Full disclosure: I wasn't happy when I first learned about your mom. None of us were. But we talked it out. It's all good now."

"What happened to your dad?" Matt only knows what Lenore shared.

"He was Liza's primary financial and health power of attorney, and the only friend she had left. They met regularly over lunch at Rosemont. He'd tried talking her out of selling her place in Beverly Hills and swore she'd regret donating her estate. But she was adamant. You know how she could get."

"I do." He knew that firsthand.

"Anyway, at lunch last month she told him her year was almost up and she was convinced she wouldn't be around much longer. She told him about Aubrey and he was furious. He drove for hours afterward and then went for a walk. He fell and hit his head, broke his leg real bad. A neighbor found him, thank God, but he's been dealing with some memory loss and he's still in a brace."

"Sorry to hear that."

"He's much better now. The memory loss was more severe right after the accident, but it's slowly returning. He's been staying here with me while he recovers, which is why Lenore Pullen couldn't get a hold of him. He lost his phone and we never got around to having it replaced."

Matt nods at everything she says, listening carefully. It's all so much. "Nothing about this bothers you, about me? My mom?" Siobhan speaks so matter-of-factly about their relations. He's having a hard time grasping she's accepting him without question.

She shifts her weight onto her hip and folds her arms. "I was angry when he first told me. He cheated on our mom. But after talking it out with my siblings, we agreed it wasn't worth getting upset over. The affair happened over fifty years ago. That man was not the man Dad is today. He's not the man who raised us. My parents had a good marriage, but it wasn't perfect. What marriage is? For all we know, Mom was unfaithful too. We can't blame your mom, or you. But we can choose to embrace you if you'll have us. There are a lot of us."

"Like how many?" he chokes out.

"I have three kids. My oldest just had a son. My brothers each have two kids, all in college right now. And my sister, she's the oldest. She has five kids and six grandkids. So yeah, a lot. Christmas is chaos."

Matt blows out a long stream of air, processing it all. He went from having no family aside from Dave and Dave's sister, who he suspects invites him over on the holidays because she feels sorry for him, to having more extended family than he could ever fathom. Arms crossed, he tucks his hands under his biceps.

Siobhan laughs lightly and pats his shoulder. "Like I said, we're a lot to handle. But you needn't worry. You'll get used to us. Oh my, look at your face. I'm scaring you."

"It's a lot to take in," Matt agrees. His heart is racing, and his palms are clammy again.

She laughs. "My dad is in the den. He's watching *Family Feud* reruns. Follow me."

Siobhan takes him down a wide hallway plastered with framed photos. Sensing excitement, Vinnie leaps off the couch and trots behind. Matt's gaze skims over the wall collage of school photos and family reunions. There are so many. At the third door on the left, Siobhan announces him.

"Dad, look who's here. You remember Matt?" She crosses the room and grabs a remote atop an ottoman, leaving Matt in the doorway. She turns off the TV and opens the blinds to a window that faces the street.

Opposite the TV are a floor-to-ceiling bookcase and a small sofa. But seated in an armchair in the corner, a braced leg propped atop a pillow on the ottoman, is an elderly man. He stares back at Matt with wide, faded brown eyes. Despite the twelve-plus years that have passed since he last saw Adam, Matt still recognizes the man who greeted him at the Burbank airport. And now that he knows this man is his mom's biological father, his mind fills in the blanks. Aubrey was built like Adam, and she'd moved like him. But Matt hadn't looked close enough. She had Elizabeth's coloring, and he'd been told his grandfather was Matthew Holloway.

Adam pushes against the chair arms until he's sitting more upright and leaning slightly forward as if he wants to get out of the chair. "Young Matt?"

At the sound of Adam's voice, Matt is immediately thrown back to his childhood. There's Adam throwing the baseball with him in Elizabeth's backyard. Adam picking him up from practices and staying to watch games when he dropped him off. Adam in the kitchen washing dishes while he helped Matt with his homework. When his grandmother could hardly stand to be in the same room as him, Adam had stepped in. He didn't replace his parents, but he tried to be the next best thing to the extent his position as a household employee allowed. And Matt had left without saying goodbye to him. Clouded with anger and guilt and so focused on ditching Elizabeth as soon as he came of age, Matt took off and never looked back.

"You're here," Adam says, astounded.

"Hello, Adam." Matt shoves his hands into his pockets and moves into the room. He looks down at the gray wool socks covering Adam's feet and the exoskeleton leg brace that spans from his heel to upper thigh. "How are you doing?"

Adam snorts. "I've had better days. Ready to get back on my feet, that's for sure. Sit, sit. Shiv." He gestures at the messy stack of newspapers and books on the couch. "Clear a space for him, dear."

Siobhan tosses the remote on the ottoman and scoops up the newspapers and books. She sets them on a desk. "I'll leave you two to chat.

Holler if you need anything." She smiles at Matt and leaves the room, Vinnie's nails click-clacking on the plank flooring as he follows her through the house.

Matt sits on the couch, angling toward Adam as if he's a guest on a talk show.

"I'm too old to put anything off, so we might as well face the elephant in the room. I didn't know you were my grandson. I had no idea, Matt. None at all. If I had . . ." Adam shakes his head, mouth pursed. "I never would have let you stay in that house."

Matt leans his weight on his thighs and loosens his breath, rocked by Adam's conviction. "But your wife."

"Oh, she would have given me hell. We would have gotten through it. We'd been in a bit of a rough patch when Liza and I—well, my marriage was touch and go there for a while."

"You had no idea about my mom? You couldn't tell she was yours?"

He looks down at his lap for a moment. "I had my suspicions. I can admit that now. But I was also in denial. Aubrey looked so much like her mother, and I wanted to believe she was Matty's, that Liza wouldn't outright lie to me about it, that I convinced myself I saw a resemblance to him in her." Adam makes eye contact. "Why not tell me she was mine, that's what I want to know. And why tell me at all? She kept her secret for so dang long. I'll never know, though." He strokes a palm over his thinning hair. "I was furious when she told me. I left in a fit."

Matt looks at his clasped hands. "I think I might know."

"You do?"

"She left me a letter."

"Oh? What did she say?"

"She wanted Matty's child from the beginning. She wanted Aubrey to be his," Matt says, wishing there were a more delicate way to put it. But he doesn't want any more secrets.

Adam stares out the window, and Matt can only wonder what he's thinking, how he's feeling.

"I think she loved you," Matt adds, recalling their relationship from Magnolia's perspective and Elizabeth's own words in the letter.

"I know she did," Adam says, his voice far away. He blinks, snapping out of his trance, and turns back to Matt. He claps the armrests. "Well, you're here now. I'm not sure I can ever forgive her, but it doesn't mean I hold it against you. I always liked you, kid. Don't know how much time I've got left, but I'd like us to keep in touch."

Matt's throat swells with emotion. He looks down at his hands. He's gripping them so tight. He's anxious, he's nervous, and he's scared this isn't real. But facts are facts. Matt has relatives and, if he's agreeable, family. He isn't alone, not anymore. "I—I'd like that."

Adam grins. "Good. That's good. That makes me happy." He leans in and drops a hand over Matt's and gives it an optimistic shake. It takes everything in Matt not to lose his shit. He takes in a deep breath and lets the air out slowly.

"Me too," he says tightly.

"Wonderful. You hungry? You must be thirsty. Shiv," he bellows, then winks at Matt. "Nice to be the one getting catered to for once."

Matt grins, highly suspecting Adam has been milking his convalescence.

Siobhan appears in the door. "What is it?"

"Two whiskeys. Neat."

Siobhan's face folds into a disgruntled frown. "You're on meds. No alcohol."

Adam blows a raspberry and says to Matt, "She's no fun."

"I can get Matt a whiskey. But you're sticking with soda water."

Adam groans and Matt laughs. It's a great feeling. "Make that two waters." Matt holds up two fingers.

"And pretzels. I want those super-salty ones," Adam orders.

Siobhan rolls her eyes and leaves the room.

Adam turns to Matt. "Now tell me, young Matt, what the hell have you been up to since I last saw you?"

CHAPTER 43

JULIA

Julia comes home after a full day of spa appointments to Matt cooking in her kitchen. Her wrists ache, her thumbs are throbbing, and she wants nothing more than to take a hot bath and go to bed. Crying might be on tonight's agenda too. But his presence, and whatever's stewing on the stove, is unexpected.

"What are you doing here?"

As soon as she asks the question, she remembers their brief text exchange from this afternoon. He planned to stay in California another night and would get a hotel but wanted to make her dinner. Julia insisted he stay at her house again. Having lived paycheck to paycheck, she couldn't justify the expense for anyone, not with a perfectly good guest room upstairs going unused. And she liked his company—him and their conversations. She accepted his dinner invite on the condition he use her guest room and told him where to find the key under the gnome with the chipped hat. Then she put her phone in the locker before he texted an answer and returned to her afternoon appointments. Matt's invite slipped her mind.

"Making dinner," he states the obvious at her surprise. "Thought it was the least I could do after what you did for me last night." He smiles at her as he stirs whatever is inside the dutch oven pot, and she glowers, irritation replacing her surprise. He's too happy for someone who watched his grandmother die.

She drops her loaded bag on the counter with a loud *thunk*.

Matt's smile falters. His stirring slows. "I hope this is okay. I texted I'd pick something up."

"I missed it." She hasn't checked her phone since this afternoon. She feels guilty for slacking on calling the facilities on Lenore's list. She's also still reeling from her visit with her grandmother and what Mama Rose said about Lea coming back for her.

Her grandmother was delirious—Julia knows that. But there's always some truth or history in everything she says and does. Whatever Mama Rose thinks and feels, one thing is clear to Julia: her grandmother has plenty of regrets. And it seems one of those has to do with her daughter, Lea.

"I can leave," Matt says, picking up on her vibe. He turns off the burner flame.

"Why are you in such a good mood?" Julia plants her hands on her hips.

Matt blinks. Then he frowns, reflective. "Do I seem like I'm in a good mood?"

"A moment ago, you were smiling. You don't smile much," she says, sourly.

Matt's chest expands with a choked laugh. "Thanks?"

"That wasn't a compliment." She's being unfair, venting her frustration on Matt. It's not his fault Mama Rose has forgotten her. But some days are too hard, and home is the only refuge where she can feel sorry for herself.

Then she remembers his plan today. "You called Adam."

"I saw Adam."

"You saw him?" She balks.

"I did." Matt puts the lid on the pot and turns to her. "Maybe that's why I'm happy. I have two aunts and two uncles and cousins, and even . . . I guess they'd be first cousins once removed? My cousins' kids?"

"And they just welcomed you into the family?"

"Surprisingly, yeah. They did. I met only one of my aunts. She was very receptive and said the rest of the family is eager to meet me."

She can tell that he's more than surprised. He's astonished. Whereas she's confused. That wasn't how she imagined his day would go. His family was supposed to have rejected him. Make him feel like an outcast. Remind him he is alone and unloved. "Even though Adam was married at the time and your mom was illegitimate?"

Matt has the wherewithal not to physically react to Julia's remark, but Julia rears back, shocked the question came from her mouth. Now she's just being mean. But she feels possessed, unable to dial down the jealousy and disbelief.

"Yes," Matt says slowly, watching her curiously. "But that was over fifty years ago. Are you okay?"

"Fine," she snaps.

"You're not fine. Your wrists hurt." He gestures at her hands, and Julia looks down at them. She's aggressively digging her thumb into the ball of her palm and wasn't aware she was doing so. She shakes out her hands and crosses them over her chest.

"They're fine. So, you're what, like, the Brady Bunch now? Are you going to invite them over for Thanksgiving dinner? Sing 'Kumbaya' around the campfire?" She wants to smack herself. Would she shut up already?

"We didn't get that far, but we are going to keep in touch. What's going on with you?"

"Nothing's going on."

"You could have fooled me. You're angry. Did I do something wrong?"

He hasn't done anything wrong. That's the problem. Everything went right for him today. He did what Julia has been too afraid to do. He reached out to his only known relative and his family accepted him on the spot. Julia has lived with her mother's rejection her whole life, and her fear of being rejected again has kept her from contacting Lea. Even after what Mama Rose said today, that Lea might have tried to come back but Mama Rose pushed her away, Julia is still too afraid.

Apparently fed up with her behavior, Matt wipes his hands with a dish towel. "Look, it seems like I should go. Whatever's going on with you, I don't need you to take it out on me."

"Says the guy who hung up on me twice after yelling at me."

"I've had enough. Nice knowing you, Julia." He scoops his phone off the table.

Julia blocks his way out of the kitchen. "Aren't you at all feeling a little anxious about today? Aren't you a little worried that your meet-cute will backfire and they'll reject you after all? All of Adam's kids can't be cool with this. Somebody has got to be upset about your mom."

"Do not bring my mom into this." Matt stares down at her.

She knows she's being cruel, but she can't bring herself to stop. She wants to hurt him as much as she's hurting. She wants him to feel just as lonely as her. She grabs his hand. "Tell me one thing you've never told anyone else."

"What?" He tries to pull his hand from hers, but her grip tightens.

"One thing you've never told anyone else. Then you can go. We never have to speak to each other again." She's goading him, backing him into a corner.

"This isn't helping my anxiety." She frowns, and he shows her his other hand. It oscillates violently.

So today didn't go as perfectly as he's letting on.

"I'm barely keeping it together," he whispers.

He's scared, which makes Julia think that he thinks it's too good to be true and he'll lose it all again at the snap of a finger.

She looks up at him, her eyes bouncing between his, and shares the one thing she's never told anyone. "I have two brothers."

"What?"

"After she left me, my mom got married and had two sons. She doesn't need me. She has a family. That's why I haven't contacted her. She gave me up and now she has them. But today—" Tears unleash. Her voice shakes. "Today—"

"What happened today, Jules?"

"Mama Rose said something that makes me think she hadn't given me up, not in the end. She said my mom came back but Mama Rose sent her away. I'm afraid, so afraid to call her to ask if that's true only for her to reject me again. And I'm sorry, Matt. I hate that it was so easy for you. That they accepted you so willingly."

"It wasn't easy. Calling my aunt was probably the hardest thing I've ever done. I dialed four times before I let it ring, and even then I almost ended the call before she answered."

"But she and Adam welcomed you, and now you've got this big family. You won't be alone anymore, and I still am. Mama Rose is going to die and it's going to be just me, and I'm scared."

Matt is quiet for a moment, then whispers, "When my mom died I told the police and everyone else she had drowned. My friends, neighbors, Liza. They all believed it was an accident."

"What really happened?"

"She killed herself in front of me."

The admission sends a shock wave of despair through her. "Matt." He was just a boy.

Sensing he wants to withdraw, she squeezes his hand and cries for him.

"That's why Elizabeth blamed me for my mom's death. We were on the skiff together. I gave my grandmother the impression my mom fell into the water. She couldn't understand why I didn't try to save her. No concern for me. Just her Aubrey."

"Did you try to save her?"

Matt shakes his head. "She told me not to."

Julia is speechless.

"She was mourning my dad. I shouldn't have listened to her; I realize that now. But it's a cold reality when you know you aren't enough for your mom to stick around, and I was frozen. I don't think I could have made myself jump into the water if I tried."

Julia knows that feeling well. Her breath shudders when his remark brings forth her own memory of Lea driving away.

"She was sick, and she should have sought help. Still doesn't change the fact she couldn't love me enough to keep living. That I wasn't enough for her."

Julia looks at him, really looks at him, his firm-set jaw and intense eyes, and she sees something there that he hasn't shown her before. The despair and self-loathing. It breaks her heart because that simple statement—that simple truth he believes about himself—sheds so much light onto why Matt is the way he is. He's alone because he believes nobody would want him. He believes he can't be enough for someone to stay.

His mother left him, and Liza neglected him.

So he pushes people away with anger and his gruffness.

In so many ways, they are the same.

Julia expects he'll push her away next. She deserves his rebuke after the way she's been acting toward him tonight. He'll walk out the door and she'll never see him again. His admission—that one thing he's never told anyone except her—will take its toll. The vibration in his hand has spread. His entire body is quaking. His skin has turned ashen, and his eyes dart from her to the doorway behind her as if he's set on an escape. Despite his habit of keeping to himself, now is not a time he should be alone. Neither of them should push the other away. Neither should bury their grief and regret and go about as if that's the way of things.

So she does the opposite. She kisses him.

Let him work his anger and frustrations out on her. She'll do the same.

Matt lurches back and grabs her upper arms, holding her away from him. Tension tautens his spine, keeps his legs braced. His eyes search her face as if looking for a place to land, from her flushed cheeks to her parted mouth and down to her quivering chin and the outline of her breasts under her uniform tunic before lifting to her eyes again. Then a different kind of tension fills him.

"Jules." Her name is an exhale of breath.

"Don't think." *Just kiss me.* She wants this. Him, his touch. To feel and to forget. To just be, and not be alone. It's been so long since a man has touched her. So long since she's felt any desire. An eternity since she's acted so selfishly.

"Don't think," he repeats. A breath. Then another.

Then he yanks her to him and his mouth lands on hers.

His kiss is hard and aggressive, filled with longing and pain. And she matches him. Her fingers tug at his hair, pull at his shirt. He drags the cotton over his head, and then he's grappling at her clothing as he spins her around and lifts her onto the kitchen table.

The old, rickety table that wobbles under a short stack of books.

"Not here," she says, dragging off her tunic. She drops it on the floor along with her bra.

Matt flicks off her Crocs and pulls off her socks, taking a hungry look at her breasts. "Where?"

"Out there." She points toward the front room.

Matt lifts her up as if she's weightless. She wraps her legs around his waist and draws her arms around his neck, feasting on his mouth as he walks them toward the couch.

"Not there either." The couch has no support. She won't have any leverage.

A low rumble in his chest. "I don't think I'll last long enough to make it upstairs," he says, tightly, and she can hear how turned on he is. She can feel his hardness against her core, and warmth floods her lower belly. She doubts she'll last long either.

"Here." She slides down him, drawing him to the floor with her between a bookcase and the coffee table. The woven throw rug is rough with age and will likely chafe her flesh, but she'll worry about that tomorrow. Right now she needs his skin rubbing against hers and the weight of him on her.

And thank God they're in tune and he's just as frantic to be with her.

They are a frenzy of limbs and lips as the rest of their clothes come off. In between gasps and sighs, strokes and caresses, Matt locks eyes with her. He cups her cheek and kneads her breasts, mumbling incoherently how beautiful she is. How good she's been to him. How much he desires her. And how incredible and extraordinary it is that they had the chance to meet.

When Julia stretches on her back and Matt settles between her thighs, she grabs his face in frustration. "That's great and I'm happy you feel that way. I totally feel the same. But would you just shut up and fuck me?"

Matt's expression sobers for one second, then another. Then his face cracks into a huge grin and he drops his head onto her chest and laughs. His whole body rumbles.

"Matt!"

"I'm here. I got you." He lifts his head and kisses her senselessly, slowly undoing her, and the entire mood shifts. "I got you," he whispers, breaking their kiss, slowing their tempo. He locks eyes with her again and arches his hips, pushes inside. And all Julia can do is watch him, feel him, breathe with him. "I got you," he whispers again, thrusting.

He rests a forearm alongside her head. His other hand cradles her cheek, his thumb drifting tenderly along her bottom lip. She feels the caress down to her toes. And what he is doing inside her . . . She feels that everywhere. She's buzzing, tightening, rising.

"Matt." She groans his name and fits her hands to his cheeks, holding his head, her eyes searching for confirmation that he's right there with her. Then he smiles. Just a little one that almost passes as a grimace. But it's enough. He's there.

He presses his forehead to hers as the motion of their hips becomes more erratic, their breathing more ragged, and then she's bursting, spiraling, unraveling into a trillion pieces as she falls back to earth.

Matt comes with a grunt and several deep thrusts, his arms squeezing her tight. Then he stops.

Then he rolls off her and takes long strides to the bathroom.

She immediately feels cold at his abrupt departure and pulls a throw blanket from the couch to cover herself. She waits to hear the water run, thinking he's getting a cloth for her. But she hears nothing. And several long, awkward minutes later, Matt is still in the bathroom.

She stands, wrapping the blanket over her shoulders, and pads to the bathroom. She lightly taps on the door. "Matt?"

He doesn't immediately answer, but after a few seconds, the knob turns. He opens the door and steps out. "Sorry."

Her eyes coast over his face. She can't read his expression. He's completely closed off.

Her heart does a little jerk. "Everything okay?"

He pushes back his hair. "I had an overwhelming urge to talk about my mom, which is wrong," he says with a bland smile. "You don't talk about your parents after what we just did. I shouldn't even be thinking about them."

"I like what we just did."

"Me too. Very much so. But I had to step away until the urge passed."

"Because you don't talk about your mom."

He nods slowly, and Julia can't help but feel let down. She wants him to talk about his mom like he started to with her over the phone, has been wanting him to since she first heard he'd lost her. And she wants to be the person he talks to when he does finally open up about her.

After telling him that she has brothers, she feels unburdened, amazingly so. She didn't realize how tightly she'd been holding on to that part of her life. She wants to tell him more. Maybe even talk it through. She wants to stop feeling scared about the possibility of her mom rejecting her again.

And she wants Matt to feel like he can do the same with her, use her as a sounding board to work through his grief. He's been hiding from his trauma almost as long as she has.

"You can talk to me, you know that. Even if you just want me to listen."

"Thank you," he says, gently. "But I don't think I'm ready. It's nothing against you. I just . . ."

"I understand." Julia looks at his chest, unable to make eye contact, worried he'd think she was overly concerned and would push her away.

He crooks a finger under her chin, lifting her face. "I didn't say never. I'm just not ready . . . yet."

"When you are—"

"I know where to find you," he offers, putting her at ease. Then his mouth pulls up into a lopsided smile, sending her heart twirling. "So, you hungry?"

Her appetite roars to life at the mention of food. "You made dinner."

"I heated up food. There's a difference." He lifts a finger to make his point, and she giggles. "I swung by Whole Foods and picked up a prepared fettuccine and pesto dish. Bought some cooked chicken we can add to the pasta too."

"Veggies?" she asks.

Pause. "My thought process wasn't that expansive," he says with a mouth quirk, and she laughs.

"I'm sure I have something in the freezer. Come, I'm starved." She grabs his hand and pulls him toward the kitchen.

"One sec." He picks up his jeans and pulls them on. "I don't cook naked in front of a stove."

Julia barks with laughter. They enter the kitchen, and as she opens the freezer for vegetables, her phone rings. It's the ringtone she programmed for Trevor, Mama Rose's caregiver.

Her gaze darts from the phone to the time. It's almost 10:00 p.m. Night calls never bode well.

"Julia?" Matt asks.

She can't make herself pick up the phone. The ringtone roars in her ears.

Matt picks it up and peeks at the screen. "You should answer this." He gives her the phone.

Julia watches herself take it. She watches herself tap the green button to answer. And she feels herself pressing the cool glass to her ear. She knows, she already knows. Something is horribly wrong.

"Hello?" She barely hears herself answer.

But every word Trevor says reverberates through her.

"Julia, it's Trevor at Rosemont. I'm so sorry. Your grandmother went into cardiac arrest. We tried everything."

CHAPTER 44

MAGNOLIA BLU

August 1, 2016

Dear Liza,

I shouldn't be surprised you wouldn't see me today. You haven't responded to the dozens of letters I've sent you. I guess I thought an in-person visit would be different, especially if you knew why I wanted to see you this one last time.

I'll admit, I felt silly yelling at you through the door, but I hope you heard me. I meant everything I said. While I don't regret loving Matty, and I could never regret having our child, Lea, I regret how you found out about us. I regret I didn't have the strength to stop seeing Matty. I regret what happened to you and me. Please know that I am so, so terribly sorry. Out of the kindness of your heart, you gave me a home, a job, and your friendship when I had nothing. And what did I do? Exactly what I'd promised you I wouldn't. I broke your trust and took advantage of your kindness and hospitality.

You were right. I not only ruined your marriage, but I killed Matty. If it weren't for me, he might still be alive today. He certainly would have lived for many more years. At least as many years as I've borne the guilt of my betrayal.

I've wronged too many people, including you, Benjie, my parents, and Lea. Other than this unsettling need to love free of constraint, I don't know why I do it. And I fear my reckoning has arrived. I am going to forget my daughter, my beloved granddaughter, Julia, and I'm going to forget you, Liza. I am mature enough now to admit that I am scared about what happens next for me. It seems my punishment before I leave this world is not only losing the people in my life, but losing the memory of them too.

Perhaps one day, this note will find its way into your hands. Or perhaps one day, you'll allow me to look you in the eye and apologize in person. My last desire is that you might find it within your heart to forgive me. I'd be so lucky.

If you heard me at all today, you know you'll find me at Rosemont.

Your humbled friend,

Magnolia Blu

CHAPTER 45

MATT

Matt arrives at Rosemont with Julia. Her fingernails bite into his palm where she grips his hand. He doesn't let go. She's sinking right now and he needs to help her stay afloat, even if she's not aware she needs him. He won't let anyone drown on his watch. Never again.

Trevor explained to Julia over the phone that he and several other nurses on staff had tried to revive Ruby Rose before the paramedics arrived, and once they got there, nothing could be done. She was pronounced deceased at 9:42 p.m. The coroner was on her way if Julia wanted to say her goodbyes before Ruby Rose Hope was taken to the morgue.

They rushed over to Rosemont with Matt driving Julia's car. She couldn't get the key into the ignition; she'd been trembling from the news and likely her new reality.

Lenore intercepts them in the hallway. "I'm so sorry, Julia." She hugs her, but Matt doesn't release Julia's hand. He half wonders if he needs her to ground him as much as she needs him. For all intents and purposes, Ruby Rose Hope was Julia's mother. Matt knows too well how great this loss is for her.

"The coroner just arrived," Lenore explains. "I'll keep her occupied while you say your goodbyes."

"Thank you," Julia says.

"Thanks for coming with her, Matt."

"Of course."

Julia glances at him, only half-aware he's beside her. But when Lenore leaves, she pulls her hand free. "She shouldn't have been alone when she died. I should have been with her."

And not with him, Matt concludes without saying.

Matt doesn't dare remind Julia that Trevor said Ruby Rose had been asleep, that Julia's presence wouldn't have made a difference to her grandmother.

But it would have made a difference to Julia, as it had for him with Elizabeth.

"I'm sorry you weren't."

"I think you should go. I have to—I have to say goodbye, and I'd like to do so alone."

It doesn't take a genius to figure out she's not asking him to leave just Rosemont.

"My things are at your place."

"Did you put the key back under the gnome?"

He nods.

"Use that."

She starts to walk away.

Just last week, he would have let her go because he let everyone go or he pushed them away. But leaving Julia like this feels wrong.

"Julia."

She stops. "Goodbye, Matt."

He nods that this is it, fighting the urge to go after her. He almost does when she hesitates at Ruby's door. Shouldn't he be here for her like she was for him? But she takes a deep breath, gearing herself up for what she has to face, and steps into the room.

Reluctantly, he leaves Rosemont for what will probably be the last time and takes an Uber back to her house. He already packed his duffel this morning, so he cleans the kitchen, puts away the food they never got around to eating, and straightens the front room. When he realizes he's looking around for something else to do, he grabs his bag and reaches for the door. But he can't turn the knob.

He can't leave her.

These last five days have been confusing as hell. The woman he spent the weekend with turned out to be a figment of his imagination. The man he grew up believing was his grandfather might be Julia's. He thought he lost his last living relative only to gain a family he didn't know he belonged to.

And the woman he spent this evening with? The only person who's ever pulled the confession about his mom from him? She's something special.

Golden, brilliant, and enchanting.

The center of his gravity.

His sun.

"Huh."

Maybe there was something real about his time spent with Magnolia Blu after all.

Matt releases the knob and sets down his bag. Then he sits on the couch, and he waits.

He'll wait as long as she takes.

Thursday

CHAPTER 46

JULIA

Julia held Mama Rose's cold, lifeless hand. She kissed her chilled, unmoving cheek. And she watched the coroner take her grandmother away.

She remained behind long afterward. She listened to the last book her grandmother had read, picking up where she'd left off. She played Mama Rose's favorite music as she removed the linens from her bed, leaving those on the floor to be disposed of and folding the quilt to take home later. By the time she could make herself leave Rosemont, it was almost dawn.

Juggling a stack of books, she unlocks her front door and finds Matt standing by the couch, rubbing his face. His shirt is rumpled and his hair askew.

"You're still here." She thought he would have been long gone by now and regretted asking him to leave. She wasn't thinking straight. But she's had plenty of time to think about last night, mulling over the time they spent together as she packed up Mama Rose's room, finding both cathartic: the mulling and the packing. She's glad he decided to stay.

"I fell asleep on the couch." He stretches his back. "There's no support."

"None." She closes the door behind her and cautiously approaches him.

"How are you doing?" he gently asks.

She sets the books on the coffee table. "I'm both sad and relieved. Is it wrong to feel that way?"

He shakes his head. "No."

"Lonely."

He lifts his hand, hesitates, then briefly touches her hair. "I'm here."

She cried most of the night, but it seems she's not done. Tears spill over her cheeks.

"Jules." Matt opens his arms, and that's all the invitation she needs. She steps into his embrace. He holds her as she sobs, murmuring incoherently, and soon enough, the well dries. For now.

She steps back and wipes her face. Matt's arms fall to his sides. "You'll be okay."

She nods. "I know. I will." She sniffles. "Why *are* you still here? I mean, I'm glad you are. I'm just surprised is all."

He looks around. "I was going to leave. I couldn't, not while you're feeling like this. I—How do I say this?" He glances at the ceiling, thinking. "Nobody helped me get through the loss of my parents. My mom wasn't any help after my dad died, and, well, you know what happened after she died. I don't know if you have someone, but I wanted to be here when you got home. I can stay. If you want me to."

He wants to be enough for her.

Julia's heart expands in her chest.

"What happened to the dickhead on the phone a few days ago?" she teases.

"I know, right?" He chuckles. Then his expression turns serious. "He met someone who helped him realize not acknowledging his grief isn't exactly healthy. He doesn't want to hide from it anymore."

He's making her ache, and he's making her fall for him.

"I'm sorry about earlier."

"You regret last night?"

There is much she regrets about last night, things that were out of her control. Namely, Mama Rose passing and Julia not being at her side when she had. But Mama Rose dying was inevitable. She's been preparing for it for a long time. Still, it doesn't make the loss hurt any less.

But she definitely doesn't regret what happened between her and Matt. What, she hopes, *is* happening.

She shakes her head. "No. No regrets. I wanted that. I think I needed it. In fact, I know I did. We both did."

"We did."

"So thank you."

He touches her hair again. "You're welcome."

They share a smile.

"I realized something last night," he says after a beat. "It's why I ran off to the bathroom."

"I thought you were thinking about your mom."

"I was, indirectly. And I thought on it more before I crashed on the couch. I realized I've been so angry about everything that has to do with my parents' deaths, my mom's especially, that I left no room to love. I want there to be love in my life. I want to feel love again."

"I want that for you too." She also wants it for herself. Hopes for it. Julia might not have grown up with parents, but she had Mama Rose. And Mama Rose showered her with love.

"That's the other reason why I waited for you to come home, so I could tell you that. That's why you found me here. I left Florida and I left California. I'm always leaving. I don't want to leave anymore. I don't want to leave you. But first, I have to go back."

"What do you mean?" She swallows nervously at the thought of him going so soon after she lost Mama Rose.

"After my parents died, I went a little insane. I don't think I've ever come back from that, but it's time that I do."

"Are you saying sometimes we have to lose ourselves to find ourselves?"

"Exactly. I have to go back to where it all started. If I want to move forward, I have to go back to Florida."

"Maybe my grandmother *was* making sense when she spoke to you."

He looks thunderstruck. "I didn't make that connection. She couldn't have been there with me," he says, alluding to Julia's fanciful thinking about memories and where they go.

"Likely not, and who's to say who she was giving the advice to when she saw you at Rosemont. But it was good advice." And came at the right moment too.

"It was."

"When are you leaving?" Six hours ago, she wanted him to leave. She wanted to be alone in her grief. Now that she's over the initial shock of Mama Rose's death, she isn't sure she's ready to be alone.

"I'm booked on a flight to Miami in several hours. I can stay if you need me to, but at some point, I have to go. I have to do this before I change my mind."

And Julia knows she shouldn't talk him out of going or convince him to stay because she doesn't feel like spending today alone. She can be selfish of her time and her needs now. With Mama Rose's death comes a freedom she hasn't had before. But she can't be selfishly uncaring of others. It isn't in her nature. She's a massage therapist for goodness' sake. She won't force him to take a detour on his own journey toward healing to get through her own.

"Will I see you again?"

He thinks on her question for a moment. "Will you hate me if I can't answer that right now? I mean, you will see me again. I hope you will. But I can't say when."

It saddens her he can't give her a straight answer, but she shakes her head. She could never hate him.

He fits a hand to her face, and she snuggles a cheek into his palm, closes her eyes, and sighs.

"May I kiss you?" he asks.

Without opening her eyes, she nods. Then his lips tenderly touch hers.

"Goodbye, Matt," she whispers into his mouth.

"Goodbye, Julia," he says, lifting his head. He slings his bag over his shoulder and reaches for the door.

"Matt."

He turns back to her.

"You are enough."

He goes absolutely still.

"You are enough for me," she whispers.

His body shudders, and he closes his eyes for a count before they lift to hers. She hopes he believes her, because she means it.

"Thank you."

She smiles softly. "You're welcome."

———

A short time after Matt leaves for the airport, the sun rises. A new day, her first without Mama Rose. Julia calls into work to take a bereavement leave and wanders the house, restless. She makes tea but doesn't drink it. She turns on the morning news but doesn't watch it, so she turns it off and puts on Janis Joplin's "Cry Baby," only to turn that off too. She tucks the books she brought home onto the shelves and sits down on the couch, wondering what to do next because with Mama Rose gone, most of her worries are gone too.

She doesn't have to worry how to pay for Rosemont. She doesn't have to worry when she can fit in a daily visit. And she doesn't have to worry if Mama Rose will recognize her, or how worse off she'll be that day.

All those worries have just been replaced with an indelible sadness.

Julia wipes a rogue tear and looks around the house, not particularly focused on anything. Outside, a car drives past and a jogger coasts up the sidewalk. Inside, she feels a palpable emptiness. There's also an empty slot on the bookshelf.

Remembering Mama Rose's diary, she retrieves the journal from her bag. She stands, and another letter, this one addressed to her, falls out.

Fury flashes through her. She doesn't want a letter from Liza. She wants one from Mama Rose. But she picks it up and unfolds the paper anyway.

> *Well, Ms. Julia Hope, I read your grandmother's last entry. For our peace of minds—yours, mine, and Magnolia's—I forgive her. If that old bat is ever lucid enough to listen to you, you can tell her that.*
>
> *While we're on the subject of apologies, Magnolia doesn't owe me one. Yes, Matty was the love of my life. Yes, she had an affair with him. Yes, I blamed her for my marriage's demise when it was already beyond salvaging. But when I confronted her, she was honest about it. I can't say the same about me.*
>
> *There is more to what I told you this evening. It is true, Adam was the father of my child. But I desperately wanted Aubrey to be Matty's, and I had everyone convinced she was. At one point, even I believed it. But it wasn't possible. The timing wasn't right. Matty was away when I became pregnant with Aubrey, and she didn't look anything like him.*
>
> *I thought for sure people could tell, and every day I expected someone to call me out. But they never did. And for a time, until Aubrey became fed up with me for forcing her to follow in Matty's footsteps, Hollywood embraced her as his. I've written a list of movies on the back of this sheet if you'd like to see my beautiful girl on the screen. For she was beautiful, the spitting image of me. Maybe that's why nobody*

questioned her parentage. People only see what they want to see.

I saw your grandmother occasionally over the years. She tended many gardens in my neighborhood. As her business flourished, I saw her trucks everywhere. I never approached her. But I missed her friendship, and once, I was tempted to stop as I drove past. Then I saw her, Magnolia's daughter—your mother. She was young, but she looked identical to Matty's boyhood photos. She was his, and the sight of her ripped out my heart. You, my dear, have the look of him. It would explain why I tolerated your company as infrequently as I have. Your presence was both heart-warming and heart wrenching.

But back to your grandmother. For years I despised Magnolia, envied her with passion. I wished I'd never ventured to the grocery store that day we met. I was supposed to have Matty's child.

I went decades without seeing Magnolia, or even thinking about her. Then eight or so years ago, after she sent me countless letters that I never read or replied to—I just couldn't—she visited my house, pleading to mend the rift between us. She'd recently been diagnosed with Alzheimer's and wanted to settle her affairs before losing her memory entirely. She didn't want to die with regrets. I turned her away. By that time, I was too lost in my own despair because Aubrey had long since left me.

It's taken me years to admit that I am as much if not more at fault for what's between Magnolia and me, that my desire to remain relevant among Hollywood's power players, where I felt closest to Matty and to the mother I lost as a little girl, and my relentless crusade and incessant push to see Aubrey succeed in Matty's footsteps drove my own daughter away. And her poor boy. How ignorant and callous of me to think ignoring him in my own home would help me ignore my grief. I might have lost my daughter, but he lost his mother.

So, my dear Julia, at the request of your grandmother when she told me where I could find her if I ever wanted to put the past to rest, I arrived here at Rosemont intent on telling her the truth about Aubrey. But we both know how that went. I was too late. I am also tired.

I don't expect we'll see each other again, but if there's one piece of advice I can impart, it is to forgive. I couldn't forgive Matty for dying, or Magnolia for falling in love with him. I couldn't forgive Aubrey for leaving me, or my grandson, Matt, for not saving her. If there is anyone who's wronged you, and I know for a fact there is—you know exactly whom I'm referring to—forgive her. You'll regret you never took the chance.

Don't live your life with regrets. Just live as fully as you can. Take it from one who knows: you can reshoot a scene multiple times, but you cannot do over your life.

My regards,
Elizabeth Holloway

CHAPTER 47

MATT

Key Largo, Florida

What Matt remembers of his parents is that their story was a love story. Aubrey and Joel were teenagers when they met. Joel had worked for the company that owned the yacht Elizabeth chartered for a weekend cruise to Catalina Island. They kept their romance secret for a couple of years because Aubrey knew Elizabeth wouldn't approve of their relationship. They ended up eloping to Las Vegas and, from there, moved to Key Largo, where Joel worked for a charter fishing company and eventually bought out the owner when he retired. Aubrey was an elementary school teacher. She was also the best mom a rambunctious, adventurous boy like Matt could have had.

His parents didn't have much. But they had a bungalow near the seawall with a dock off the back deck in a canal that fed into the Atlantic. They had neighbors they treated like family. And they had each other until Joel died in a boating accident during a tropical storm that had moved in faster than meteorologists predicted. His body was never recovered.

Matt could say he lost both parents in that storm. Joel's death broke Aubrey. Matt didn't get a chance to mourn his father because he'd been forced to care for his mother. Neighbors helped. They brought over frozen meals Matt reheated, and they made sure he attended school. But they didn't see the worst of Aubrey's grief. Only Matt had been privy to her depression.

For over a month Aubrey spent her evenings seated atop the seawall, staring at the open ocean. Matt brought her dinners that she didn't eat, and he brought her blankets she didn't seem aware of when he draped them over her shoulders to ward off the night's chill. He sat with her, listening to her stories about where she thought his dad had ventured off to and why he hadn't yet returned. The story she told the most was the one where Joel was living on a small island with an abundance of coconuts, its waters alive with shrimp. He had plenty to eat, but his boat was broken. He had no way to return to them. It was up to her to save him, for she possessed a certain magic. At will, she could turn into a mermaid. She said that's why she loved living by the ocean. And in her story, when the moon was full enough to guide the way, she would swim to the tiny island that was a speck in the vast sea and rescue him.

Matt knew these were just stories. He didn't believe in them. But she must have, because one evening he heard the motor of his dad's skiff. It had been over a month since Matt heard that sound, and for a moment, he thought it might be his dad. He rushed outside.

"What are you doing?" he asked, panicked to find his mom in the boat.

"Your dad needs me." She tossed the oars onto the dock, alarming Matt.

"He's gone, Mom. He's not there. You're not going to find him."

"Don't be silly. Of course I'll find him." She smiled, but the light in her eyes had long gone out, and that worried Matt.

He couldn't convince her to get out of the skiff, so he jumped in just as she pushed away from the dock.

She barely acknowledged him. But off they went, winding through the neighborhood and out into the open ocean as the sun dipped below the horizon.

It grew dark fast, but from what Matt could see, they had a full tank of gas. Yet he couldn't talk her into turning around, and his sobs didn't deter her. She navigated at cruising speed for just under an hour until the skiff sputtered to a stop, the tank empty. Then she stared at the star-filled sky.

"There's no moon tonight," she said, sadly. Matt could barely make out the outline of her head.

"How are we supposed to get back?" There was an emergency kit on the skiff with a radio, but since the boat hadn't been used for some time, Matt had neglected to keep it charged. They had no way to contact anyone on land.

"Sweet boy, I'm not going back."

"W-what?"

The boat rocked under her weight as she shifted forward. She grasped his face, and he saw the flash of her white teeth when she smiled at him.

"I'm going to be with your dad. I'm going to turn into a mermaid and swim away to him."

He grabbed her wrists. "No, Mom. No!"

"Don't you dare jump in after me. Stay in the boat."

"Moooommmm."

She shook his shoulders. "Promise me." He whimpered and she squeezed his shoulders hard. "Promise you'll stay in the boat."

"Don't go, please don't go."

"My brave, sweet boy." She kissed his forehead, then his mouth.

Then she was gone.

She left him without fuel or oars, food or water. She left him an orphan.

Matt recalls screaming for her until he lost his voice. He recalls crying until his tears dried up. He recalls being too afraid to jump into the water, and he's always regretted that he didn't. He recalls thinking he hadn't been enough for his mom to stay. And by the time a fisherman found him two days later, sunburned and dehydrated, after it occurred to Matt to send up a flare, he recalls what he believed about himself: he wasn't lovable enough for the person he loved most to stick around.

It's almost sunset when Matt arrives at the spot where his mom had spent most of her last days. He sits on the seawall where he once sat beside her and looks out at the ocean, trying to imagine what his mom must have seen. In some ways, he never left this spot. He's been sitting here for twenty years. He's held on to his grief and anger and regret and loathing for so long that they've kept him glued here.

Matt still has dreams of his mom turning into a mermaid and swimming away to be with his dad. He closes his eyes and dreams of her now. Then he pictures himself saying to her what he never has before.

"Goodbye, Mom." He hopes she found peace.

The breeze carries his words over the water, taking his grief with them as he lets it all go. And with that release, he forgives Elizabeth for being incapable of loving him. He forgives his dad for dying. And he forgives his mom for not being strong enough to stay.

Then he forgives himself.

He knows he has a long road ahead of him, but he's already moving in the right direction just by coming here.

Then there's Julia, the woman who helped him get to this point. He smiles at that, thinking of the weekend he spent with her when he'd hit rock bottom. He could argue he was hallucinating. He could argue Julia's wild theory that he was living out one of Ruby Rose's forgotten memories. What he can't argue is the truth. Julia was the one on the phone with him. The one who kept calling back. The one who talked him through it all. The one who stayed.

———

After sunrise, Matt strolls the wooden planks toward his old house. The rears of the homes look over the private waterway, and he can see families getting ready for their day through the windows.

He stops when he reaches the back of his house. He doesn't know who sold it on his parents' behalf or what happened to the money. It probably went to Elizabeth. The house has since been remodeled and is home to a new family. He can see three kids packing their lunches in the kitchen. One waves to him. He probably thinks Matt is a neighbor. He's pleased to see his former house is a home bursting with life. He remembers feeling warm, safe, and loved inside its walls. No wonder moving into Elizabeth's estate had been a shock to him.

Next door an older woman appears on her deck. She hums as she waters her plants before retreating inside to return with a coffee mug and her iPad. She notices Matt staring at her. She frowns at him, and it clicks. She's the woman who helped him pack his suitcase for California. She drove him to the airport.

"Mrs. Kinsley?"

"Yes?" Her response is wary. He is a stranger in a private neighborhood.

"It's Matt. Matt Gatlin," he says, approaching her.

She blinks, then gasps. "Matt? Is that really you?"

"Yeah, it's me."

"Well, I'll be. I always wondered what happened to you. Come sit." She pulls out a chair for him. "And for goodness' sake, call me Kathy. We're both adults."

His mouth quirks. "All right, Kathy."

"Would you like a cup of coffee?"

"I'd love one."

"Cream?"

"Black."

She smiles sweetly. "Just like your father. Never could understand how he drank it that way. He and Hal used to take their coffees out here every morning before they went off for work." Matt frowns and she clarifies, "My ex-husband. We divorced years ago."

"Ah." He takes a seat. She goes inside the house and returns a moment later with another mug.

"Thanks."

"Did you move back to Florida?"

He shakes his head. "Just visiting."

She gives him a knowing look. "California, then? Are you still there?"

"New Mexico." He gives her a few brief highlights of his life: his photography, assignments, and travels.

"No wife?" she asks when he finishes.

"No wife."

"Girlfriend? Partner?"

"Neither. One day." He says that with surprising ease, amazed he feels excited at the possibility.

"I miss your parents."

"I do too."

"They were good people."

Matt nods, sullen.

"I think of them every so often, especially your mom. I really liked her."

"She was wonderful."

After a beat, Kathy throws up her hands. "I just remembered. Wait here."

While she's gone, Matt looks around. Many homes have been updated, but much about the canal hasn't changed. He can almost picture his dad tossing their fishing rods into the skiff. He can see his mom correcting test papers on the rear deck. And he smiles. He regrets not returning sooner than he has, but he's glad he finally did.

The glass door slides open and Kathy returns. "I've kept this for years, not quite sure what to do with it. Maybe I hoped you'd come back someday. I found it after the estate company moved everything from your parents' house. It must have fallen off a shelf or out of a drawer. It belongs to you. You should take it."

She gives him a photograph, and Matt stares at it in stunned silence.

"Do you know who they are? I could never tell but figure it must have been important for your mom to keep it."

He flips the photo over. Penciled on back is *Liza & Magnolia Blu, Beverly Hills, 1972.*

"It's my grandmother," he says, not taking his eyes off the photo. "And her friend, Magnolia Blu." The photo is almost an exact replica of the one Ruby Rose had at Julia's house. They're so similar that the pictures must have been taken in sequence.

Kathy's smile is smug. "I knew it was important. Glad I kept it."

"Me too." Because his memory is slowly returning. His mom kept the photo in the middle drawer of her desk. Matt recalls finding it when he went looking for a sharpened pencil once. He'd asked his mom about it, and she told him, "That's your grandmother and the only genuine friend I think she ever had." It was the only photo of her mother Aubrey had.

Matt releases a shaky breath and settles back into the chair. Turns out he had seen Magnolia Blu before. He remembers returning to this photo on numerous occasions just to look at it. And sure enough—he peers closer—Magnolia is wearing the crystal pendant.

Well, I'll be damned.

Magnolia was buried deep in his subconscious.

Last weekend might have been hell, and aspects of that psychedelic experience—one he cares not to repeat—may always remain a mystery to him, but there is one thing he's certain of. Had he not seen Magnolia's photo and heard her story, had Julia not been persistent with her concern, he never would have acknowledged that he needed to address his past trauma. Ignoring it was storing it, and doing so was impacting his life. Most especially, his relationships.

Matt might have forgotten about the photo, but his subconscious sure hadn't. While the memory of Magnolia's image had been buried deep, she was enough to trigger him to confront his grief.

Whoever said God works in mysterious ways wasn't kidding. Matt would add that the human mind does the same.

"Thank you for this," he says, thanking Kathy also for the coffee when he rises to leave.

"Don't be a stranger," she tells him before he goes.

"I won't. I'll be back." One of these days he'll be brave enough to take a boat out to the spot where his mother left him.

Until then, one step forward at a time.

One Week Later

CHAPTER 48

JULIA

Lea Hope lives in a four-bedroom, three-bathroom craftsman-style home with a pool and a professionally manicured yard in Culver City, where she and her husband of eighteen years are raising their two boys, aged sixteen and fourteen. Both boys play for the high school junior varsity football team and are honors students, while their parents comanage a residential real estate office downtown. Lea and her husband both drive Teslas, which they park in tandem on their driveway. By all appearances, everything about Julia's mom is disgustingly perfect.

She wonders if her husband knows Lea had a baby before she married him. Do her sons know they have an older half sister?

Since she learned to search the internet, Julia has devoured all public information about her mom, from her real estate listings to her street address. She's stalked her on social media. But she never tried to make contact. Two reasons: she didn't want Mama Rose to think she wasn't enough for Julia, and she was afraid her mom would reject her again.

Lea had ample time to come back for Julia. The fact she hadn't told Julia everything she needed to know. Lea didn't want Julia in her life.

Or so Julia had been led to believe by Mama Rose.

But now, after what her grandmother said to her, mistaking her for Lea, Julia isn't so sure. Was it possible Lea hadn't abandoned her?

Could her last memories of her mom be wrong? They were those of a three-year-old child.

Either way, and at the risk of Lea's indifference, Julia's mother has a right to know her own mother has died.

Julia rings the doorbell and nervously straightens her blouse. She could have called Lea, but she wants to see her mom's face when Lea hears Mama Rose is gone. Her reaction will be telling. Did she ever care? She wants her mom to hurt, and shamefully, Julia wants to hurt her, as much as she has been hurting.

Julia timed her arrival for right after the boys get home from their after-school activities and around when Lea would be starting dinner. It's taken Julia a week to work up the courage to come. She spent just as long mapping out Lea's schedule and route home from the office to make sure she came by at a time that her mother would be here.

When nobody comes to the door, Julia glances at the driveway, wondering if she miscalculated. One Tesla is there, her mom's. She should be home.

Julia rings the bell again, and this time a voice bellows, "Coming." It's followed by the sound of heavy feet running down a staircase and the front door swinging open. Julia involuntarily backs up at the sight of her half brother. His eyes narrow and he blurts, "We already have solar."

Julia barks a laugh. She wondered what kind of greeting she'd get. That was not what she'd imagined.

She takes in the unfamiliar yet familiar sight of this boy-man with floppy hair and acne, feeling a flutter in her chest as her heart rate quickens. He's built solidly, with broad shoulders under a loose, worn-out T-shirt and thick thighs filling the legs of his board shorts. And his eyes, his cheekbones . . . He resembles his grandfather, Matthew Holloway. Julia has spent the week digging into his history too. She even brought herself to watch a few of his old movies.

Her half brother starts to close the door on her, and she quickly finds her voice. "Not selling solar. Is your mom home?"

"Who's asking?"

"Julia Hope."

The door opens wide again, as do his eyes. He drags his gaze up and down her. He then looks askance at her and yells, "Mom! Julia's here!"

From within the belly of the house, Julia hears a crash. The boy-man doesn't leave the door. "You okay?" he yells into the house.

There isn't an answer, and he hesitates. Julia's nerves prickle. Why would he shout her name through the house like that? He can't know who she is.

"Ah, one sec." He starts to close the door again when the click-clack of heels approaches.

"I'm okay," a woman says, breathless. A hand appears on the boy-man's shoulder, and then the woman—her mother—is there. Dressed in a pale linen pantsuit and heels, she looks exactly like her professional photo online. Better, even. Healthy. The woman who dumped her on Mama Rose's doorstep had been filthy and strung out, unnaturally thin from a poor diet of handouts and drugs. That had been Julia's last impression of her mom.

Now, she looks like a mom, as well as a professional, and a business leader, and the doer and achiever Julia has read about, with Matty Holloway's features and Magnolia Blu's frame. She's beautiful.

Lea's chin quivers, her eyes buzzing over Julia's appearance as Julia tries her best to put on a brave face. "Julia?"

"I have news about Mama Rose. Your mom, Grandma Ruby," she clarifies, when her mom just stares at her. The boy-man is gawking at her too.

"You're really Julia?" he asks.

She looks at him, surprised. "You know who I am?"

"I've known about you my whole life."

Lea shakes off her shock. "Both my sons know about you; so does my husband."

Her half brother grins. "'Bout time you showed up. We've been dying to meet you."

Julia's gaze darts between the mother and son.

"I know what you must be thinking," Lea starts.

"What am I thinking?" Julia snaps back. Her brothers have known about her? Nobody bothered to include her in their little family? Did they find it funny leaving her to care for Mama Rose on her own?

"Come in, please." Lea gestures Julia inside. "You must have so many questions, and I'll answer all of them. But you obviously came here for a reason, so let's address that first. Kit, go find your brother. I'll call you boys down soon enough, but give Julia and I a chance to talk."

"Nico, you're never going to guess who's here," Kit shouts, running up the stairs.

"Sorry about that. Can I get you anything? Coffee, water?"

"I'm fine, thanks."

Lea leads her into a sitting area that shouts Restoration Hardware. They settle across from each other on a pair of couches framed by a large fireplace on one end and an opening into the dining room, which looks out into the backyard. Lea doesn't waste a moment. "Mom?" she clears her throat. "Your grandmother?"

"Cardiac arrest. Last week," Julia says with as little emotion as she can manage, just as she practiced a dozen times. "She passed in her sleep."

Lea studies her before abruptly turning away. She looks out the window into the back, then down at her hands clasped tightly in her lap. She doesn't say anything for at least a minute, and then she releases a shuddering breath. She swipes a finger under her eye and looks at Julia square on. Her eyes are glassy. "I am sorry for your loss."

"She was your mother." Julia's tone is abrupt, and Lea flinches.

"She was. She and I . . . She was more of a mother to you than I ever could have been."

Julia's eyes dart past the family portrait on the wall she doesn't dare look at toward the stairs. "You could have fooled me."

"I was in a different place when I had you."

"And since then? It never occurred to you to try again with me? Did you ever think of me?" The questions fire out of Julia. This isn't how she intended this meeting to go. But all the despair from Mama Rose's death, and the longing she kept bottled for years for the sake of her grandmother's feelings, come pouring out.

"Not a day has gone by that I haven't thought of you. Not. One. Day."

"I don't believe you." Julia's chin quivers like a petulant child's.

She looks down at her lap to collect herself when she'd rather scream at her mom. Does Lea know how hard it was watching Mama Rose deteriorate? Does she know how lonely Julia's been, how inadequate she's felt? Does she have any idea how much Julia has sacrificed for the sake of *her* mother? But her sons are upstairs, and as contorted as Julia's reasoning might be, she doesn't want twenty-seven years of uncorked rage to be her brothers' first impression of her.

She wants them to know that she's strong and brave and has survived on her own. That without her mother—their mother—she still grew into a kind, compassionate, and decent person.

"I returned for you on several occasions."

Julia shakes her head. "I don't believe you." That would mean Mama Rose lied to her. But that last thing Mama Rose said to her . . .

"You're wearing the necklace I bought you," Lea says.

"What?" Julia lifts her head, startled. Lea's cheeks glisten from her tears.

"The rose pendant. I bought it for your thirteenth birthday."

Julia's fingers flutter to the necklace. She looks down at the pendant. "Mama Rose gave this to me on my thirteenth."

Lea sighs.

"Why would she lie to me?"

"It's going to take more than one evening for me to explain everything that's happened. I can give you the highlights right now if you'll listen."

Julia nods, tightly clasping the pendant.

"Where to begin?" Lea briefly closes her eyes. "My mother and I weren't always like this, at such odds."

"That's an understatement," Julia says. "I remember the day you left me. I remember what you said. You didn't want me."

Lea wipes her face with a shaky hand. "I was hoping you wouldn't remember. Unfortunately, I can't take any of that back. It won't change what I did, or what I said. I am sorrier than you will ever know." She sits back down and squeezes her knees. "I was at my worst then, and it took me a long, long time to fix myself. I'm still fixing myself. It never stops, not when you're as bad as I was. But that's a story for another day. For now . . ." She takes a collective breath. "I loved my mother, and we were very close until I was around ten. That's when my father died. And before you say anything"—she lifts a finger when Julia opens her mouth to interrupt—"I've known about my biological father, Matthew Holloway, since I was old enough to remember. Benjie Stromski was my adoptive father, the one I called Dad. He raised me, and I adored him. His death destroyed both Mother and me. We were never the same.

"I'd like to blame it on the drugs. We both had problems. But I think we were suffering from broken hearts. The drugs made it easier to cope. She was a recreational user. I don't think she ever stopped."

"She didn't."

"She was still hosting her parties?"

Julia nods. "Until she was diagnosed."

"Wow." Lea forces out a breath. "My teenage years were chaotic. I can't recall if she kicked me out or if I left. Probably a little of both. But I moved out when I was seventeen. Had you at twenty-one. Left you with Mom when I was twenty-four and landed myself in the hospital more than once. I had to be revived twice."

"Jesus."

"I was not fit to be a mother, and when your grandmother approached me to give up my parental rights, I didn't think twice. Chris, my husband, cleaned up before me. We weren't married then, but he helped me find my way back. Then we held each other accountable. Got our GEDs, passed our real estate exams. Married, had kids."

"And lived happily ever after." Julia's mouth pinches, her mind turbulent with envy and anger. "Where did I fit in during all this? Or didn't I?"

"These are highlights, Julia. So much more was going on. I don't want to overwhelm you."

"I'm already there."

"I'm afraid if I tell you everything right now, you'll never want to see me again. I've waited twenty-seven years to speak with you. Seventeen years for you to come see me."

"Then why didn't you come to me? Why didn't I see you when you came back for me? How am I supposed to believe you? This necklace proves nothing." Julia shoots to her feet and dangles the charm for Lea to see.

"Because your grandmother didn't want me to," Lea says, impassioned as she rises. She stands face-to-face with Julia. Their posture is defensive, identical. Any doubts about whom she came from are eradicated this instant. She sees much of herself in her mom. She doesn't know if that makes her proud or disgusted. She's definitely confused.

"Why wouldn't Mama Rose let you see me?" Giving up her parental rights is one thing. But for her to stay away entirely? "Would you have been that bad of an influence?"

"I would have been horrible. Those first five years after I gave you up, when I kept coming back." She shakes her head. "You would not have wanted me anywhere near you. But after I cleaned up? I don't think your grandmother believed I'd stay that way. And by the time I showed up around your thirteenth birthday, she considered you hers. It wouldn't have mattered how sober or successful I was. At the heart of it, I think she was afraid of losing you too. She'd lost her parents. She'd lost my biological father, then Benjie. Then me. I don't think she would have survived if I'd taken you away."

"Didn't you at least try to fight for me? What about joint custody or visitation rights?"

"Oh, we tried."

"We?"

"Chris hired attorneys. He was ready to go to battle for you."

"Chris? Your husband? Why would he—?" She stops, and Lea's gaze darts over Julia's shoulder as the tumblers fall into place. *Click-click-click.* "Who's my father?"

"I am." The voice comes from behind her. Julia pivots to find a man dressed in suit pants and a buttoned shirt, the sleeves rolled up his forearms, a blazer draped over an arm. He must have come in through the garage. Darn stealthy electric vehicles. She hadn't heard his arrival. She'd hoped to be gone before he got home. She wasn't sure she could handle meeting Lea's entire family at once. But this man, the blank spot on her birth certificate, is her father.

Lea must have a grasp of what she's thinking because she says, "Your grandmother didn't know. I never told her. She wouldn't have believed he'd turned himself around either."

"Lea didn't tell me about you until you were ten or eleven, after we'd sobered up." The edge of his mouth tilts upward, and his gaze darts to his wife. "Kit texted me."

"I thought he would," Lea says.

Chris sits next to Lea and drapes his arm over her shoulders, pulls her to his side. He kisses her cheek. "I came as soon as I heard," he says, quietly.

Realizing how unsteady her legs are, Julia slowly sits back down. She stares at them. *Her parents.* Those two boys upstairs are her full brothers.

"I don't understand." She hears the shock in her voice. Mama Rose kept this from her, and she almost took it to her grave. Julia wonders if she would have shown up here if Mama Rose hadn't planted seeds of doubt about Lea.

"I'll get you some water." Lea is quick to her feet and heads into the kitchen.

Chris leans forward, knees spread, forearms on his thighs. "I listened to most of what Lea said to you from out there. I'm sorry this is coming as a shock. We knew it would. What we didn't know is if we'd ever get the chance to explain."

"Why?"

"That's a loaded question." Lea returns with a glass of water and puts it in Julia's hand. Julia drains half the glass and sets it on the table, worried that she'll spill the rest. She clasps her hands, squeezing them on her lap to control the tremors circulating through her arms.

"One she deserves an answer to," Chris says. "We wanted to fight for you; we almost did. Lea convinced me otherwise."

Lea touches his arm. "We agreed, together," she says, making a point. "I already disrupted your life by giving you up. Going to court to get our rights back would have disrupted your life further. Your grandmother gave you a wonderful life. She raised you beautifully. She did for you what I never gave her the chance to do with me. After I tried to see you when you were thirteen and your grandmother wouldn't let me, I realized she was right. By that time, you were hers. We figured you were already thirteen. In five more years, you'd be a legal adult. If you wanted us in your life, you would reach out. If you didn't—and it seemed you didn't—we'd have to be all right with that. I didn't give you a choice when you were three. The choice had to be yours this time."

"Did you know Mama Rose was sick?"

Lea shares a glance with Chris, and she nods. "Eight years ago, she came to tell me. She explained everything had been arranged, that she knew where she wanted to be when it became too much for you to care for her, and she insisted that she had enough financially."

"She didn't have enough. I had to volunteer—" Julia covers her mouth to stop herself. "Nothing I say will change the fact that you weren't there, that you didn't help."

"She didn't want my help. She'd come to say goodbye to me. Had I known you were struggling . . ." Lea shakes her head. Chris folds her hand between his.

"You didn't know," he whispers to Lea. She cups her free hand over his.

Jealousy burns inside Julia. How many times did she wish she had someone to hold her hand?

Lea sniffles and lifts her chin. "I shouldn't have listened to her. I should have helped. I'm sorry I didn't."

Julia closes her eyes and takes a moment. "I'm not sure I would have welcomed it," she tells her mother truthfully. She stands, unsure how much more she wants to hear.

Chris and Lea stand with her. "Please don't leave yet." There is a note of desperation in her mother's voice.

"Lea," Chris softly speaks, a suggestion, Julia is aware, not to push her.

Julia digs out her keys. "I need time—"

"Can we come down now?" Kit hollers from upstairs.

"Not yet," Chris answers, but it's too late. Two sets of bare feet come bounding down the stairs. Kit and Nico land on the bottom step with big eyes and nervous smiles. Her brothers look almost identical, but Nico is noticeably older.

"Is she staying for dinner, Mom?" he asks.

Lea glances nervously at her. "We haven't had the chance to ask her."

"I'm not sure—" Chris starts before Kit interrupts.

"Stay for dinner. Dad's grilling steaks."

"I am?" Chris chokes. He looks at Lea. "I guess I am. We have enough in the freezer."

"Just don't sit next to Kit," Nico says. "He hasn't showered for three days."

Kit blushes. "Not true." He punches his brother in the arm.

"Boys." Chris orders them to behave.

Julia watches their interaction, and her chest aches. This is her family, one that she wasn't a part of. She's angry and hurt and confused, and she has every right to walk out the front door and never speak with them again. Her mother—no, her parents—would be devastated, and she feels a sickening sense of satisfaction that she could hurt them as much as she's been hurting. Exactly what she came here to do.

Then she remembers what they said to her and realizes they have been hurting. Perhaps as long as she has been. They could have moved away. They could have made it difficult for her to find them. But they've been here all along, and they're all over the internet, easy to track down. As if they've been wanting her to find them. Just waiting for her to come around. She recalls how envious she'd been when Matt's grandfather and his aunt embraced him. She felt it shouldn't have been that easy for him. But here is her family, welcoming her into their fold as if they've been holding their breaths until she was ready. Until she no longer wanted to go through life alone.

This isn't at all how she expected this meeting to go.

The decision is hers. She could walk out that door. Or . . .

Her family looks at her expectantly.

She nods, smiling shakily when the tears make her brothers look fuzzy. "I'll stay."

Two Months Later

CHAPTER 49

MATT

Matt stands in his garage, ready to embark on a task he's put off long enough. He went to Florida and made peace with his parents and himself. He joined Dave in France just in time to photograph Ford's cars in the final six hours of Le Mans, and when he returned, he found a therapist as he promised himself he would do. He's been keeping in touch with his family—still getting used to that. And he's been talking with Julia. But he's been avoiding the boxes in his garage.

His therapist advised him the longer he put it off, the more difficult the task; that sorting his grandmother's boxes was part of his journey to reconcile their past relationship. One step more on his journey to move forward.

This week's homework: one box. That's all he has to do.

With his Porsche parked in the driveway, he drags the nearest box to the center of the garage and slices open the top. Again, the scent of her trips him up. Musty and powdery, but her. He also recognizes a lingering odor that reminds him of Rosemont.

He dives into the box, quickly sorting shoes and clothes. More items for him to donate.

That was easy, he thinks when he finishes.

He grabs another box and does the same. Then a third box. Slowly, a pile of clothes builds. He slices open a fourth box expecting much of the same, but it's filled with paperwork. The contents of her desk, Matt presumes.

He takes a breath and starts sorting. It doesn't take him long to come across a small hatbox filled with letters, each addressed to Elizabeth Holloway from Magnolia Blu. All unopened.

Matt frowns. How did Julia miss these?

She packed Elizabeth's room, but she might have done so quickly and failed to look inside the letter box.

He flips through the envelopes, debating whether to open them. The time he spent in the motel with her seems more like the acid trip it was with every passing day. But Julia told him about the letter Elizabeth had written her and how she wished for a letter from her grandmother.

Matt is holding a stack of them. They aren't addressed to Julia, but they'll give her something.

He and Julia have been texting back and forth, and they exchange calls almost daily. He wants to give her time to get to know her family, and he couldn't be happier for her. He's trying to be patient about seeing her. But these letters warrant an in-person delivery. He's also due a visit with his grandfather. Mostly, though, he misses Julia. He's been wanting to be with her since he left Florida.

Matt pulls out his phone and books a flight for tomorrow.

The Next Day

CHAPTER 50

JULIA

Julia is waiting on the porch steps when Matt's cab pulls up to her house. She's on her feet and striding toward him before he's fully out of the car. When he sees her, he drops his bag and catches her up in his arms.

"I've missed you," he says into the crook of her neck. The rumble of his voice and the scent of him send a burst of excitement through her.

"Me too." She squeezes him tight, and he sets her back on her feet. His hands cradle her face, and he kisses her. Her fingers dive into his hair. "I'm so glad you're here."

"Mmm." He groans into her mouth.

"'Bout time you got your ass back here."

He chuckles and kisses her lips, her cheekbones, her jawline. Julia's breath comes in short gasps, and she squirms in his arms. "We should go inside or Mrs. Marston across the street will get an eyeful," she says between kisses. "Besides, my family wants to meet you."

Matt stops. He lifts his head and stares at her, his eyes bouncing between hers. "You want me to meet your parents?"

"And my brothers. They're kind of part of the deal."

"Wow," Matt mouths. "You sure?"

She nods, and then she's smiling. It's something she never thought she'd be able to say. "Yeah, I'm sure. They've invited us for dinner if we're free."

"Are we free?"

She trails a finger down his abs. "That depends on what happens next."

He grabs her hand, his eyes flashing with heat. "One condition."

"Oh?"

"You have lunch with me and my grandfather tomorrow."

Julia's grin broadens. "I'd love to."

"Then dinner with your parents it is." He pushes out a rough breath. "I've never had a girl bring me home to her parents."

"Nervous?"

He thinks about it for a moment. "Nah. They're gonna love me."

Julia barks a laugh. Lea and Chris won't be the only ones. She's already fallen hard for him.

She hugs him again because she can't help herself. They sway side to side, holding on to the moment and to each other.

"I have something for you," he whispers against her ear.

"You do?"

He picks up his bag, and she grabs his hand, leads him to the porch, where they sit on the steps.

"What is it?" She watches curiously as he unzips his bag.

"Letters." He hands her a stack of them. Julia slowly flips through them, realizing what she's looking at.

"She wrote to your grandmother for years. They're unopened," she says as she lifts one up, deeply moved.

"You mentioned you wished your grandmother had written you a letter. These aren't written to you, but they belong to you."

"They belong to you too." She slides the envelope back into the stack. "We'll read them together." The way she says it, he knows the matter is settled.

"I'd like that."

"I like you too." Julia smiles tenderly at him, touches his cheek.

His gaze caresses her face. He fits a hand to her jaw. "I more than like you, Julia Hope."

He smiles back at her, and in that smile, Julia feels his love.

EPILOGUE
MATT

Five Years Later

Matt stands over the grave site of Ruby Rose Hope. Laid to rest beside her is her late husband, Benjamin Stromski. Nearby lies Elizabeth Holloway, and beside her, her husband Matthew Holloway. And across the cemetery, his grandfather Adam Nulty. It was his burial that had brought Matt here today. Five years wasn't as much time as he would have liked with his grandfather, but he's grateful he got those years.

He touches the granite block before him and smiles at the bouquet of daisies Julia left. He has to laugh that all of them—Matty, Elizabeth, Adam, and Magnolia—ended up in the same place. Life certainly is weird.

He often thinks back on who or what he picked up alongside the road that day. While he understands he was hallucinating, he still goes back and forth between believing she was a ghost or a memory released to the universe as Julia once said. One thing is clear: his mind certainly showed him he couldn't keep the pain from his past bottled up forever. He's also never forgotten the advice Julia gave him, advice passed along to her by none other than her grandmother, Magnolia Blu. *Life isn't worth living if we don't allow ourselves to love.*

"I have loved," he says out loud, thinking of Adam. "And I love." He glances over his shoulder and smiles at the woman waiting for him by the car. Julia waves back just as their daughter rushes over to him, waving a daisy.

"Daddy, I found this in the car." She joins him at the gravestone and tucks the wilted daisy into the bouquet. "There. Now Gammie Ruby has all the daisies. She's going to love them." Proud, she claps her hands.

"She'll love them, Rosey, because they're from you." Matt picks up his four-year-old daughter. "Ready?"

"Mom says we're going to be late if we don't leave now, and Aunt Shiv wants me to help make the tater salad."

"Yum," Matt says, playing along. He'd never eaten a Tater Tot salad until he met his aunt Siobhan. She's hosting the family for Adam's celebration of life, and they're already late, Matt thinks, noticing the time.

But first . . .

He touches the cool stone and whispers a thank-you to the woman beneath his feet.

"Who you talking to, Daddy?"

"A very wise woman," he says of his daughter's namesake as they return to the car.

Julia touches his cheek. "Are you going to be okay?"

He kisses his wife, the love of his life. "I will be."

Not only because he has Julia at his side. He let love back into his life.

DISCUSSION QUESTIONS

1. You could say *Find Me in California* is four stories in one. Matt, Julia, Liza, and Ruby Rose each have a unique journey. Whose story is your favorite? What about their story did you find appealing?

2. Which scene is your favorite?

3. Do you have an estranged family member? How does this person treat you and your family? Have you thought about reconciling?

4. Matt and Julia both desire family, but due to circumstances beyond their control, they find themselves on the brink of facing life alone. Compare and contrast their situations. How do their past experiences help them understand each other? What draws them together?

5. What do you think happened to Matt during his weekend in the motel? Was he hallucinating? How did the experience propel him on his healing journey?

6. Do you think Julia was too meddlesome with Matt and Liza, or did she do the right thing by getting involved?

7. Multiple themes are woven through this story. These themes include forgiveness, family, secrets, self-worth, and love. Which theme resonated with you? What other themes did you find in the story?

8. Were you surprised to learn the truth about Matt's and

Julia's grandparents?

9.   Have you ever lost a loved one before you had a chance to say goodbye? What would you have said to this person?

10. What are your thoughts about the ending? If you learned of relatives that you never knew about, would you reach out to them?

11. For fun, what is the significance of the date on Magnolia Blu's last journal entry, August 1, 2016?

Acknowledgments

First and foremost, a huge thanks to my readers. Thank you for picking up this novel—my tenth!—and every novel beforehand. Knowing you're out there devouring my stories brings me great joy.

My agent, Gordon Warnock, has been one of my best supporters since my debut novel, and I really wouldn't be writing stories for you without him. Thanks to him and Laurie McLean and everyone else at Fuse Literary for having my back. You don't just ignite publishing careers; you keep that flame burning.

I've been incredibly fortunate to work with the Amazon Publishing team on all ten books, and I'm grateful for everyone's support. I especially want to thank my acquiring editor, Danielle Marshall, without whom I might never have been published. Thank you, Melissa Valentine, for taking me on so that I can continue telling my stories. *Find Me in California* shines because of you. And the title! You couldn't have come up with one more perfect.

From editing to production, thank you, Jodi Warshaw, Haley Miller Swan, Kellie Osborne, Sossity Chiricuzio, and Angela Elson for helping me get this book into shape. Thank you, Ploy Siripant, for designing the beautiful cover.

Thank you to my early reader and influencer teams and that boost you give my books. Thank you to every author who's endorsed my books (this one included) or in some way supported me when I needed that extra nudge of encouragement. There are so many of you, and I'm lucky to consider each of you a friend. Thank you to those of you who shared their personal stories with me about the struggles that come with caretaking for elderly family members. It's never easy, but know that I understand.

And finally, thanks to my family—Henry, Evan, and Brenna. I am a better person because of you.

Love exclusive content? Join my top reader group (www.facebook.com/groups/kerrystikilounge) and subscribe to my newsletter, Kerry's Beach Club (https://www.kerrylonsdale.com/beyond-the-book/beach-club/).

About the Author

Kerry Lonsdale is the *Wall Street Journal*, *Washington Post*, and Amazon Charts bestselling author of *Side Trip*, *Last Summer*, and *All the Breaking Waves*; the Everything Series (*Everything We Keep*, *Everything We Left Behind*, and *Everything We Give*); and the No More trilogy (*No More Words*, *No More Lies*, and *No More Secrets*). Her work has been translated into more than twenty-seven languages. She resides in Northern California with her husband and two children. You can visit Kerry at www.kerrylonsdale.com.